Blue Skies

Lynette Rees

Whilst most of the places in this story exist or existed at some point, most of the character names mentioned in this novel are fictional. Some details of the story have been changed for dramatic purposes. To the best of my ability I have kept the dates as accurate as possible of when the buildings existed in accordance with local historical detail.

Dedication

To 'The Evans Family'of Cardigan, from whom I am proud to be a direct descendant.

When I was a child, my paternal grandfather, Myddrin Evans, spoke about the family from that area, referring to them as 'Cardis'. They were farming people, and the reason I'm who I am today is that one of them, my great grandfather, John Morris Evans, chose to marry and settle in Merthyr Tydfil.

To SallyAnn Cole for your proofreading skills and to all those who have supported me whilst writing this book.

Many thanks.

Chapter One

Merthyr Tydfil November 1896

Nurse Rebecca Jenkin walked briskly along the Nightingale Ward at the Merthyr General Hospital, checking on the welfare of her patients. It had been a long night shift and now as the first embers of dawn were about to break, the patients would soon be awake and in need of their medicines, toilet care and breakfasts. It had been a hard shift. During the night a man had been brought in from a nearby coal pit with crush injuries from a collapse at the coal face. A young woman had got badly burned at the iron works. She worked as a rubbish tipper at Cyfarthfa. And a young child had been admitted, malnourished and uncared for. She despaired sometimes at the thought of how hard life was for some folk in the town.

It wasn't that she'd had a particularly privileged life style, but it was a lot better than some people in the area. Her father, Dafydd, was the chief Inspector of the Merthyr branch of the Glamorgan Constabulary, and her dear mother, Kathleen, who'd sang like a song bird in the local theatres to much acclamation now led a very quiet life. She was very proud of her parents, who'd worked hard to provide for her and her seventeen-year-old brother, James.

"Nurse, please help me?" Rebecca turned for a moment to see an elderly woman, stretch out her crepe-like hand.

Rebecca walked over to her patient. "What's the matter, Martha?" she asked gently. She tenderly stroked the old woman's brow.

"I'm afraid I must have had an accident during the night," Martha whispered.

Rebecca spoke softly to the woman. "Please don't worry about that, I shall clean you up and give you a new under sheet."

She pulled a portable screen around the bed and filled a bowl with warm water and washed the elderly lady down, all the while reassuring her it was just an accident. Incontinence was a problem for Martha during her elderly years and Rebecca realised what an embarrassment it must be for her. She was a very lady-like sort of person, who had once owned a sweet shop in the town, and would be absolutely mortified if any of her customers knew about her little accidents.

Rebecca dried her off gently with a towel and gave her a fresh night gown to wear. Quickly removing the soiled sheet and replacing it with a clean one that smelled of starch and detergent. "There we are now, would you like me to escort you to the lavatory?"

The elderly lady nodded gratefully. Rebecca helped her on with her dressing gown and slippers, led her to the lavatory and then later settled her back into bed.

"Nurse, you are so kind, I won't forget this," Martha settled herself back under the covers.

"It's all in a day's, or should I say night's work," Rebecca smiled. Soon she would be finishing her night shift and couldn't wait for her head to touch the pillow. Her parents had moved from their cosy little house on the cobbles of Upper Abercanaid a few years ago at Chapel Square, and now resided in a much larger house in The Walk area of Merthyr. Rebecca liked living there as it was close to Park Chapel, which she attended twice a day on a Sunday, and helped out at various groups in the week there, shift work permitting.

She had just settled Martha down in her bed, when Doctor Daniel Evans, strode into the ward. She found his short manner the height of arrogance at times.

"How did the burns and the crush injuries do during the night?" he asked brusquely.

She shook her head. "If you mean Miss Jennifer Edwards and Mr. Howard Clark, then they did quite well, Doctor."

He raised his brow as if he could not believe the way Rebecca addressed him. "Yes, that's who I meant." He cleared his throat.

"Neither has slept of course. I've given them some tincture of laudanum, but it will take some time. How deep do you think Miss Edwards' burn is, Doctor?"

"I would say thankfully, it's a surface burn, though Mr. Clark might not be so fortunate with his crush injury. I'm anticipating a possible amputation if gangrene starts to set in, and if it does, would you be prepared to assist me later today?"

Rebecca stiffened. It unnerved her somewhat at the thought of assisting Doctor Evans. He wasn't her favourite person to work with. "Of course," she replied, hoping that an amputation would not be necessary. She had witnessed during the course of the night, the way

Mrs Clark had sobbed pitifully. It broke Rebecca's heart to see such young children clinging on to their mother's skirts with trepidation and fear.

"My shift shall finish within the hour and I will be going to sleep straight afterwards. But if I'm needed before tonight, please send someone to my home address, I will write it down for you."

He nodded. "Thank you Nurse Jenkin." He smiled, realising for the first time she'd never seen a smile light up his face before. It made him look quite handsome. His dark hair, swarthy skin and olive eyes, gave him some sort of Mediterranean appearance. Unlike the pale, washed out appearance of many of the men in the town, who did hard manual labour in the pits and at the ironworks.

"Doctor..." she said thoughtfully, "I was just wondering where your family originates from?"

His eyes came to life with light and expression. "My mother is Spanish. She came here when her father came to the Dowlais Ironworks seeking work. She met my father and fell in love..." he hesitated, his eyes almost filling with tears. This was a far cry from the abrupt, efficient doctor she usually worked with. "Now where is that address? Please write it down for me as I have things to do, Nurse!" he said sharply.

Shocked by his sudden change of tone, she picked up a fountain pen on the Nurses' station, dipped it in an inkwell and wrote her address on a scrap of paper. Handing it to him, she searched for his eyes, but now they were cold like steel, a barrier firmly in place once again.

The nurses began to arrive for the morning shift in their capes and uniforms, rosy-cheeked and prompt, to begin their shift for the day. The nursing ward sister ushered them to her office to inform them of the patients' progress, and tell them about the new overnighters.

She glanced across at Martha who was now sitting up in bed, trying to read an old book she'd brought in with her. "You like that young man, Nurse, don't you?" Martha said, with a small smile and a twinkle in her hazel brown eyes.

A hot blush spread over Rebecca's cheeks and toward her neck. Changing the subject, she said, "Do you need to be taken to the lavatory again before I finish my shift, Martha?"

7

Martha shook her head. "I'm fine, dear. And if I do need to go again, I'll ask one of the nurses when you've gone. Though none are as nice as you."

***

By the time she got home, Rebecca's mother was already in the kitchen with a large pan of porridge on the boil. She turned when her daughter came in through the back door. "Had a hard night? You look tired, Becky."

"Not really, Mam. No harder than usual, though I might be called back in to work later as there might be an amputation necessary for one poor man who suffered a crush injury during the night at the coal mine."

"Well, sit you down then and I'll call your father for his breakfast 'tis time he got up for work." Rebecca's mother had lost none of her Irish accent, it was something Rebecca could listen to all day, her voice was so melodic, just like her singing voice was too.

"Where's James this morning?" It was unusual not to see him around first thing, if he was not up helping with the chores then he was over Cyfarthfa Park feeding the ducks or birdwatching, he had a keen interest in wildlife.

Her mother smiled. "You've obviously forgotten, he starts work this morning at 'Johnson and Goldstein', the solicitors in town." It was a legal Jewish firm that had recently been set up on Merthyr High Street, and James was fortunate to get a job there, instead of going down the pit or toiling in the ironworks like many of contemporaries. He was a studious young man, both parents insisting that neither the pit nor the ironworks were suitable environments for their son.

"Oh my goodness, I've been so busy with work that I'd forgotten that was today. How did he look setting off to work?"

"Very smart indeed in his new suit, quite the young gentleman."

Her mother left the room and called up the stairs. "Dafydd, your breakfast is ready, come on or you'll be late for work, for sure!"

"I'm coming!" he shouted back down the stairs.

A few moments later he joined them at the table, already dressed in his work trousers, shirt, braces and boots. As Chief Inspector at the police station, he had a very responsible job.

8

The three sat and ate their porridge in silence until her father said, "So what's this I hear our Rebecca, that a doctor might be calling to the house later to escort you into work?"

Rebecca swallowed, there was not much that her parents did not share with one another, they were that close. "It's not for definite, Dad. But there's a possible amputation lined up for later; a collier had his leg crushed underground."

Her father set down his spoon and furrowed his brow. "Which pit was that?"

"Castle Pit in Troedyrhiw, I believe."

"Terrible thing to happen," her mother chipped in. "That happened to your father once at Gethin Pit in Abercanaid."

She looked at her father and watched his eyes glaze over. "That was a long time ago, Kathleen..." he muttered, shaking his head as if his wife's revelation was too much to bear.

"I never knew that Dad, I mean I know you walk with a slight limp sometimes, but I never liked to ask you about it."

"Yes, he has some blue battle scars from that filthy old pit too, Rebecca." Her father shot her mother a glance as if telling her to heed her mouth. Colouring up, she carried on, "Anyhow that was a long time ago and fortunately for your father, he didn't lose his life like those other men and boys in that pit explosion."

"How long ago was that?" Rebecca looked at her father.

He lowered his head. "Thirty one years ago this Christmas..." he said sadly. "That was how your aunt Lily met your uncle Evan on the day of the disaster."

Rebecca blinked several times. "I had no idea. How romantic."

"Romantic?" Her father raised his voice a notch, then glowered at her. "I wouldn't say meeting in those circumstances was like a fairytale, more like a nightmare!" He banged his fist on the table and stood suddenly, scraping his chair on the hard flooring and left the room.

Her mother patted Rebecca's hand. "Pay no heed," she advised. "He gets like this sometimes. It's almost as though the mere mention of it brings back such bad memories for him around that time. 'Tis silly me saying anything."

Rebecca managed a wan smile. She had heard her father have outbursts before, but not one like this for some time. Mostly she was a daddy's girl and had been since the day of her birth. They exchanged glances as they heard the front door slam loudly as he left for work without even saying farewell.

"He's doing such a difficult job, Becky," her mother explained. "Such a lot of responsibility and it all gets to him sometimes."

Rebecca had to agree, he did have a responsible job upholding the law and she was so proud of both of her parents: her father as head of a team of policemen at the Merthyr branch of the Glamorgan Constabulary, and her mother with the voice of an angel, having performed at local theatres and even on the London stage many moons ago. And then there was her younger brother James, almost a young man with a good head on his shoulders. Really she could ask for no better family then she already had.

***

Doctor Daniel Evans did not call to Rebecca's home to urge her to assist him with an amputation, nor did he dispatch anyone else. The call just did not come and by the time she entered the ward for her night shift, it was in great upheaval. Martha was wandering around like a lost soul, barefooted and in her nightdress, as wails and screams could be heard from somewhere down the corridor.

"Let me escort you back to bed, Mrs Griffiths…" She draped her arm around the elderly lady's shoulders, guiding her back into bed.

Two nurses were in the process of drawing portable curtained screens around a bed in the far corner. Then she saw Doctor Evans striding toward her. She hadn't even had time to remove her cape, but she had to know what was going on. "What's happened?" She searched his face.

"Mr. Clark died unfortunately. I had been ready to operate and was going to send someone to fetch you, but he had a massive internal bleed…" His lower lip trembled.

"So those screams I just heard?"

"That was his wife. She's been inconsolable since hearing the news and fears now she will lose the children as she can't afford to keep them without his wage."

"Poor mites. I suppose the Parish might help?"

He shrugged. "Possibly. Though my guess is they'll all end up at the workhouse…"

St Tydfil's Workhouse had been operating for some time and most folk in the town dreaded the thought of their nearest and dearest ending up in such stark surroundings. There were tales of people going insane after entering that place and many were never seen by friends or family ever again, almost as though they had disappeared down some vast dark hole with no means of escape.

Rebecca shuddered to think that this time yesterday evening everything was fine for the family, they had their bread winner, but then within an hour or two of the pit collapse, everything was to change. If Mr. Clark had been working a different shift, then he would not be dead now, leaving behind his young family. It was then she realised how fortunate her own father had been during the Gethin Pit Explosion.

It was a tough shift on the ward that night. Rebecca spent a lot of time consoling Mrs Clark and her children, and managed to find a couple of pallets for them all to share to sleep on. The younger children managed to get some rest but the elder, and the widow herself, were awake all night long, seated on two wooden chairs with blankets draped over them. By the time dawn broke, she felt they had all cried a river and although unable to eat, had drank copious amounts of tea.

"Nurse!" Martha was calling again.

"You would like me to accompany you to the lavatory, Mrs Griffiths?"

"No, Nurse. I'm fine. I'm just concerned about those children and their mother." The old woman grimaced and her eyes shone with tears.

"Yes it's difficult, it will be hard for them that's for sure. Do you know them?"

Martha nodded. "The children used to come into my shop very regularly. Lovely they were and all. Very respectful. Their mother often came in to buy a quarter of humbugs or mints as a weekly treat."

Rebecca suddenly had an idea. She knew that the Clark family's home was rented and that they could now lose the roof over their heads. Martha, on the other hand, owned a nice size house, but had no one to look after her if she left the hospital due to her needs. Wouldn't it be a good idea if the Clark family moved in with the elderly lady? Mrs Griffiths was reasonably well off, if the family were to move in with her, Mrs Clark could work as her carer and cook and clean, then Martha could be allowed home. She decided to put her idea to Matron before asking Martha what she'd like herself, not to raise her hopes.

The shift breezed on by, and she even had chance to join Matron for a cup of tea and put her proposal to her in the office.

Matron Steed was a tall, thin woman, with angular bone structure and piercing sapphire blue eyes. Her grey hair swept up in a tight bun, in a style that always looked tidy and graceful. She had never married and some said it was because she had to care for her elderly mother. She studied Rebecca's face in a kindly fashion. "It certainly sounds a good idea, Nurse Jenkin, but we cannot be too idealistic about this, the elderly need a lot of attention…"

Rebecca guessed that Matron was drawing on her own experience. "But Matron, it would solve two problems in one fell swoop…"

Matron stood and began to stare out of the window, she turned with tears in her eyes, a rare sight indeed, this steely strong woman showing such emotion. "Very well, we shall put your proposal to Mrs Griffiths herself in the first instance and then to Mrs Clark to see how they both respond. It could work I suppose…" she said thoughtfully.

And so it was arranged eventually after some discussion between both parties, Martha would leave hospital and Mrs Clark would become her full-time carer, on the provision that Mrs Griffiths put a roof over the family's heads. Feeling pleased with herself, Rebecca walked the short journey home to find James in the kitchen. "Are you going into work later this morning?" she asked.

He nodded. "Yes, I was asked to start earlier yesterday as it was my first day." He ran his index finger under the collar of his white shirt.

"You'll get used to it," she said with a smile. "Mam must have starched that collar good and proper." She straightened his tie. "That's much better."

He laughed. "Yes, she's been making a big fuss over me since I started working. She even gave me a bigger supper than Dad last night when you were in work and he wasn't too pleased about it either."

"I can well imagine. Tell me James…" she seated herself at the kitchen table and her brother followed suit. "Have you noticed any change in Dad lately?"

"What do you mean?" He frowned.

"Oh nothing really, it's just he seems to lose his temper awful easily…has Aunt Lily mentioned anything?"

"No."

"I might have a word with her."

James's bottom lip protruded. "I don't much care for that sort of thing, Becky."

"What is it you're implying?"

"Talking about Father behind his back. He's a proud man…"

Yes, that was true, she knew all about that. Their father had his pride and had worked hard for everything he had in his life. "Don't worry, it shall not be tittle-tattle I can assure you, it's just that I bear some concerns about him. Now where are Mam and Dad, anyhow?"

It was unusual not to find them all seated around the table for breakfast when she came home from a long night shift.

James yawned. "Mam has gone into Merthyr, and Dad walked with her into work, he said he did not want her to go alone."

A feeling of dread that was hard to describe seeped through Rebecca's veins. It all sounded so strange. Her mother never went to Merthyr shopping this time of a morning. She feared something was wrong, and thinking about it, her mother had looked quite pale lately, maybe their father feared she was ill. That might explain his moods. If he should ever lose his dear Kathleen, she knew it would rip his world to shreds.

"If that's the case, then I shall make us both some breakfast. How about a nice boiled egg and some toast?" Her brother nodded eagerly. "Right I will slice some bread and you can toast it on the fork in front of the fire, meanwhile I'll boil the eggs and make us a nice cup of tea." James smiled gratefully, and waited as his sister sliced the bread, then took it on a plate to the living room to toast. Another thing that concerned her was that it was so unlike her mother to leave her brother to fend for himself. And that worried her greatly.

***

The ticking of the mantel clock appeared to be getting louder by the minute. James had already departed for work, and now, Rebecca could not go to sleep after her night shift knowing there might be something amiss with her mother. Usually her mother kept the parlour room immaculate: the fireplace with the chenille runner across the top, all the china ornaments in the exact same places above that, various paintings adorning the walls in a symmetrical fashion, antimacassars over the chair backs and arms, and in pride of place was an old black upright piano in the corner. James had been having lessons at a neighbour's house and was becoming quite accomplished. It appeared, though, her mother had left in a hurry this morning without time to straighten things out. Rebecca tidied around the room and then she added a few more lumps of coal to the fire and stoked it up. Dirty dishes remained in the kitchen sink, so she washed and dried those to keep herself occupied. It was another hour before she heard the front door opening. She roused herself from the settee to see her mother in the living room, removing her bonnet.

"What's going on our Becky, why haven't you gone to bed yet?" Her mother asked, cheeks reddened from the cold.

"I…well we, I mean, James and myself, we were worried as to what was going on? It's so unlike you to not be here when I return from work."

Her mother frowned momentarily and then smiled a smile that had a look of uncertainty about it. "I needed to get some shopping, t'was all..." She laid her heavy-laden basket down on the living room table.

Somehow Becky sensed there was still something amiss. "Mam?"

Her mother turned toward her. "Yes?" She blinked several times.

"There's nothing wrong is there?"

"No, why ever should there be?"

Her mother seemed to be avoiding eye contact with her and Becky thought she answered a little too quickly. "It's just a feeling I have."

"Now, don't you be worrying. I'll just put these few things away and we'll have a nice cup of tea and then you can get to your bed."

Rebecca nodded and rubbed her eyes. She must have dropped off again as the next thing she knew her mother was stood beside her with a cup of tea in her hand.

They drank their tea in silence until Rebecca finally asked again, "Mam, what is the matter?"

She caught her mother's gaze and watched her eyes brimming with tears. "I was waiting to tell your father tonight…"

Rebecca was on her feet and by her mother's side in an instant, wrapping her arm around her mother's shoulders. "Are you ill? Is that what it is?"

She shook her head. "Thankfully no, but I was gone so long as I walked to Abercanaid. Your father took me part of the way, but he had to go to work. I stopped off to see Old Dr Owen in the village and he's confirmed it…"

"Confirmed what?"

"Oh Becky, what am I to do? I am pregnant and at my age too!"

Rebecca could hardly believe what she was hearing. Her mother, whilst not exactly being elderly, was not that young any more. "Oh Mam, are you all right?" Her mother nodded. "So that's why you haven't been feeling well!" It was all beginning to make sense now.

"I'm afraid so. I was waiting to break the news tonight, but to be honest, I needed to let it out."

"What does Dad think is wrong?"

"He thinks I have some sort of stomach complaint. That's what I thought too as I have been having problems keeping my food down lately. Pregnancy was the furthest thing from my mind." She shook her head.

"Well, I tell you what you will need to do now, Mam, is rest. We can't have you up early carrying coal and lighting fires. From now on, we shall do all we can to help you."

Her mother smiled. "There's good you are to me, our Becky."

"But how do you feel about the fact you are to have another baby after all this time?"

Her mother paused for a moment. "'Tis not something I would have planned. But God has granted me good health and with all the wages coming into this house, we shall manage well enough." She smiled almost nervously, as if trying to convince herself all would be well under the circumstances.

"That's the spirit, Mam. It'll work out, you shall see…" Rebecca hoped she sounded more confident than she felt. "Now I am going to bed as I need to sleep off this night shift. Is there anything I can do for you before I go?"

Her mother shook her head and closed her eyes for a moment. "No, you get to your bed and I shall have a short nap here, that walk to Abercanaid has taken it out of me."

Becky stooped to kiss her mother's cheek, then left for her bed, her mind a whirl at the thought of what her mother had told her.

***

Later, she heard voices from downstairs and realised that both her father and brother were home from work. She wondered if her mother had told them the news yet. From the sounds of her brother's laughter drifting towards her, she guessed not.

In the semi-darkness, she poured some water into a bowl and quickly washed and dressed herself and then joined everyone downstairs, who were already seated around the kitchen table.

"How did work go today?" Rebecca asked James.

"Good. I'm beginning to like it there. I was left to deal with some clients on my own…" James declared proudly.

"What about the partners then?" Their mother asked as she ladled the steaming stew into the bowls set before them.

"They were out today, on business in Cardiff…" James explained.

"The way you're going they'll end up making you a partner there, I'll be bound," their father said, gruffly. "Just watch they don't put on you, son."

James nodded. "I will."

"It's all good experience for you," Rebecca chipped in. Then locked eyes with her mother, who shook her head as if to indicate she hadn't said anything as yet about her predicament.

They ate their meal in a convivial manner, then Becky turned to her brother. "Come on, let's go into the parlour and play chess…" she said gauging his response. Immediately his eyes lit up. She wanted to give her parents a chance to speak in peace.

She caught her mother's thankful gaze and rose to follow her brother. "I'll beat you this time, you see if I don't, Becky!" He laughed.

As they sat in front of the fire with the chessboard between them, Becky strained to see if she could hear anything coming from the kitchen, but the voices were low and muffled.

"Concentrate, Becky!" James said, as he took one of her pawns. "What's the matter with you, you seem far away?"

"I'm sorry I just have a lot on my mind, can we play this some other time?"

He frowned and reluctantly said, "All right. I suppose you're still tired after that night shift?"

She nodded. It was one way out of it without having to explain. It wasn't her place to tell her brother the news, and she had no idea as yet, how her father would react.

A few moments later, she heard the front door closing and went to find her mother who was sitting at the kitchen table. "How did he take it?"

Her mother shook her head. "It's hit him for six, Becky. You know what he's like. He's not very good sometimes at dealing with things, so he's gone out for a walk."

Rebecca guessed that during his walk, he might end up at a pub for a pint, somewhere. That's how a lot of working men dealt with things. She seated herself opposite her mother at the table. "Well at least now he knows…" she took hold of her mother's hand and softly squeezed it.

Her mother nodded. "Yes, it will need time for it to sink in for him. I can hardly believe it myself."

"Believe what?" James said brightly. Neither had noticed his entrance into the kitchen.

"Are you going to tell him or shall I?" Becky searched her mother's eyes.

"I will of course," their mother said.

James joined them at the table as his mother related the news, his eyes widening with surprise. "I can't believe it!" he said. Then his face broke out into a smile. "I hope it's a boy as then I can take him fishing and bird watching. But I won't much mind if it's a girl either…"

Rebecca and her mother exchanged glances with one another. At least someone was pleased with the news.

Chapter Two

Rebecca's father did not come home that evening before she went to bed. She had the evening off from her nursing shift so had gone for a stroll with her friend and nursing colleague, Jane. They walked as far as Cyfarthfa Castle and sat for a while chatting on a bench near the lake. She had not told Jane about her mother's pregnancy as she wanted her father to digest the news first.

When she returned home, her mother was sat at the table rifling through an old biscuit tin, she was wearing specs and appeared to be holding a newspaper clipping in her hand.

"What's that, Mam?" Becky asked.

"Oh 'tis just an old article 'bout when I sang at the Temperance Hall. The time Doctor Joseph Parry was present."

"I remember that time quite clearly, it was a wonderful evening. I remember how proud you were when Joseph Parry came back stage to speak with you and said how well you'd sang his song, Myfanwy."

Her mother clasped her hands with pride. "They were good years, to be sure."

She studied her mother's face. "You yearn for them don't you? You miss singing on stage?"

"I do, yes. But I had a family to attend to, and now even if I wanted to sing again, I am pregnant."

Becky nodded her head. "Yes."

"Don't look so forlorn, Rebecca. I am not upset about the pregnancy just a little shocked that's all."

"And what about Dad? What are you going to do if he doesn't hold with this?"

Her mother shook her head and sniffed. "He has little choice. This baby is on his or her way whether he likes it or not. After all, he did play a part in all of this."

Rebecca didn't like the thought of her parents being intimate at their time of life. They were after all, just her parents. She wasn't stupid though, she knew they had a phenomenal love for one another. And love could heal many things.

"How about I make us a cup of cocoa each before I get off to bed?" she said, wisely changing the subject.

"Aye. That would be nice. I find it easy to eat and drink of an evening, 'tis the morning times that are worst for me."

Rebecca patted her mother's shoulder. "Well from now on, Mam, you're going to take it as easy as possible.

"T'will be little chance of that I fear." She chuckled.

"Well anyhow, when I'm around, I shall help. Dad will get used to the idea, you'll see."

After drinking their cocoa together at the kitchen table, Rebecca made for her bed. She had a restless sleep as she strained during the night to hear her father's key in the door. She did not hear him return home and by the morning was up early to speak to her mother, who was still dressed in the same clothing she'd worn the night before. The dark rings beneath her eyes, testament to the fact she had not slept well either.

"He didn't come back then?" Rebecca peered into her mother's emerald eyes.

She shook her head. "I don't know what can have happened to him."

Rebecca didn't say what she was thinking, but feared her father had taken to the drink again. He'd been pretty sober for years, but she had heard tales of many years ago from Aunt Lily that her father had taken their mother's death badly and gone missing for some considerable time. It seemed if things got too much for him he wandered off to escape it all.

"Might he have gone to stay with a friend for the night, Mam?" Rebecca whispered.

Her mother shook her head and with a haunted look in her eyes replied, "No, he can't handle this, he's probably been in an ale house all night."

The front door slammed causing both to startle.

Her father stood at the kitchen doorway, looking steady and sober.

"Where have you been, Dad?" Rebecca accused.

"Well, I have not been drinking if that's what you both think..." he rubbed his chin. "I stayed with our Lily and Evan at Abercanaid. Sorry, I should have returned home last night, but it was late and I was tired, they offered me to stop over for the night."

Relief flooded through Rebecca's veins, but her mother stood stock still and through narrowed eyes said, "Well that was good of them both to put you up for the night."

"Yes, it was. Now if you don't mind I'm going to my bed and will be up at lunch time for my afternoon shift."

Neither woman said a word, but when her father was out of earshot, Rebecca said, "What's wrong Mam?"

Her mother frowned. "I know when your father is lying, Beccy. He's been elsewhere."

"I don't understand."

Her mother cleared her throat. "Never you mind, now let's get on with breakfast as your brother will be up shortly and he can't do a full day's work on an empty stomach."

Rebecca nodded, and lifted the heavy kettle from the stove to fill it with water for a cup of tea while her mother busied herself putting a pan of porridge on to boil.

"Mam…" I was thinking," Rebecca said tentatively, "you're going to need some new clothes now. How about if this afternoon, we take a trip into Merthyr to buy some nice material from the market? I could run up a couple of new dresses for you on the Singer sewing machine." The sewing machine was a treadle one that sat in the corner of the living room. It had little use of late, but when Rebecca was young, she remembered her mother sitting there, her foot tapping away on the treadle after she made lots of pretty dresses for her.

Her mother smiled. "There's a good girl you are, our Rebecca. Yes, I'd like that. But I thought you were working the afternoon shift?"

Becky shook her head. "No, I changed it. Jane needs the night shift off, so I've swapped the shift for a night one instead and have got her afternoon off."

Her mother frowned. "But you seem to have done a lot of night shifts lately?"

"I know, but I don't mind though. It means I can be around in the day if you need me and Dad will be here at night."

Her mother rolled her eyes as if she now doubted that prospect. "Well, we'll see. He's busy with his work and has the odd night shift himself, but at least James will be here should I need him."

***

20

Both women left for Merthyr town before even Rebecca's father had risen from bed. She had a strong feeling of dread as if her parents were somehow drifting apart. Something needed to be done to get both back on course.

When they arrived at the town, it was market day, so full of hustle and bustle. Rebecca was glad in a way as it helped take her mother's mind off her problems. They ended up choosing a dark brown tweed material so Rebecca could make her mother a skirt and some cream coloured cotton for a blouse.

"I'll make you some more garments as and when you need them, Mam," Rebecca advised.

They stopped off at shop for faggots and peas, which the stall vendor scooped into an earthenware bowl the women had brought along, before taking the journey back home. It was easy enough for Becky, but her mother being in a pregnant state so late in life, found the walk strenuous and every so often had to stop for a breath.

"Are you all right, Mam?" Rebecca asked, when they reached the Brecon Road near St Mary's Catholic Church.

Her mother nodded. "I'd like to go inside and speak to the Father, if you don't mind?" she looked to her daughter for affirmation.

It had been a long time since her mother had been to the Catholic Church. Although brought up as Catholic in Ireland, since marrying Rebecca's father, she had attended various chapels in the town.

"I understand, Mam. I'll wait here for you, if you like?"

Her mother nodded gratefully. Rebecca guessed she wanted to discuss the news of the pregnancy with a priest.

"No, you go on ahead, Becky. I'll be home soon."

It was only a short journey to their home in The Walk area of the town. "Well I'll get back home and prepare the vegetables for tonight's meal."

"Tis good you are to me," her mother said, turning towards the gates of the church.

Rebecca watched her walk up the drive way and ascend the steps of the church all the while hoping all would be well.

***

A couple of months later, Rebecca was about to take her break during her shift at the hospital as she brushed past two women in the corridor who had been visiting a relative on the ward. She vaguely recognised them as being neighbours in the area. One of the women glanced at her and whispered something behind her gloved hand.

"Is anything the matter, ladies?" Rebecca asked.

The woman dropped her hand and shook her head. So Rebecca thought no more of it and made her way to the canteen for her evening meal. Cook made a lovely hearty stew a couple of times a week and she was looking forward to the beef and dumplings in a rich sauce. It helped to sustain her for the rest of her shift.

On the way back to the ward feeling sated, she noticed the women still hanging around in the corridor, occasionally glancing in her direction.

"Whatever's the matter with those two?" Jane, who was working the same shift, asked.

"I've no idea, but I intend finding out." Rebecca marched over to the women again.

"Visiting time is over now so why are you both hanging around here, don't you have homes to go to, ladies?"

"I suppose one could ask the same of your father, Rebecca!" one of the ladies smirked.

The other tittered.

"Whatever do you mean?"

"Well he's been spending a lot of time lately under Mary Kinney's roof!"

Rebecca could hardly believe her ears. It was true that her father had been spending a lot of time away from the home since her mother's pregnancy but another woman, surely not? Widowed Mary Kinney had the reputation of being a warm-hearted woman, but she also seemed to attract the men. It was rumoured that many a married man had passed that way leaving her supplies of coal and food so she could take care of her four young children to save them from going into the work house.

Rebecca paused a moment, took in a deep composing breath and let it out again. "Yes, well we all know about that," she said firmly. "My father goes there to help a widow in distress. It's not what you think at all."

She said that to save face, not really knowing anything about it at all. Both women exchanged glances and the one who'd spoken, looked Rebecca up and down as if to say, "Poor deluded girl." They turned on their heels and left the ward, their footsteps echoing along the corridor leaving Rebecca wounded to the core. Now she was left with a dilemma of whether to tell her mother of the circulating rumour or not.

When she arrived home her mother was getting ready for bed, James was already fast asleep. "Where's Dad?" she asked, as she removed her cape, hung it up on a hook behind the door and sat down at the kitchen table.

Her mother glanced at her and turning her back said, "He'll be home soon enough. Would you like some cocoa our Becca?"

"Yes, but please sit down first, Mam," she said softly.

Her mother turned and with lowered eyelids, sat down at the table opposite her daughter. "What about the cocoa?"

"That can wait. I need to talk to you, Mam." She touched her mother's pallid hand across the table. "Have you heard what people are saying?"

Her mother shook her head and looked at her daughter. "I don't want to listen to gossip, Becky."

"Please, Mam. I heard something today and I feel there might be something in it. Two women at the hospital told me that Dad has been visiting Mary Kinney's house lately."

Her mother's mouth fell open. "Oh Becca, I didn't realise you were going to say that. I thought you might have said he'd been staying late at the pub." Her hand flew to her mouth.

"So you had no idea?"

She shook her head. "I just thought maybe he'd taken to the drink again like he has done in the past when he has a few problems."

"It might only be gossip though, Mam. So we need to be careful, but I couldn't live here and not say what I heard this evening."

"No, you were right to tell me of this, Rebecca." Her mother nodded.

Rebecca studied her mother's face. She looked so pale and worn out these days. "So what will you do? Have words with him?"

"I don't know if I have the fight in me anymore. I am so tired with this latest pregnancy."

"Mam, you have got to fight. Don't give up. You can't allow him to think he can spend all that time with another woman. You are his wife. You gave up a lot for him and left your family for that man…" She hoped her words were hitting home.

Her mother remained quiet for a moment, then a spark ignited her emerald eyes. "Yes, you're right. I went against my family's wishes and left Utah and the Mormon faith to come here. I've been a good wife and now he should be here at my side. He should be home by now not out there in the arms of another woman. Right, I'm going to make the cocoa then I want you off to bed so you don't hear what I have to say to him when he returns."

"That's the spirit Mam. But take care as we don't know if the Mary Kinney story is true or just gossip."

"No, don't worry. I won't accuse right away, I'll give him a chance to explain himself."

Rebecca stood and walked over to her mother's side of the table and planted a kiss on top of her head. "You stay put Mam and I'll make the cocoa."

Her mother patted Rebecca's hand. "There's good to me you are…"

***

Rebecca strained to listen from her bedroom to hear her father's key in the door and her parents speaking downstairs, but she was so tired after her long shift at the hospital that she fell into a deep sleep without knowing what happened.

When she awoke the following morning a shaft of sunlight was filtering in through the window and the smell of bacon cooking wafted up the stairs. Her father loved bacon, so her mother must have been making his breakfast.

Rebecca walked quickly down the stairs, stopping in her tracks to see James at the stove, flipping some bacon rashers over in the frying pan.

"What's going on?" She wrinkled her nose.

"I'm making breakfast for Mam."

"Why didn't you wake me instead?"

"I did want to but you looked in such a deep sleep, you work too hard, Becca…"

She smiled. "Yes, but where are Mam and Dad?"

"I don't know where Dad is, but Mam is tired, so I told her to stay in bed."

"Look I tell you what. Go get some coal out of the cwtch and set the fire to keep the living room warm. I'll finish breakfast." She'd never seen James cook a thing in his life before and feared he might

24

spoil the breakfast, though he did tend to have a lot of common sense and had probably seen their mother do it often enough.

"Thanks." He seemed happy with that and left through the back door. Before too long there was a plate of eggs and bacon each for the three of them and a steaming pot of tea brewed.

James washed his coal-dusted hands in a tin bowl in the scullery, then dried them on a towel on the hook. "Shall I take Mam's breakfast up to her?"

"No, you go on ahead and eat yours, else you'll be late for work. I'll take Mam's to her." She placed the plate of eggs and bacon and a cup of tea on a tray and tentatively carried it to her parents' bedroom. Her mother was sitting up in bed when she arrived, her long auburn hair now down over her shoulders. Rebecca set the tray down on a bedside table and sat on the bed.

"There's good to me you are…" Her mother said, her eyes filling with tears.

"Mam? What happened last night? Did Dad come home?"

Her mother shook her head. Rebecca took her in her arms allowing her mother to cry. This was all getting too much. "Eat your breakfast Mam. I'm going over to that woman's house as soon as I've had my breakfast."

"No Rebecca. If you go I'm coming with you!" Her mother stated firmly.

Rebecca softened. "All right, but take your time. There's no need to rush." Somehow though she knew her mother needed to speak to that woman as soon as possible.

***

After James had left for work and both women were washed and dressed, they marched down to Mary Kinney's house. It was a dry morning and the weather was beginning to improve a little. The Kinney house was well known on Brecon Road. The houses there were much smaller than their own nicely-fronted house on The Walk. As they passed St Mary's church, Rebecca noticed her mother close her eyes and cross herself.

As they rounded the corner just after the church, turning right, they saw several children playing in the street and a couple of horse and carts passed them by. They neared the house, Rebecca's heart racing as she took her mother's hand and paused. "Whatever happens I am here to support you, Mam."

Her mother nodded. Her pregnancy now very much in evidence.

Rebecca took a deep breath and rapped sharply on the door. The sounds of children's excitable voices reverberated from the inside, and then the door swung open. A woman stood there, hair messed up, rings beneath her eyes, carrying a child in her arms who was wrapped in a blanket, Welsh fashion.

Relieved, Rebecca took a step back. There was no way anything was going on with this woman, she looked haggard and bedraggled. "What do you want?" the woman barked.

"Mary Kinney?" Rebecca's mother asked.

"No. I'm her sister…" she turned behind her and yelled down the passageway. "Mary!"

A younger looking fair-haired woman, with glittering blue eyes and a voluptuous bosom, showed up at the door. "Mrs Jenkin?" she said in recognition.

Rebecca stood there open-mouthed. How did this woman know her mother?

"Yes, I am," her mother said sharply.

The woman smiled wickedly. "Come in, I've been expecting you…"

***

Rebecca and her mother followed both women into the darkened passage way. The house reeked of ammonia and carbolic soap. As they entered what appeared to be some sort of living room, Rebecca realised why. There were baby's nappies drying on a large wooden clothes horse in front of the coal fire. Two infants were sitting in the corner pushing a toy train back and forth making 'choo, choo', noises and an older boy and girl were clearing a small table near the window.

"Please sit yourselves down," Mary advised.

Rebecca brushed her skirts down before sitting on a wooden chair at the table and her mother took the other. The woman with the baby, ushered all the children into the scullery, while Mary herself pulled up a wooden stool and seated herself. The furniture in this small house was sparse with not even enough for comfort or to seat the entire family.

"So you know why we're here then?" Rebecca studied Mary's face. It was pretty, her eyes being her best feature, though years of hardship had ingrained her skin with a couple of wrinkles. But it was evident, she was years younger than her mother, maybe not that much older than herself.

"Well I guessed you'd come to look for your father, Rebecca." Mary straightened her pose.

"How do you know my name?"

"He talks about you often."

Rebecca's mother narrowed her eyes. "All of us?"

"Yes, you too, Kathleen. He's told me all about how you used to sing at the Temperance Hall and on stage in London too…Very proud of you he is."

"Now look here," Rebecca's temperature rose. "What has my Dad got to do with a woman like you?"

Mary had the good grace to look down for a moment and then she brought her gaze to meet with Rebecca's. "I'm his mistress. I have been for some time now…"

Rebecca's stomach turned. She wanted to slap the woman across her pretty face and ruin all her features, how dare she take away her father. As if sensing what her daughter was thinking, her mother shook her head and said, "Aye, 'tis all well and good you claiming to be his mistress, but what kind of hold do you have on him? He's only here because I'm pregnant. Men are like that. They'll go elsewhere if needs be."

Mary shook her head. "I'm afraid you're wrong. You both are. The baby my sister is nursing in the shawl is his."

Rebecca gritted her teeth and got on her feet towering over the woman. "You liar! My Dad would never have a child with another woman. It's just not possible."

"Of course it's possible," Mary said straightening. "Your mother is pregnant, isn't she? It proves he is capable. He was only here crying to me the other night that he couldn't cope with another mouth to feed!"

So her Mam was right, her father had been lying about his whereabouts that night he failed to return home. Rebecca sat back down and glanced at her mother, who she expected to be crying with emotion, but instead she sat there with a steely look of determination on her face.

After letting out a breath, finally Kathleen asked, "Well, what is it you want from my husband, Mary?"

Mary looked at them both. "Love," she said sadly, shaking her head. "It's the one thing he can't give me and that's because he loves you, Kathleen." For a moment Rebecca thought the woman was about to cry.

Kathleen nodded. "I understand."

Rebecca stared at her mother hardly believing her own ears. Why wasn't she slapping this woman hard across the face?

"How long has it been going on?" Rebecca demanded.

"About three and a half years, I suppose," Mary nodded as if her calculations proved correct.

"Three and a half years? Even before I trained as a nurse? I can't believe this."

"I can…" Kathleen said. "It was around about the time he started drinking again."

Rebecca turned toward her mother. "But how did we never work it out before now, Mam?"

"Because as he works shifts, we never question if he's late from work, has to change them or works extra hours. He's probably been staying at your house all times of the day and night, Mary?"

Mary nodded. She was no longer full of herself as she had been when they came to the front door. "I'm sorry Mrs Jenkin and to you too, Rebecca."

"Sorry isn't good enough in my book!" Rebecca snapped.

"Now don't go blaming Mary," her mother advised. "She's had it hard by all accounts since her husband died at the ironworks. She's only trying to survive like the rest of us. Life in Merthyr can be hard especially with young children. It's your father who has done wrong here by all of us. He's wronged me and he's wronged his own children too. Though what made him do this is anyone's guess and to think that I trusted him so. I must have been a fool."

Rebecca heard the crack of emotion in her mother's voice. "No, not a fool Mam, you were just blinded by love."

Her mother looked up through watery eyes and addressed Mary. "Do you love my husband?"

"Yes, I believe I do," Mary answered truthfully.

28

"Well if that's the case you shall have him. He's all yours…" Her mother stated firmly.

Rebecca's mouth fell open. "I can't believe this, Mam. Why aren't you fighting for him?"

"What's the use, Rebecca? He made a choice when he betrayed us with Mary. I don't want him under the same roof anymore."

It was true and now as it began to sink in, Rebecca realised her mother was right.

***

When the women returned home, Rebecca's mother sent her to the loft to find the old trunk to pack her father's belongings. It was hard for them both as they emptied it to find her mother's, now yellowed wedding dress. "Such happy memories of that day," she said, as a tear coursed down her cheek. "We married in Cardiff after that long gruelling journey from Utah…I bought that dress at a beautiful gown shop in the area before we travelled to Merthyr to live near your Aunt Lily and Uncle Evan. Where did it all go wrong for us?"

Rebecca hugged her mother. Not knowing what to say as they carried on unpacking the trunk. There were creased programmes from her mother's performances from both her days at the Temperance Hall and on the London stage. Old black and white postcards as the infamous, 'Kathleen O'Hara', as she twirled a parasol and raised her skirts. Her mother blushed with embarrassment, but Rebecca rather liked to see that side of her mother, carefree and happy.

When they'd finished, they set about packing her father's police uniform, day clothing and best suit in the trunk along with his books, boots, shoes, and other items. Rebecca felt like crying herself as it seemed as though he'd died. And maybe in a way, the father she knew, had.

Finally she closed the lid and secured the lock. Then following her mother's instructions, she called to Bill's, a discreet neighbour's house, who loaded the trunk on the back of his horse and cart and delivered it to Mary's home. Now all that they had to do was wait for her father's return.

James was dispatched to a friend's house when he'd had his tea, much to his amusement. He had no idea what was going on.

Then just after six o'clock they heard her father's police boots on the path outside. "I'll go to my room Mam, but won't be far away if you need me," Rebecca said wisely.

Her mother nodded, lips set in a firm line. This time Rebecca realised she meant business, she wasn't about to take any lies or excuses.

Straining to listen from her room, she heard her mother's raised voice and then she thought she heard the two of them sobbing downstairs, and within the half hour the front door slammed, and her father was gone. Rebecca rushed to her mother's side. "Well done, Mam!"

Her mother turned toward her, "Oh Becca, what have I done?

***

The following months were not easy at home and it was not the same without their father. The house was quiet and it was as though something were amiss. James took his father's infidelity to heart but refused to speak about the situation. The family just carried on almost as though the head of the house were dead. But to his credit, he left adequate money for the family to survive on each month when he received his pay, even though both Rebecca and her brother were already contributing toward the home.

Rebecca worried about her mother, who was now in her eighth month of pregnancy. Bill, the next door neighbour, called in every so often to check she was all right when both Rebecca and James were at work. Many a time he either took Kathleen on his pony and trap to town to get shopping or offered her some vegetables from his flourishing allotment. He was a nice man, who had been widowed for the past couple of years, but Rebecca knew her mother was still grieving for her father.

The weather was scorching hot. It was difficult to get comfortable at home, all the windows were open and they all tried to dress as coolly as possible. Sometimes Rebecca longed to take the short walk to the Brecon Road with a view to pleading with her father to return home as her mother needed him. They all did really. He was sorely missed. His empty chair around the table and favourite armchair their mother would not allow anyone to sit in, a testament to that.

When Rebecca arrived on the ward for her afternoon shift, the atmosphere seemed extremely tense. Doctor Daniel Evans approached her as several nurses rushed this way and that.

"We've got some important visitors expected this afternoon, Nurse Jenkin," he declared. "I need you by my side to accompany me on a ward round."

She wrinkled her nose. "Yes, that's fine Doctor Evans. But who are these important visitors might I ask?"

"They're from the Hospital Board of Inspectors. They'll be checking for both efficiency and cleanliness here. Matron managed to persuade the nurses to do a very thorough job cleaning every possible nook and cranny earlier today; and to work longer hours to get the ward up to speed, but then again Matron already has high standards."

"But why is it me you wish to accompany you, Doctor?" She blinked several times, genuinely surprised he'd chosen her as they tended to not get on with one another. She could not pander to any whims and found herself standing up to his constant demands when the ward was over worked.

He stared hard at her. "Because Nurse Jenkin, you are efficiency itself. I shall expect you at my office at 3 o'clock sharp."

That was compliment indeed from Doctor Evans. A hot flush spread over her cheeks and she hoped he wouldn't notice. "Yes, Doctor. I shall be there. You can count on me."

He smiled and turned on his heel to head off in the direction of Matron's office.

Daniel Evans was quite handsome when he smiled, his brown eyes lit up, yet he did not smile that often. Most of the nurses feared him, but sometimes she noticed the mask slip as a sliver of humanity shone through. That said, he was a fine doctor. One of the best.

She carried on with her tasks giving out medicines, checking bandages and making sure the patients were clean and comfortable. Matron was extremely picky that afternoon as though under duress from the thought of having important visitors inspecting her ward. So fussy, she sent one of the new nurses off to iron her uniform. As she put it, "It looks as if a litter of puppies has slept on that apron and dress, Nurse Williams!"

The Inspection Board showed up on the ward at a half past three. They comprised of: an elderly gentleman, dressed in black from top-to-toe, with a white crisp shirt and black cravat; two doctors from London; and a well-to-do looking lady who peered down half spectacles beneath her very silly feathered hat. Around her neck, she'd draped a fox fur which made Rebecca shiver as the beady brown eyes bored a hole into her.

They asked a lot of questions on the ward round, which a pale Doctor Evans answered methodically, and when he was at a loss for words, Rebecca herself chipped in with her own knowledge of the patients and the hospital.

When the group departed to take tea with Matron in her office, Doctor Evans sighed deeply.

"How do you think that went?" Rebecca looked at him as the colour returned to his face.

"I don't know to be honest. I answered as best as I could and thank you for helping me out. Sometimes they asked difficult questions."

"That's all right. I was pleased to and I think you coped remarkably well. That lady with the fox fur and silly hat unnerved me somewhat."

Doctor Evans began to chuckle and carried on laughing like he couldn't stop. She'd never seen him laugh so much before. "Oh yes, that hat was extremely silly, wasn't it?"

"Sshh…" Rebecca scolded good-humouredly, "in case Matron hears…"

He stifled a giggle. "Oh you have cheered me up, Nurse Jenkin." Then he stopped laughing and his eyes took on a serious expression. For a moment she feared he was going to reprimand her, but then he said, "Rebecca, would you please do me the honour of allowing me to take you out some time?"

Her cheeks suffused with heat and her mouth became dry. She didn't know what to say. "With you, Doctor?"

"Yes, don't be so surprised. What do you say?"

She hesitated before replying, "Yes, all right then. I was surprised at you asking me as I thought you might already have a sweetheart?"

He shook his head. "Up until now I haven't had that much time for one, but there's a special evening on at the Temperance Hall next week I'd like to take you to."

"That sounds lovely," she enthused. It would help to take her mind off her worries as she was so worried about her mother and how she'd cope when the baby was born. She'd have to ensure James helped out that night. Or if he couldn't, maybe Bill from next door could keep an eye on her. She couldn't leave her mother alone at this stage.

The Doctor smiled one last time and left the ward in the direction of the canteen. Rebecca tidied up all the patients' notes on the trolley and wheeled them towards the nursing station. She wondered what was going on with the visitors in Matron's office and what they were saying to her.

It was a full hour before they emerged and nodding politely, pushed past her as they departed, no doubt on their way back to Cardiff or London from whence they came.

Tentatively she knocked on Matron's door.

"Enter!" Matron Steed boomed. There was still evidence of the discarded tea cups and cake crumbs from the visitors on the desk.

Rebecca walked into the room. "Would you like me to clear those for you, Matron?" she asked.

"Yes, thank you, Nurse Jenkin." Matron averted her glance and began writing in a large ledger. Rebecca cleared her throat. "Was there anything else?" Matron looked up.

"Yes. I was just wondering how it went with the Board?"

Matron glared over her spectacles. "They shall be filing a report soon enough no doubt. But I have no feedback to give as yet. Can you close the door on your way out please, Nurse Jenkin?"

In other words, *"Shut up Nurse Jenkin, your services are dispensed with!"*

She hefted the heavy tray and managed to manoeuvre her way out of the room, whilst pushing the door shut with her elbow.

There was no one around to do the washing up but herself, so she boiled some water and made about washing the cups, saucers and plates in the steaming, soapy water. She had just wiped up and put the crockery away, wiping her hands on a towel when Jane, her colleague, popped her head around the door.

"Coming to the canteen for your break?"

She nodded. "Yes, I'll just be a moment."

Jane edged her way into the room and closed the door behind her. "Any news on the report from the Hospital Board?"

Rebecca hung the towel back on a peg beneath the counter. "No, and if there is, Matron isn't prepared to say so."

"Hmmm if you ask me I think she's concerned. Although I can't see what there is to be worried about."

"Me neither. But fair play to her, although she keeps us on our toes, she only wants what's best for everyone. She has high standards."

Jane giggled. "Yes, but she is an old battle axe at times. How did it go accompanying Doctor Daniel Evans?"

Rebecca noticed a gleam in her friend's eyes when she mentioned his name and wondered if she had designs on him. "Oh, fine. He was highly professional throughout the whole inspection..."

"I thought he would be," Jane admitted, "but you have to agree he's the most handsome doctor in this hospital."

Rebecca smiled and nodded, knowing her friend's words were true. "Come on, let's go and have something to eat. I'm famished."

As they paced the corridor towards the canteen, Rebecca couldn't help smiling at the thought of spending the evening with the handsome Doctor Daniel Evans next week.

"What are you grinning at?" Jane stopped in her tracks and studied Rebecca's beaming face.

"Oh nothing," Rebecca lied. There was no way she wanted to share this news. There were enough gossips around, and she had no idea how things would turn out, but they should prove to be most interesting. "I'm just in a good mood that's all…"

Chapter Three

The following week seemed to drag along, but soon it was time for Rebecca's date with Doctor Daniel Evans. "It's the Cyfarthfa Brass Band playing there tonight," he said, when he met her at the end of the road to accompany her to the Temperance Hall for the evening. Rebecca held her breath. He looked astonishingly handsome out of his doctor's white coat. Now he stood in best twill suit, sharp shirt and bow tie. He also wore a bowler hat which she'd never seen before, as inside the hospital of course, he never wore a hat. Rebecca had chosen to wear a long black skirt with white frilled blouse, buttoned up to the neck and pinned with a pretty pearl brooch.

Around her shoulders she wore her best stole and a fetching wide-brimmed hat with pink silk ribbon and artificial tea roses, on her head.

"You look very nice tonight," he said linking arms with her as they walked past St. Mary's Church.

"Thank you, kind sir. You look very smart yourself. The hat and stole belong to my mother, she used to wear them when she appeared on stage.

He stopped a moment and looking at her, quirked a brow. "Your mother was an actress?"

"No, a singer. Actually she once sang at the Temperance Hall in front of Doctor Joseph Parry, and also for a time on the London Stage. Kathleen O'Hara as was. She kept it as her stage name even after marriage."

"Well, well. I do believe I've heard that name, by all accounts she sang like an angel."

"Yes that's her. She doesn't bother now of course..." They both fell into step once again.

"Why's that? Has the voice gone all together?"

"No. It's just that she's busy at home and now she's about to have another child."

"I see, so she will be an older mother."

"Yes, and I worry about her now that she and my father are living apart."

He stopped to look at her. "Living apart?"

"Yes, he has another woman and fathered a child by her, we were shocked to discover this only recently. Actually he's living down the road just there." She pointed in the general direction.

His features softened. "Oh, I think I understand. So that must be difficult for you all?"

"Sometimes it is, yes. Although he still provides for us all, sends some of his wages per month, but doesn't set a foot inside the door."

"Maybe he regrets his actions?"

"Possibly. I think my mother would have given him another chance if it wasn't for the fact he had fathered another child."

"Yes, that is a difficult step to overcome I am sure, Rebecca. But tonight you must put such thoughts out of your mind and enjoy yourself at the concert. It will do you good."

They began walking once again, and then, she smiled as they turned the corner. It was nice to be in Daniel's company and he seemed more relaxed when he was away from the hospital.

***

The band played well that evening, blasting forth a selection of Quadrilles and Polkas. The piece de resistance was, 'The Tydfil Overture' which was composed and arranged by Joseph Parry for the Cyfarthfa Band. As Rebecca and Daniel, passed through the foyer on the way out amongst the throng, he turned to her and said, "How would you like to dine with me?"

She blinked. "Right now?"

"I can think of no better time than the present."

She nodded and he took her arm and led her to The Bentley Hotel, which was a fairly new establishment in the centre of the town. It was a large imposing building with brass light fittings outside, large windows and an opulent reception area.

Daniel led her to the restaurant area which was dimly lit and plush in appearance where other diners, who were very well dressed, sat enjoying their meals.

They were shown to a window table which had a small flickering candle and arrangement of red roses around it. Rebecca had never been anywhere so grand before. "Do you often eat this way?" she asked.

He stroked his chin. "Not that often in all honesty, but my father has made friends with the proprietor, Mr. Thomas Bentley from

Dublin. We've been told to expect a generous discount when we come here." He laughed. "Your expression Rebecca, is priceless."

She snapped her mouth shut. "It's just such a fine establishment; no one I know would come here."

"Maybe not. But does that bother you?"

In truth it didn't. It was just all so new to her. "No, not at all. Anyhow, you said the owner comes from Dublin, so how does your father know him?"

"From Lodge meetings."

"Oh, the Masonic Lodge you mean?"

"Yes. The local Cambrian Lodge."

She had heard of that mysterious society of business men who gathered to meet, but wasn't sure exactly what it was all about. All she understood about it was that they somehow helped one another out as well as several charitable causes in the town. She wrinkled her nose. "What does your father do exactly?"

"He's a jeweller to be exact. He owns a small shop in Aberdare selling watches, rings, that kind of thing. It's not a big business but it ticks along nicely, if you pardon the pun."

She giggled, then composed herself. "But he comes to Merthyr often?"

"Yes, he was brought up here but my mother is of Spanish descent."

"Ah I remember you telling me now."

At that point a waiter arrived to take their order.

"What would you like to have, Rebecca?" Daniel asked, as he studied her features.

"You choose for me, please." Her heart was beating so quickly, she feared it might burst and hoped that he couldn't hear it.

"We'll both have the sirloin steaks with new potatoes and a selection of seasonal vegetables. Oh and a bottle of red wine, the house speciality," Daniel said, snapping shut the menu.

"Happy with that choice?" he asked as the waiter departed.

"Yes more than happy," she beamed, and then she gazed out the window to see people passing on by the high street, beneath the glow of the street lights. There was a kind of magic in the air tonight and Doctor Daniel Evans had more than a little to do with that.

***

Rebecca felt heady with something she could not quite put her finger on, maybe it was due to a romantic evening or maybe just the wine, but she was in a relaxed mood as they walked home toward the Brecon Road. Daniel had offered to hail a Hansom for her, but she declined saying it was such a lovely evening she preferred the walk.

As they rounded the corner by the Catholic Church, her heart thudded. There were several people outside the garden gate of her house. The street now flooded with darkness apart from the odd street gaslight and oil lamps inside several homes. "Mam!" she shouted, as she ran in the direction of her house with Daniel in attendance behind.

Two women and a man were outside shaking their heads. "What's happened?" she asked frantically. The old woman, she recognised as Mrs Henry from up the road.

"Your mother's gone into labour..." the elderly woman replied.

"Is James still with her?" Now she felt guilty for having been out so long.

"Yes," the man replied. "He's sent Bill from next door out to look for your father."

Rebecca and Daniel pushed past them and went into the house where James was one side of the bed in their mother's bedroom tending to her with a cold flannel, and there was a matronly woman the other side.

"Sorry, but who are you?" Rebecca asked brusquely.

"I'm Gwen Richards. I've delivered a few babies in my time, Bill came to fetch me."

"Thank you," Rebecca let out a composing breath.

Their mother appeared to be slightly out of it as if keeping her eyes tightly shut might push away whatever it was that had been happening to her.

"How long has Mam been like this?" she questioned her brother.

"About two hours now, Bec. She started getting pains an hour or so after you left. I think the baby's on its way, but it won't come out." He turned his head away.

Becca realised this wasn't something he should see. "James, go downstairs and boil a couple of kettles and make sure you light a fire. Even though the weather has been warm, we need to keep that room heated for the baby."

He nodded and let out what she assumed was a breath of relief. Then turning towards the trio and his mother, he asked, "What about if Bill finds Dad, am I allowed to let him come up here?"

"Yes…" Their mother answered quickly and then she groaned as if in pain. It was as if the mere mention of her husband brought her back to life.

Daniel removed his jacket and turned to face James. "When the kettle is boiled, please bring a jug of hot water up here and a bowl, soap and towel, as I will need to assist in this delivery.

James's eyebrows shot up. Realising that her brother didn't for the life of him know who Daniel was, Rebecca explained, "This is Doctor Daniel Evans from the General Hospital…"

Their mother smiled weakly. James nodded and left the room.

"I've never delivered a baby before," Daniel explained, "but I have witnessed a few deliveries during my training in Cardiff."

He set about removing his jacket and rolled up his shirt sleeves. Rebecca hung the jacket on a hook behind the door. She took Gwen to one side of the room and whispered, "Do you think this might turn out to be a difficult delivery?"

The woman nodded. "I think it's due to your mother's age. It's not easy childbirth when you're over forty. It happens to so many women though."

Now Rebecca was beginning to worry, she hadn't taken much account of her mother's age before as she was so fit and healthy usually, but the past couple of months had really taken it out of her.

They heard the front door slam and then footsteps up the stairs. Then there was a knock on the bedroom door and Rebecca went to answer to find Bill stood there with his cap in hand. "Sorry Bec, I couldn't find your father, but have left a few messages with the neighbours down on the Brecon Road and in a couple of the pubs in case he shows up there."

She nodded. He strained to look over her shoulder. "Is your Mam all right? Anything else I can do?"

"Nothing for now," she bit her lip, "not unless you can take the pony and trap and go to my aunt's house in Abercanaid? She's married to the minister, Evan Davies. They live next door to the chapel. Her name is Lily. If you can knock them up and ask if they know of my father's whereabouts, that would be a big help. Thanks for all you're doing, Bill."

"It's nothing," he said modestly. "If anything should ever happen to your Mam, I would be most upset."

"SShh keep your voice down," she warned. But in all honesty she didn't think her mother heard a word of it.

"Sorry. I'm just a bit sweet on her that's all..." he lowered his voice.

Rebecca stopped in her tracks. Why hadn't she realised it before? Bill really cared for her mother, he had helped her a lot this past few months, and for all she knew, when she and James were both at work, they might have spent their days together too.

She laid a hand on Bill's shoulder. "Try not to worry too much," she whispered. "I've got a doctor here with me and a woman who has delivered several babies. You just go and find my father so he can be here, too."

Bill nodded eagerly and he turned to make his way back down the stairs.

The next few hours were horrendous. Her mother was spiking a temperature, her skin hot to the touch and her night gown clinging to her slight form. Rebecca had to keep her cool by bathing her with cold wet flannels on Daniel's orders. She also gave her mother plenty of water to drink.

Rebecca asked Gwen to prepare a crib from an old chest drawer, which was lined with a clean torn sheet and a couple of blankets.

James made them all a cup of tea to calm their nerves and at 3.30 am Bill returned to report he had been unable to find their father. Lily had told him that she suspected he had left Merthyr all together. She said she would be up first thing in the morning if they needed assistance. Evan had said he would encourage his congregation to offer prayers for both Kathleen and the baby.

There was nothing else anyone could do but hope and pray that both mother and baby would be spared.

As the sun rose, something began to happen, and her mother said she felt like pushing.

"Okay," Gwen said, rising from the chair she had been seated in. "Take my hand one side and your daughter's the other, Kathleen. Now don't push too soon. Take nice deep breaths and go with each contraction.

Daniel stood at the bottom of the bed monitoring the situation.

"I can see the head…" he said finally. "Now when you give a nice big push I am going to pull and turn it slightly. That's called, 'crowning'. Then hopefully we'll get a shoulder through one at a time."

Kathleen nodded, and began groaning loudly as she pushed. "That's it…" Daniel said.

The head appeared and he turned it slightly and one shoulder slipped out, then another, and there was a large gush of blood and liquid as the baby was delivered onto Kathleen's stomach.

"My baby, my baby!" she cried.

Rebecca frowned as Daniel stared and said, "Hang on something else is happening…"

Rebecca's hands flew to her mouth in horror. "What's wrong?"

"There's nothing wrong," he smiled. "There's another one here!"

Tears filled Rebecca's eyes as Daniel instructed Kathleen to push again and this time another was delivered, even before they had the chance to check over the first baby.

"Twins!" he said brightly, as he handed the second over and both babies were placed on Kathleen's chest.

"Of course I should have realised," she wept. "Your father is one of a twin, Rebecca."

"They're both boys too, Mam. Just like Dad and his brother Delwyn, in Utah."

Both women began to cry as Daniel delivered the afterbirths and Gwen took the babies away to wash them. She tied a length of twine tightly around the cords and Daniel who had earlier instructed James to boil up a pair of scissors, snipped the cords. Gwen cleaned the babies, and James, who was extremely excited, quickly got another drawer prepared as a make shift bed for the second baby.

Later, when all was calmed down, and they all enjoyed another cup of tea, Rebecca asked her mother, "What are you going to call them, Mam?"

"Benjamin and Daniel," she replied. "It's a pity we never found your father so he could see them both." A tear coursed down her mother's cheek. Rebecca wiped it away with her handkerchief and squeezed her hand in reassurance.

A fine pity indeed! Rebecca silently cursed the man who had abandoned his family and walked out on his young sons before they were even born.

***

Having an extra mouth to feed had really shocked the family, they'd been expecting one new addition, but not two. Also now that their father could not be located, there was no extra money coming in. Rebecca had even called to see his mistress, Mary Kinney, but she had no clue where he was either. Rebecca hesitated from calling in at the police station to check his whereabouts, not to cause further trouble for her father.

It was only the help of her own Aunt Lily that stopped her from giving up her job as a nurse. She was always on call to help her sister-in-law with the care of the twins while Rebecca worked shifts. James did all he could too, but life had become hard.

It was while she was in work, one afternoon a few weeks after the birth of her twin brothers, that she was summoned to the matron's office.

She entered tentatively as Matron Steed asked her to take a seat, closed the door and seated herself at her desk.

Rebecca twisted her hands on her lap, her palms beginning to perspire as she wondered what she had done wrong.

"You can relax, Nurse Jenkin…" Matron said, gazing over the rim of her spectacles. "I've asked to see you here as I have some news for you that you might in fact quite like." Rebecca sat up in her seat. "Remember the Hospital Board were here recently?"

Of course she did, how could she possibly forget? "Yes, I do, Matron Steed."

"Well, you'll be pleased to know we were awarded a high grade for the efficiency and cleanliness of this ward."

"That's good to hear, Matron." Rebecca let out a long breath.

"That's not all. The Board was so impressed by you, Nurse Jenkin, they'd like to offer you a job as Ward Sister on the Isolation ward here. As you are well aware, it's a ward for serious diseases like tuberculosis and a variety of fevers. There is talk that eventually an Isolation Hospital will be built in this town, and should that day come, then your experience here should stand you in good stead."

Rebecca's mouth popped open, she closed it again. "I...I don't know what to say." This had completely taken her by surprise. It wasn't something she'd considered before.

"Don't say anything for now, just take your time to think about it as there will be a lot of work involved, running your own ward mainly. It would be a step up the ladder for you, but would be more work for you to take on board."

She relaxed her posture. "I shall certainly bear it in mind, Matron."

"Very well then, Nurse. But please if you can let me know by the weekend so I can inform the Board one way or the other, it would be most courteous of you."

Rebecca left Matron's office with her head in a spin, it was all she could ever dream of and more, but she needed to bear in mind that it was more helpful for her to be close by for her mother and the twins with this promotion of position, at least it would be at the same hospital. The twins were thriving well, but her mother was extremely tired. She reminded herself that it wouldn't always be that way. As the boys grew up and became more independent, it would get easier.

She decided the best thing to do would be to consult with Daniel. She'd hardly seen him since the birth of her baby brothers and would be eternally grateful to the man who had delivered them safely into the world. He'd been away for a couple of weeks on a course in London at a large teaching hospital and now he was due back this evening. He was in lodgings at a house near the hospital with another doctor. Their landlady, Elsie Bevan, was widowed and took the utmost care of them both. Daniel had said it was like having a second mother.

Rebecca called there after her shift was over to see if Daniel had returned from work. She knocked on the door and waited, then a white haired lady, with an extremely tight chignon hairstyle, opened the door. Her black high-collared dress was pinned at the neck with a Cameo brooch. When she saw Rebecca on the doorstep, the edges of her cornflower blue eyes, crinkled into a smile.

"Hello, Mrs Bevan. I'm Rebecca from the hospital, a friend of Daniel's. I was wondering if he was back from London as yet?"

Elsie nodded. "He came back an hour ago, dear. He was just taking a nap and then I was about to serve tea in the parlour, would you like to join us?"

"That would be most hospitable of you Mrs Bevan. I would like that, thank you very much."

Elsie showed her into a parlour which was adorned with large green foliage, such as aspidistras and other ferns. The embossed wallpaper and lace curtains made it appear very smart and well kept. The table already set for tea with an arrangement of Welsh cakes, miniature sandwiches, and a large china tea pot with matching, cups, saucers and plates.

Rebecca warmed herself by the fire as she waited for Daniel. She gazed at herself in the mirror over the mantelpiece, pinching both cheeks to make them appear pink. Then as the door opened she swung around to see Daniel stood behind her with a huge grin on his face.

He stepped forward to greet her, taking both her hands in his. "Oh Rebecca, I have missed you so. If you hadn't called I would have gone to your house this evening."

Before Rebecca had a chance to respond, Mrs Bevan poured the tea and invited them to the table, then she discretely left the room and closed the door behind herself.

As they sipped their tea, Rebecca turned to Daniel and asked, "How was London?"

His eyes lit up as he spoke animatedly. "London was amazing, so different to the Welsh Valleys, but St. Bartholomew's Hospital something else. The General Hospital would fit into a small corner of it. I learned so much whilst I was there, there were lectures from prominent surgeons and physicians every day, we got to see operations and post mortems, and made several visits to the wards. It was a breath taking experience. Now you, Rebecca, what about you?"

Her cheeks suffused with heat. She hesitated before answering. "Matron called me into her office this afternoon..."

"And?" he blinked several times.

"And, she said the Board was so impressed with me that they've offered me a job as ward sister on the Isolation Ward..."

He frowned, his dark brown eyes studying her face. "That's truly great news, but you don't sound very sure about it?"

"That's because I'm not. It will be a lot more responsibility and extra working hours. And what about the twins if I took any infectious illnesses home to them?"

"Hmmm," he rubbed his chin. "That could be a risk for sure, but then you risk that every day already working in a hospital. Who knows what diseases people carry these days? But something you could do to resolve your concerns about bringing any disease home is to move into lodgings close by."

"Yes, that's an idea. I'd also get extra wages as a ward sister, so I could send more money home to Mam."

"How long have you got to make up your mind?"

"Only a few days at most."

"Well if I were you, I would weigh up the consequences most carefully. Now how about a Welsh cake?" He passed the plate over to her. "I missed these when I was in London."

She laughed. "I bet you did. But what did you miss most, those or me?"

He smiled. "You, of course." Then he took her hand and planted a kiss upon it.

***

Over the following days, Rebecca did little else except think about her options, and all things considered, it was her final thought that she should take the job as a sister on the Isolation Ward. The extra income for her mother would come in handy, but the drawback was she wouldn't be around so much to help with the twins. James would pitch in of course along with Aunt Lily. Bill next door, promised he would do what he could by taking the trap to the markets and getting the best fruit and vegetables.

Another thing that concerned her though was the thought that she would see less of Daniel. He tried to reassure her that wouldn't be the case, but she knew in her heart it would. She managed to find lodgings at a house near the hospital along with another nurse to share with. It was decided she would call home on her days off to help with the twins, but only after bathing well and wearing fresh clothing, that way she could maintain contact but it would reduce the risk of passing on any infectious diseases at home. The house, she now lodged at, was owned by a Mr. and Mrs Baker, a nice elderly couple who had never had any children but seemed to like to fuss

45

over her and the other nurse, Della. She even had her own room which was very convenient as it afforded her privacy. Mr. Baker had a lovely garden, where she liked to sit of an evening, it was so peaceful, and sometimes all she could hear was birdsong and the distant sound of someone playing a harp in a neighbouring property, so melodic it made her heart sing.

***

Rebecca settled into a pattern of work, rest, and helping her mother with the boys. It wasn't easy for her and her new-found relationship with Daniel suffered as a result. He didn't seem to make so much effort to see her and claimed to be busy far too often for her liking.

One day, when she was at home with her mother washing clothes at the sink, she turned and asked, "Do you think we'll ever see Dad again?"

Her mother, who was seated at the kitchen table, took a sip of tea and then rested her cup, and looked up into her daughter's eyes.

"Maybe. Now don't go thinking your father's a bad man, Bec, because he's not. He's provided well for this family."

"Until now," Rebecca turned back to the sink to rinse a baby's night shirt, squeezing with all her might. The more she thought of them all and their predicament, the harder she squeezed.

Taking a deep breath, then turning toward her mother, she said, "Mam, it's time you faced facts. Dad has been gone a while now. You, we, can't carry on like this. It doesn't look like he's coming home. He hasn't even seen his own offspring, and as well as abandoning us, he's left his new found family in Brecon Road."

"Well, what do you suggest I do?" Her mother surprised her by raising her voice an octave.

"What I think is irrelevant. It's what you think that counts." She flung the last rinsed item into a bowl, wiped her hands on her apron and seated herself at the table opposite her mother.

"There are some shortbread biscuits in the cupboard…" her mother pointed.

"Please Mam, don't change the subject. You can even get a divorce these days. I've read of such things in the newspaper."

"A divorce?" Her mother's neck reddened. "I was born a Catholic. We marry for life. In any case, divorces aren't that easy to come by and they cost money."

In a softer tone, Rebecca said, "That's as maybe, but I'd love to see you settled and happy again."

Her mother sat bolt upright. "And in any case, what sort of a man would take on another man's offspring?"

Rebecca smiled and then took a sip of tea, setting her cup back down on its saucer. "I know someone not a million miles away who would."

Her mother's eyes widened. "You can't be suggesting Bill next door?"

Rebecca nodded. "Yes, I am."

"For sure we like one another, but marriage 'tis an entirely different thing. We are just good neighbours to one another, that's all."

Rebecca looked her mother in the eyes. "That man would be forever at your side if you allowed him to be."

"'Twill never happen, I'm still married to you father, and you won't catch me living tally with anyone. No, thank you very much indeed!"

Rebecca sighed and then went in search of the biscuits. Aunt Lily had baked them. If it wasn't for her and Uncle Evan and of course, Bill next door, she wondered how they'd cope at all.

***

A couple of weeks later, a letter arrived with a strange stamp on it addressed to her mother. Rebecca handed it over as her mother stood there trembling, her face a deathly shade of puce. Rebecca guessed what her mother was thinking, that maybe her father was dead.

Passing it back, her mother said, "Please, will you read it to me, Bec?"

From upstairs they heard a faint cry from the twin's room. Her mother glanced at the ceiling and made to leave the room.

"Please leave them a minute or two longer, Mam. While I read out the letter."

Her mother nodded. "Go ahead, Bec."

"The address is somewhere in Great Salt Lake City in Utah. It reads:

My dearest Kathleen,

It has been many years since we last corresponded with one another. But I feel I should let you know that your husband, Dafydd, is here with myself and his brother, Delwyn, at our home.

He arrived here last week and travelled via the Trans Continental Rail Road. The journey is still a long one, but nowhere near as dangerous or arduous as the previous Saints had to endure.

He has explained his plight to us and wishes to make amends. Delwyn was surprised to see him turn up at the door and has missed his twin so much over the years. We have both welcomed him with open arms.

He was looking thinner and older than when we last saw him, but that is understandable under the circumstances. Although he is a broken man, we feel the Lord guided him here to Zion. It is Delwyn's intention to school him in the ways of the Saints.

Whatever happens, he is safe here with us for time being. He might well return to Merthyr, his home town, one day. But for now he is away from any sin and suffering.

I hear you were pregnant and I expect by now the baby is born. Should you ever wish to make the journey here, we would welcome you and the family. We would love to see husband and wife reunited and are praying it shall be so.

Your own family, Kathleen, are fine and faithful members of the Church. Dafydd intends to make amends with them too for taking you away from them and your new found faith. He is plagued with tremendous guilt over all sorts of things…"

Rebecca stopped reading as she heard her mother sniff and watched her dab her eyes with a lace handkerchief. "Shall I carry on, Mam?"

Her mother nodded.

"I hope to hear from you when you have the chance to reply. If only to give Dafydd a glimmer of hope. We send our warmest regards from Great Salt Lake, where the skies are blue and the mountains rugged, not black like back home in Merthyr Tydfil."
Rebecca paused, "It's signed by Rose and there's a Biblical verse written here, Mam. *'For there is hope of a tree, if it be cut down, that it will sprout again, and that the tender branch thereof will not cease. Job 14:7'"*

She passed the letter to her mother, who read it to herself, open mouthed. "I cannot believe this…" she said finally as she folded the letter and slipped it into her apron pocket. "I'm going to see to the twins. I don't have the luxury of travelling miles and miles on some Trans Continental Railroad to escape my problems!"

Rebecca nodded, knowing in her heart her mother was right. She'd stayed to face her problems. But she had to admit she was glad her father was safe with Delwyn and Rose. What a turn up for the books indeed.

***

The following day, Rebecca called at Aunt Lily's house in Abercanaid. "Come in, Bec," she welcomed. "I was just about to make a cup of tea for your uncle, he's writing his weekly sermon in the parlour. Would you like a cup?"

Rebecca nodded eagerly. She had walked all the way from the family home and later, would need to go into work at the hospital for a night shift. "Yes please, Auntie."

Her aunt poured three cups of tea, and took one on a tray with a fruit scone to her husband. "I won't be long," she explained. "Help yourself to a scone, Bec."

When she returned, she seated herself in the kitchen opposite her niece. "And to what do we owe the pleasure, young lady?"

Rebecca's heart beat wildly at what she was about to tell her aunt. "It's about Dad…"

Lily's hands flew to her face. "Please don't tell me he's had an accident or worse?"

"No, no, Auntie. It's nothing like that. Mam received a letter from Aunt Rose in Great Salt Lake. Dad is out there!"

"Pardon?" Aunt Lily blinked several times her mouth agape.

"Yes, he is staying with them. Apparently he took the Trans Continental railroad to get there. I expect maybe you'll receive a letter soon."

Aunt Lily's mouth snapped shut as she digested the information. Then she took a long swig of tea. "Oh, I don't know what to say, I honestly don't Rebecca. He went missing years ago after the death of your grandmother and I feared he'd be found dead then, but at that time it was only local, not thousands of miles away."

Rebecca sat on the edge of her seat. "I remember you once mentioning that, but where did he show up?" She took a sip of tea unable to eat a thing.

49

"In China…"

She almost spluttered on her tea and set her cup down on its saucer on the table. "China! That rough side of our town! But that's full of drunks and undesirables!" She said, in total disbelief that her father would go there of all places. He'd spoken of it often enough in his role as a policeman.

Lily nodded. "Yes, and it was even worse in that hell hole back in those days."

"But what was he doing there?"

"He took to drinking and it seemed as if he wanted to escape his life. He had a good job working on the barges, but lost it as a result."

Rebecca could well imagine. "So what happened in the end?"

He came back home and then followed Rose and your Uncle Delwyn to Great Salt Lake, which is where of course, he met your mother."

"Please tell me more about that, Auntie?"

Lily paused a moment. "He said he heard her sing for the first time in a tavern before they boarded the ship at Liverpool for the journey to New York. He told me she had the voice of an angel. Then during the passage he made sure he got to speak to her on deck when her father and brothers weren't around…"

Rebecca frowned. "But why does there always seem to be so much secrecy surrounding their marriage?"

"Because, I think, your father truly fell in love with your mother from first sight and he made it his duty to find her and bring her back to Wales with him. Her family, who had converted from Catholicism to the ways of the Saints, did not approve. They wanted their daughter to remain with them. But instead your parents came to Wales and got married in secret."

"I didn't realise that was the case. I mean I knew they encountered one another in Great Salt Lake, but not that they'd run away together…"

Lily watched as her aunt gazed out of the window into the distance, then she turned and facing Rebecca said, "Do you know what I think, Bec? That maybe your father has returned to Salt Lake as a place of safety, you know as he's prone to leaving when things get difficult. Maybe being there is a way of him remembering the good times with your mother?"

"Possibly. Though that doesn't help us much does it? There are two extra young mouths to be fed back home."

Aunt Lily's face flushed red. "Yes, that is the worst thing of all. It was bad enough him abandoning your mother and his grown family, never mind those two young mites, he knows nothing of as yet. And don't get me started on that Jezebel from the Brecon Road and his love child! I was mortified when you mother told us about what had been going on under her very nose for the past few years!" She narrowed her eyes.

Rebecca realised what an embarrassing situation her father had put Aunt Lily and Uncle Evan, a member of the cloth, in.

They carried on drinking their tea, both engrossed in their own thoughts on the situation.

***

Later at the hospital, Rebecca was able to take her mind off things by being too busy to indulge herself in such thoughts. She had left Abercanaid with promises from both aunt and uncle that they would pray in earnest that her father would eventually come to his senses and return to the town he was born in, and most of all his family duties.

A young boy had been rushed onto the ward and put into isolation. It was thought he had contracted Scarlet Fever from his red pink tongue and all over body rash. He seemed listless and his body ached from top-to-toe, his mother had informed the medical staff. One moment he was too hot, then he shivered from the cold. He was placed in isolation and monitored. It was a new illness for Rebecca to encounter and it never ceased to amaze her how ill people became at the hospital. It was a ward very much needed in the town. Some died of course, and it was particularly a tragedy when they were so young.

Doctor Mansell Owen, a son of the family Doctor Owen from Abercanaid, was the doctor on call that night. He whispered to Rebecca when they were out of earshot, "We should know within the next twenty four hours or so what the prognosis is, Sister."

"So you think it is Scarlet Fever, Doctor?"

He nodded. "What I meant is, we should know if he's in danger or not."

Rebecca shuddered at the thought that the young boy could die. He was only eight-years-old.

"Would you like a rest and some refreshment in my office, Doctor?" she enquired. "You've been working for hours without a break."

"Yes. I could use one and so could you, Sister." His face broke out into a smile. He was easier to talk to than Daniel had been at work. Doctor Owen was a married man with several young children. He seemed an easy going sort of chap in the short space of time she had worked with him. His wife was a very lucky lady.

Rebecca instructed another nurse to take over and monitor the young lad, while she took a break.

As they sat facing one another in the office, Doctor Owen looked into her eyes. "So tell me Sister Jenkin…what made you take a job on this ward?"

"It wasn't something I'd thought about in all honesty."

"Oh?" The Doctor's eyebrows shot up. "Well how did it come to pass then?"

"The Hospital Board visited this hospital a few months ago and apparently, I made some sort of impression on them, so it was suggested I transfer here."

Doctor Owen smiled, his blue eyes lighting up. "Well it sounds to me like you were big game hunted, young lady." He chuckled. Then taking a gold watch on a chain from the top pocket of his tweed jacket, said, "I think it's time I knocked off for the night. I'll be back first thing in the morning before you go off duty."

He stood and before she had a chance to say goodnight, he left the office making her feel some emotion she didn't quite understand.

Chapter Four

Rebecca's night shift went quite quickly as she made regular observations on the young boy called William, who had scarlet fever. By the time Doctor Owen had returned the following morning, the boy was sitting up in bed trying some porridge.

"That's good to see, Sister Jenkin," Mansell Owen beamed. Although he was smiling, Rebecca noted the dark rings beneath his eyes.

"Yes, he seems to be picking up nicely. His mother is pleased." Rebecca gestured toward the woman slumped on the wooden chair beside her son's bed. She had been awake all night and only just fallen asleep. "I'll give her something to eat when she wakes."

"Good. She'll need to keep her strength up to take care of her boy and the rest of the family. It's been a bad time for them all, that's for sure. But now, thankfully, the lad is out of danger..." He paused a moment, before adding, "There's a hospital meeting this afternoon, though I doubt you'll be able to attend as you'll need your bed."

"What's it all about?" Rebecca studied the Doctor's face as if she could garner a clue from it.

"It's the Hospital Board, they just want some feedback how all the wards are doing here as this hospital has only been open for a couple of years."

"What time will it be?"

"Three o'clock sharp."

"That's all right. I'll go home for a few hours sleep and return for the meeting, I'm not working tonight anyhow."

The Doctor let out a long breath. "Oh that's good. So no young fellow then to take you out in the evenings?"

She bit her lip. "There was one actually, a doctor working on one of the other wards, but since I've been working on this ward, it's been difficult for us to meet with one another due to my shift pattern."

Doctor Owen raised a brow. "Which doctor would that be?"

"Daniel Evans."

"Oh I know the man of course. He's a splendid chap. By all accounts an excellent physician. I tell you what, if you can arrange it with him I'll get the housekeeper to cook a nice meal on Friday night and we can all dine together."

Rebecca swallowed a lump in her throat. Her go to Doctor Owen's home? She hadn't been expecting that. "Thank you very much, Doctor. I will send a message to Doctor Evans to see if he can attend, and we shall let you know as soon as is possible."

She smiled as she made to leave for her bed and Doctor Owen held her gaze for a little too long, which made her cheeks burn with embarrassment, causing her to turn away.

"Goodbye for now, Nurse," he said, as she left the ward. She smiled inwardly to herself, surprised at the emotion induced within.

***

Following her shift, unable to find Daniel, Rebecca located Jane in the corridor to give her a note she'd written for him, inviting him to accompany her to the dinner party at Doctor Owen's home.

"What's this all about?" Jane asked, blinking.

Rebecca hesitated before replying. The note wasn't sealed, so Jane could read it anyhow. "Er...he's been invited to the home of Doctor Mansell Owen."

Jane frowned. "So? Why should you do Doctor Owen's dirty work for him?" She narrowed her eyes to slits.

Rebecca took a deep breath, then let it out again, she was too tired to try explaining so to shut her friend up, she said, "Because I've been invited there, too. Now I'm exhausted and have a meeting to attend this afternoon, so need to get to my bed!" She snapped thrusting the note in Jane's hand.

Jane's eyes widened and she took a step back. It was becoming evident she had become jealous of Rebecca's promotion to ward sister. She'd hardly had any contact with her friend for weeks. Whenever Rebecca asked Jane to meet up to go for a walk or to go to her favourite coffee tavern in town, Jane had some sort of excuse ready. It was almost as if Jane were avoiding her.

Rebecca slept fitfully in her bed as all sorts of issues ran through her mind. There was the case of her father being safe and well, but miles away from home, worry how her mother was coping with the twins and now this, Doctor Owen, a married man, who seemed to be getting too close for comfort. Yet, she didn't feel she wanted to push him away either.

By the time she arrived for the afternoon meeting with the Board, she was worn out and her heart slumped when she realised the Doctor wasn't there. As a man with a ruddy face and bushy beard, read out the minutes of the last meeting, he mentioned that Doctor Owen was delayed as there had been some sort of last minute family emergency. So he might not be in attendance at all. The meeting dragged on and she was far away in her thoughts until she was jolted back in time and place when one of the Board members asked her a question about the ward she ran.

"Yes, it's all going well but I feel we could make use of a couple more nurses, especially during the night shift," she answered truthfully.

The sharp dressed man, who had asked the question, twiddled a fountain pen in his hands. "Hmmm that's not as easy as it sounds, we need more funds first."

The hairs on the back of Rebecca's neck bristled. In indignation, she straightened in her chair. "And what should happen if there were a lack of nurses to attend and we should lose lives?" She enquired.

The man set his fountain pen down and rubbed his bearded chin. "Very well. We cannot assign you a few nurses but we could assign you one extra for the ward."

"But we need more than one, the other night it was very busy here," she protested. "Ask Doctor Owen..."

"Well unfortunately he's not here to back you up, Sister..." the man glared at her. "Very well, we can assign you three nurses, but they'll have to be taken from other wards."

"But that's not what I want. You can't go robbing Peter to pay Paul!" She straightened in her seat.

Rebecca could feel her eyes filling with tears of frustration, but she didn't want to give the man the satisfaction of seeing her upset. She took in a deep breath and let it out again and was just about to say something else, when a voice said with a tone of authority:

"I, for one, agree with Sister Jenkin about this matter!"

She looked up through misted eyes to see Doctor Owen stood there.

The man held Mansell's gaze, and slowly nodded. "Well, if that's in your professional opinion, Doctor Owen."

"Indeed it is….." he strode over to where Rebecca was seated and took the empty chair beside her, as if in support of her plight.

"Very well," the man carried on. "I shall see to it that three new nurses are assigned here. Make a note of that please, Mr. Caudle, and mark it a priority."

The red-faced man making notes, nodded.

Doctor Owen smiled at Rebecca, and when no one was looking, patted her hand under the table.

She became a little breathless and took a sip of water and the Doctor removed his hand.

"And that concludes the meeting," the man said. They all stood and left the room, leaving the Doctor and Rebecca together.

"Thank you for that," Rebecca said.

"No problem. He should have taken more notice of you, Rebecca."

It was the first time he'd used her name and it made her tremble slightly.

"It's probably because I am a mere woman…"

Doctor Owen nodded, all the while gazing into her eyes. "I can see why you were chosen to work here, Sister Jenkin. You shall be an asset to this ward..."

He stood, leaving her with that thought hanging in the air as he left the room.

***

Word had got through to Daniel Evans that they were invited to the home of Doctor Mansell Owen and his wife in Abercanaid. So at least for all Jane's jealousy, she had done the decent thing and passed the message on. Indeed, it would have reflected badly on her had she not done so. Daniel arrived at Rebecca's door to escort her for the evening. There was a slight chill in the air as they walked the distance to the small village.

Doctor Owen's house was a three-storey, Georgian-style house, set beneath the canal bank, surrounded by large lawns and privet hedges. Rebecca had never been anywhere so grand in all her born days and felt totally underdressed for the occasion. She had worn her new gown which had a high ruffled collar, synched in waist, and leg of mutton sleeves. Daniel looked astonishing handsome in his dark suit, with silver-grey cravat set against his white well-starched shirt, causing her to reflect that his house keeper looked after him well.

On the journey to Abercanaid, he'd been fairly quiet not making much conversation, and mainly only speaking when spoken to, which made her feel ill at ease. The only time he'd shown any interest was when he asked how she was settling on the new ward and would she be expecting to stay there permanently.

As they stood outside the house, a gentleman attired in a black suit opened the door and welcomed them inside, causing Rebecca to draw in a breath. This house was opulence itself with its rich embossed wallpaper and green shrubbery, there was even a large glass conservatory with even more plants at the rear of the house.

From Rebecca's understanding, Mansell Owen was the infamous, son of, 'Doctor Owen of Abercanaid', whom her mother often referred to. He was still a practising family physician, though quite elderly these days. Mansell Owen seemed to have loftier ambitions than his father. It had been rumoured he'd once thought to set up a clinic in Harley Street, London, but that had fallen through on his wife, Hannah's protestations.

In the background from somewhere above, she heard the sound of childish giggles and whispers and guessed that Mrs Owen might be putting the children to bed, or else it was a nanny of sorts.

The manservant showed them into the drawing room and Rebecca gasped when she saw the high marbled fireplace, beneath the ornate, large gold mirror. Catching sight of herself next to Daniel, she had to admit they looked an attractive couple together.

"Take your stole, Madam?" the gentleman enquired.

She nodded as Daniel handed the man his hat and cane.

A maid appeared with a silver tray with two glasses and a crystal cut decanter of something.

"What's that?" she whispered to Daniel.

Bemused he replied. "I would imagine it's sherry."

The maid offered them the aperitif, which they gratefully took to warm the blood.

There was still no sign of Doctor Owen nor his wife, the only sound now being Rebecca's heart beat and the ticking clock.

"Please be seated, Miss, Sir..." the maid advised.

They did as requested, seated opposite one another on two high-backed but comfortable armchairs, either side of the fire.

Rebecca licked her lips and took a sip of the sherry. She was not that used to alcohol except at Christmas time. After the drink had warmed her through, she said, "Daniel, is anything the matter?"

He averted his gaze and shifted about in his chair. Then appearing to look at her, but somehow she felt looking through her, he replied, "Whatever makes you think so, Rebecca?"

She took a deep breath and let it out again. "I just feel you are not quite so friendly toward me anymore."

"I have just been working long shifts this week, that's all. *You* of all people know how things can be."

Relaxing, she took another sip of sherry, deciding not to probe any further. They had not seen much of one another since she'd been working on a different ward, and now she sensed a gulf between them. He had not even made the effort to visit her.

Her thoughts were interrupted as the door to the drawing room swung open and a large ruddied-face woman walked toward them. "Good evening to you both," she said with a beaming smile that lit up her china-blue eyes.

Rebecca guessed she was a little older than her own mother. "Good evening," they both replied

"I expect you're wondering who I am. I'm Mary Jacobs, Hannah's mother. Doctor Owen's mother by marriage. I'm afraid they are not here as yet, but a message has been sent for me to keep you company until they arrive. I am sorry I was unavailable to greet you both but I was putting the children to bed and they kept asking me to read them the same story!" She laughed, making Rebecca immediately warm towards the woman.

"I am very pleased to meet you, Madam," Daniel said, rising and offering her his seat, which she gratefully took. He sat himself on the sofa a little distance from both women.

"Likewise," Rebecca added.

"I understand you work at the hospital with my son-in-law?" Mary enquired beneath her silver haired brow.

"Yes, I do indeed and he has been kindness itself, Mrs Jacobs."

Mary smiled. "I am glad of that, he is a good man." Turning to Daniel she asked, "And you work there also?"

Daniel nodded. "Yes, Ma'am but on a different ward to Mansell. I used to work with Miss Jenkin until she absconded to the Isolation Ward."

Rebecca could hardly believe her ears. What was he trying to say? Before she had a chance to respond, Mary stood.

"I do believe I can hear a carriage drawing up outside, they must be here at last..."

There was a sound of the front door opening and slamming quite violently, causing the trio to glance at one another in trepidation.

Mrs Jacobs forced a nervous looking smile. Daniel busied himself checking out some novels on the bookcase, and Rebecca stared out the window.

It appeared as though Mrs Jacobs were about to say something when Doctor Mansell burst in the room.

"Please, I must apologise to you both. We were unavoidably detained..."

He glanced up at the ceiling as there was the sound of hurried footsteps on the stairs and then the sound of what appeared to be muffled sobs.

"No matter," Daniel said, turning from the leather bound novel he was inspecting. "Is there anything wrong, Mansell?"

Doctor Owen shrugged his shoulders and his mother-in-law stood by his side. "Tell them, Mansell..." she urged.

He removed his top hat and seated himself as the others followed suit. "It's my wife Hannah...for some time now, she has been having 'women's problems' since the birth of our last child, who is now almost one-year-old. We were late, as I took her to see a well-respected physician in Cardiff..."

"What are her symptoms?" Daniel asked, stroking his chin.

Doctor Owen let out a breath. "Oh malaise, feeling generally unwell, a strong element of melancholia, other times she's on the edge of hysteria. I really do not know what to do with her anymore."

Mary Jacobs stood and placed a reassuring hand on her son-in-law's shoulder, while he sat in the armchair. "Mansell has been very good," she explained. "But my daughter is not herself anymore and we fear she might end up in some sort of asylum."

"Not if I have anything to do with it, she won't!" Doctor Owen said forcefully. "If things become impossible to contend with, then I shall open up the attic, refurbish it and employ a nurse to look after her."

"That's very commendable, Mansell," Daniel said, with a note of camaraderie, "but your family life and work might suffer as a result."

"He's right," Mary agreed. "I think it might be an idea if we sent Hannah to my sister who lives in Cardigan. She would get good clean, fresh air then. My sister and her husband live on a farm and they are childless, so she would get plenty of attention. Only yesterday, I found Hannah walking the streets of Abercanaid in bare feet. It was bitterly cold too. It's so dangerous for her here. I fear she might get run over by a horse and carriage or fall in the River Taff. Llanbadarn Fawr in Cardigan would be far safer for her. No polluted air from the iron works there, just lots of green countryside and it's near the coast too."

Doctor Owen appeared to mull the thought over in his mind. "Maybe, Mary. But that would have to be a last resort for me."

"Very well," said Mary, rising. "How about another glass of sherry, everyone? You all look like you could do with one?"

They all nodded eagerly. It would probably be a long time until they got to eat their dinner, if they got to eat it at all and she suspected Mansell could do with a sherry after all he'd been through.

Rebecca rose and followed Mary. "Please may I sort the sherry out for you, so you can see to your daughter?" she asked.

"Thank you, dear. That's very thoughtful. I can see you and I are going to get along well. Just go into the kitchen and ask the cook to hold the dinner over for another hour and to take some nourishing soup up to Hannah upstairs, then ask the maid to bring the sherry into the drawing room, would you, please?"

Rebecca did as requested, as Mary went in search of her daughter and by the time she had arrived upstairs, the sobbing appeared to have stopped.

Rebecca let out a breath, what a lot of strife poor Doctor Owen had on his plate. He had four children, a highly responsible position at the hospital, and a wife who seemed to have some form of hysteria, bordering on madness.

When she entered the room, Daniel averted his eyes. What was the matter with him? If he didn't want to come here this evening, he might have said so, if that was what was troubling him?

She couldn't go on like this and made up her mind to confront him on the journey home. They ended up dining much later than expected and the company was agreeable. Hannah remained upstairs throughout. At the end of the meal, Doctor Owen insisted on getting the driver of his carriage to take the pair home. Once inside the cab, Rebecca asked, "Daniel I cannot go on like this any longer, are we still stepping out with one another, or not?"

He shrugged.

"I'll take your non committal as a 'no' then, shall I?"

"Take it whichever way you wish, but you cannot have expected me to wait around for you while you pursued you career. A wife of mine would be required to stay at home and keep house," he replied curtly.

"A wife of yours? You were planning to marry me?"

"Yes, I was, but not now. To be truthful, I have found someone who is far more compliant. One of your former colleagues actually."

She tried to digest the information, but it was swimming around in her mind. Marriage, career, someone else? It was all too much. "Then who is the unfortunate lady, might I ask?" She finally found the courage to say.

"Jane Worthington."

A shiver skittered along her spine. "Jane? But I have known her for years and she has not told me any of this. She knew that we were dining together tonight and said nothing of it. I cannot believe it. You are just trying to make me jealous, aren't you?"

He shook his head and although it was dim in the carriage, she could tell by his tone of voice he was telling the truth. "No, I am not, and to be perfectly honest, I don't much care how you feel any more."

Hot tears of humiliation welled up and a lump in throat made it difficult to breathe. She must not allow him to see he had upset her. She took in a composing breath and let it out again. "Very well," she said coolly. "It is all for the best as I do have my career to think of."

They sat in silence for the remainder of the journey. When the carriage drew up outside Mr. and Mrs Baker's house, she rose without glancing at him. The driver opened the door and allowed her to dismount.

"Goodnight to you, Rebecca!" Daniel called after her with a note of merriment in his voice.

She didn't answer, but instead headed for the house, and once inside her room, behind the closed door, broke down in tears.

***

The following day Rebecca went to help her mother with the twins. She had lain awake half the night running matters through her mind and sobbing at the thought it was all over between her and Daniel. It had been a couple of weeks since she last visited the family home as her shift work kept her so busy. When she arrived, her mother seemed to be in a flummoxed state, mixing up her words and distracted.

"What's the matter, Mam?" Rebecca asked, gazing at her mother's weary face. Her hair was slightly messed up and she had deep rings beneath her eyes.

"It's your father," she replied, sitting down at the kitchen table.

Thankfully the twins were taking a nap, so Rebecca seated herself opposite. "Yes, go on..."

"He's written me a really long letter begging my forgiveness. He has now become one of the Saints. Saint indeed! After what a sinner he has been. Can you believe that?"

"Well, it's a start that he's remorseful Mam, I suppose."

"'Tis too little, too late, if you ask me!" Her mother's lips were set in a grim line. During the past year she seemed to have aged a lot and no wonder after all Rebecca's father had put her through.

"So you wouldn't give him a second chance then, Mam?"

Kathleen shook her head vehemently. "Certainly not! And to top it all, 'tis a cheek that he's asking me and the boys to join him in Utah!"

Rebecca took in a sharp intake of breath and let it out again to compose herself. Her mother and brothers sailing half way around the world? If they went she might never see them again. "What about James?" she asked.

"Yes, he has asked if you and James would like to come too, Bec?"

"My life is here, Mam, but you and the boys and even James, as he is still young and not settled, could go if you want to, but I would miss you so very much."

Her mother stood and hugged her daughter's head to her breast, as Rebecca remained seated. Smoothing down her daughter's hair, she murmured, "No, Rebecca. Don't even think that way. I would not go there. I've been there once and it's a beautiful land, but Merthyr Tydfil and Wales are home now, even above Ireland."

Rebecca nodded gratefully with tears in her eyes. Her father had been a selfish man indeed, but at least it sounded as if he wanted to make amends. "So will you reply?"

Her mother shook her head. "By all accounts I should ignore him like he did to me, but then that wouldn't be the Christian thing to do, would it? I shall reply and tell him I am not interested and he is free to take on a new wife. The Saints allow that kind of thing. It almost happened to your Aunt Lily when her and Evan became parted."

Rebecca furrowed her brow. "I don't understand?"

"Evan suffered a blow to the head after visiting China looking for your father. To be sure it must have been bad as he lost a lot of his memory and appeared to not know his wife in the Biblical sense any more. Lily got upset and took your cousin, Mollie, to Utah to live with Delwyn and Rose in order to start a new life. Uncle Delwyn arranged for Lily to be married to a business man called, Cooper Haines. But Evan, when his memory returned, raised the money to follow his wife to Utah and reclaimed her!"

Rebecca's mouth popped open and snapped shut again. "I can hardly believe my ears. So you think it's possible Dad will remarry under the present circumstances?"

"I do think it's a possibility. If I had no children then maybe I would have considered going, but 'tis not realistic to take the twins on such a gruelling arduous journey. Believe me, I've made the trip there and back."

Rebecca nodded. Her mother was probably correct. "So, what will you do now?"

"Well money is becoming a problem, Bec. Although I have your brother's wages helping to support us and some of yours, thankfully, 'tis not enough. I would like to return to the stage."

Rebecca blinked several times. "But where?"

"The Theatre Royal at Pontmorlais. I've already been to speak to the manager there who remembers me from my early stage days. I won't be top of the bill of course, but it will help me raise a little money from time-to-time. Your aunt Lily has offered to help with the twins and Mollie will help too."

Mollie, Rebecca's cousin, was older and happily married with two children of her own and living in Cefn Coed.

"Well Mam, if that's what you want to do then I have no objections, and will help when I can. Now how about I make us something to eat before the twins wake up?"

Kathleen nodded. "There's a good girl you are our Bec, I don't know what I'd do without you."

***

On Monday morning at the hospital, Doctor Owen called Rebecca into his office. His face looked grim and he gestured for her to sit down.

She took a seat and looked at him in expectation as he seated himself opposite her. "I feel I need to apologise for Friday evening, Rebecca. I should have warned you about my wife but I was hoping she might have been lucid that evening, but as you could tell she wasn't."

Rebecca nodded. "Please don't trouble yourself about it, Doctor Owen..."

He looked deep into her eyes. "There is something I've been meaning to ask you, how would you like to take on a little extra work?"

"Doing what?"

"Working for me. I know your mother has a lot on her plate at the moment, so the extra money might come in handy for you all. It would mean working for me a few hours a week to care for Hannah. I need a companion of sorts for her to keep her mind active and take her out for walks. She needs some healthy air in her lungs. I want to send her to Cardigan as my mother-in-law suggested and hope maybe you can accompany her. I can arrange for another nurse to cover your duties here in the short term, it won't be for too long a period."

Rebecca didn't know what to say. "I'll certainly think about it, Doctor Owen."

"Please don't take too long as I have to arrange this as soon as I can."

"How about I sleep on it tonight and let you know tomorrow?"

His face broke out into a smile for the first time that morning. "It would be a heavy weight off my mind if you accept my proposal. I have a lot of faith and trust in you."

She nodded, stood and brushed down her uniform with her hand, before leaving the room she turned and said, "I shall certainly give it some consideration..."

Chapter Five

Rebecca decided to accept Doctor Owen's proposition, and the following week she found herself sitting in a carriage accompanying Hannah to Llanbadarn Fawr. It would be the longest journey she had ever made in her life and she wondered throughout how her parents had managed to go all the way to Great Salt Lake and back again. Or even why her father should choose to make the journey one more time.

The Doctor's cook had made up a wicker basket of food for their journey, which was mainly crusty bread, cheese, and fruit. There was also a small bottle of homemade ginger beer and some water to sustain them.

So far Hannah had not uttered a word. It had been heartbreaking seeing the Doctor say goodbye to his emotionless wife with tears in his eyes. Once he realised Rebecca had noticed his upset, he quickly looked away and bade them a safe journey. Now they were off to the village of Llanbadarn Fawr for some fresh clean air.

As they took the Brecon Road, Rebecca watched the grey clouds belching from the chimney stacks of the Cyfarthfa Ironworks in the distance, as she breathed in the sulphurous air. Why people left places like Cardigan to come to dirty smelly Merthyr Tydfil, she had no clue. But her mother had always told her they came for the money as they thought the streets were paved with gold. Poor farmers who had almost lost their livelihoods and struggled through hard times, got the shock of their lives when they came to Merthyr having to live in hovels where diseases like Cholera were rife, or else had little choice other than to bed down with lots of others in doss houses peppered around the town. There had been an explosion of the population. Merthyr had once been a farming community itself. Now no more. It was something entirely different. A boom town, a heaving metropolis where iron was King and coal its Queen.

When the coach driver announced they were stopping for a rest a couple of hours later, Rebecca tried to rouse a sleeping Hannah, who appeared extremely irritable.

"Please Hannah, you must eat and drink something to keep your strength up..." Before she had a chance to finish her sentence, Hannah lashed out with her hands, scratching at Rebecca's face.

Instinctively, Rebecca's hands flew to her cheek, and on close inspection there were a couple of droplets of blood on her fingertips. She dabbed at it with a clean handkerchief she extracted from the pocket of her dress, all the while thinking, "It's true what they say, let sleeping dogs lie."

She decided to let Hannah be, eating and drinking a little herself, though she did not much feel like it, but there was no use both of them starving. She offered some to the coach driver, who gratefully accepted as they sat on a verge of grass next to a furrowed field.

"'Ere Miss, I don't know how's to tell you this..." He did not have a Welsh accent—it was one that was new to her.

"Yes, please go on. What's your name by the way?"

"Tobias Cookson, Miss. What I was going to say is that you'll have your work cut out with that one..." He pointed to the coach where Hannah lay fast asleep once more.

"I gathered that," Rebecca said, not wishing to gossip about the good Doctor's wife.

"Yes. She's a rum sort she is. Really mad. Totally off the wall. She gives Doctor Owen and that mother of her's a hard old time I can tell you...always showing her drawers to all 'n' sundry!"

"Mr. Cookson, where were you born?" she asked, changing the subject.

"Malvern, Miss."

"How did you end up in Merthyr then?" She took a sip of ginger beer and poured a tin cup full for the driver and handed it to him.

He took a long swig and swallowed, then made a rasping noise of appreciation. "That were me parents, see. They got married and decided to seek their fortunes in Merthyr Tydfil. They did quite well and returned to the family farm and told me all sorts of stories when I was a boy. I quite fancied the adventure of coming here myself, but didn't care for working in the pit or the ironworks, though I did for a spell. Then I found out the Doctor was looking for a coach driver, I'd done a bit of that in me time back in Malvern."

Rebecca smiled. "Would you like to go back some day?"

"Oh aye, I would indeed. I miss those Malvern Hills with that clear air and sparkling spring water, but I have to say living with Doctor Owen has been most entertaining..."

Before he had a chance to say anything more about Mrs Owen, Rebecca rose and brushed down her skirts. "I think we need to be on our way if we are to reach Cardigan before nightfall," she said with some authority.

He nodded soberly and rose, then taking a last swig from his cup handed it back to her. "Thank you kindly. I just need to relieve myself Miss, and I suggest you do the same as we still have a way to go yet. You might think of waking Mrs Owen. I wouldn't want no accidents in the back of the cab."

She knew full well what he meant, not realising Hannah did that sort of thing, but then again she was used to people soiling themselves in hospital, it was nothing new to her.

She found a large tree to hide behind to urinate, and after adjusting her clothing, went to rouse Hannah, who this time did not lash out but went with her placidly behind the same tree. She noticed the carriage driver staring at them.

"Please avert your eyes, Mr. Cookson!" she shouted at him, prompting him to turn his head away.

When she was quite sure Cookson was minding his own business, Rebecca explained to her charge what she needed to do and Hannah complied with a small grin on her face as if she was doing something all together naughty. Before she had a chance to rearrange the woman's clothing, Hannah began dancing around the tree, but Rebecca managed to contain her and ensure her clothing was in place.

Oh dear, this was going to prove to be hard work on this so called holiday break.

She escorted her charge back to the carriage, and once on their way again, offered her something to eat. This time Hannah took a piece of bread and cheese and consumed it in a very unladylike manner, shoving large pieces into her mouth, causing Rebecca to shudder in horror. But being the understanding person that she was, she said nothing for time being, handing the woman a cup of water. There would be time to correct her manners later.

As darkness fell, Rebecca snuggled back against the leather squabs, resting her head against the window as the coach trundled along. What had she let herself in for?

***

After the coach driver had lost his bearings several times, it became completely dark by the time they arrived at Llanbadarn Fawr. Hannah was in a drowsed state as her husband had given Rebecca a special tincture to medicate his wife. It was a spoonful to be taken four times a day for the relief of melancholia. Rebecca couldn't work it out as on some occasions Hannah acted childlike, bubbling over with life, and other times after the tincture, she slept and became docile as a lamb. She guessed the tincture must be some kind of sedative but was not really happy about giving it to the woman. Of course, there were times when his wife lashed out and could be violent, so she supposed the Doctor must know what he was doing.

The coach drew to a halt, lurching the carriage forward, causing Rebecca's head and neck to whip back violently. One of the horses whinnied loudly, and then there was the shout of male voices.

Frightened to leave the carriage, Rebecca tentatively put her head outside to see the coach driver in a heated discussion with two men, who appeared to be intoxicated. "They're demanding money from me, Miss Jenkin! Remain seated in the carriage!" Peeping out the window, by the help of the moon's silvery beams, she noticed a middle-aged man with a younger man beside him, dressed in a scruffy looking tweed jacket, waistcoat, and flat cap, both were mounted on horseback. Almost before she had a chance to sit herself down she felt the coach being pulled away at an alarming rate. By the sound of his cracking of the whip, she realised the driver was frightened for their safety. The shouts became louder, as the men banged on the carriage door. But, whoever the interlopers were, they couldn't compete with the strength of the Doctor's horses that were fine thoroughbreds, and soon they had broken away into a gallop and Rebecca could breathe easily once more. When they were well on their way the driver pulled in against the roadside and dismounted to explain what had happened.

"I think they were highway robbers of sorts, Miss Jenkin. That was hair-raising I can tell you..."

Rebecca's heart went out to the man. Being careful not to wake her sleeping charge, she took the wicker basket and removed the stone bottle of water and handed it to Mr. Cookson, who gratefully took a long swig and returned it to her. "Well you did a very fine job there, Tobias. I shall be mentioning this to Doctor Owen."

He shook his head. "No, Miss. I was only doing my job, we don't want to alarm him none."

"Very well, then. But I wish to express my deepest gratitude to you for keeping Mrs Owen and myself safe."

He touched his cap as a sign of respect and left to remount at the foot of the cab. It had been a close call that was for sure.

By the time they drove further along the rickety road, Rebecca felt ready for sleep. In the distance she spotted some sort of building with an oil lamp in the window and guessed it must be the farmhouse belonging to Mary Jacobs' sister and her husband. There was a pungent smell of manure in the night air wafting into the cab, causing Rebecca to gag slightly. It was an odour she was going to have to get used to, realising maybe it was better than some of the smells around parts of Merthyr.

The farmhouse door swung open. A rotound woman stood there, silhouetted, holding a lantern in her hand. As they dismounted, Rebecca could see the likeness to Hannah's mother there, but this lady was plumper and shorter in stature.

She stepped towards them, her lantern swinging in the breeze. "Welcome to Crugmor Farm!" she announced in a very Welsh, West Walian accent. There's good to meet you and all. And where is my darling, Hannah?"

Hannah stepped out shyly from behind Rebecca, and in a moment was in her auntie's arms, trusting. It was such a sight to see. In the short time Rebecca had known Hannah, she had not once seen her hug anyone, not even her own mother or husband.

"I am Mrs Evans. You can call me Mable, *bach*," she addressed Rebecca. "It is good to see you all."

If Mable was shocked by her niece's appearance, then she wasn't showing it. She led them all inside to her flagstone kitchen and they seated themselves around a large pine wood table, while Mrs Evans made them all a cup of cocoa.

"I am sorry my husband Gwyn is not here to meet you. One of the cows has been sick and he's been up all night with her. She was a good milker too, so we don't want to lose her."

The kitchen door opened and a young man stood there, inebriated, his face blackened. He wore a tweed jacket and flat cap. The hairs on

70

Rebecca's neck bristled as recognition dawned, it was one of the men who had earlier tried to hold up the carriage. She glanced across at Mr. Cookson, who by the look of his narrowed gaze had also realised the same thing.

Seeing the pair, the young man showed no emotion, just stamped back out of the room and out through the front door.

"Who was that, Mrs Evans?" Rebecca asked.

"That was Jake Morgan. One of our farmhands. He's going to help Mr. Evans with our best milker."

Rebecca let out a breath. It certainly made her feel unsafe knowing he had not an hour since, tried to rob them. She had a feeling he might not even realise who they were, for surely many carriages passed that way at night and he was inebriated. Tomorrow she would speak with Mr. Cookson and ask his opinion on what they ought to do about the matter.

**

Mrs Evans ladled them all a bowl of homemade rabbit stew with some crusty bread which they ate ravenously, Hannah spooning the stew into her mouth as fast as she could. Rebecca thought to ask her to slow down, but didn't wish to upset the woman's mood, so remained quiet. After a nice chat by the fire, they were shown to their bedrooms. The farm was quite spacious, so Rebecca got a small room to herself next to a slightly larger one with an adjoining door for Hannah. Mr. Cookson was allotted the old horsehair sofa downstairs with a few Welsh blankets to keep him warm, seeming more than happy with that arrangement.

When Rebecca had helped Hannah wash and undress for bed, and was sure she was settled for the night, she crept downstairs to find Tobias. He was already snoozing in front of the fire, it seemed a shame to wake him but she knew in light of what happened, she needed to do so.

She gently shook his arm to rouse him. "Er wassa matter?" he mumbled.

"Mr. Cookson, I need to speak with you as you'll be leaving early in the morning..."

He blinked several times, then pulled himself up on his haunches. "Oh yes. I noticed the lad too, that's what you wanted to speak to me about and you're right I will be gone first thing."

"What shall I do?" she twisted her hands together as she stood in expectation. "Shall I tell Mr. and Mrs Evans?"

"I wouldn't for time being, lass. You don't want to cause no trouble and you're only staying with them for a few weeks. If I were you, I'd give the lad the benefit of the doubt, but if he does anything untoward, then tell his employers."

She nodded, it seemed sage advice under the circumstances. "Very well, Mr. Cookson. Now you get back to sleep, you'll get a good seven hours if you get right back to it."

He grabbed hold of her arm, causing her to stumble and then smiled. "Don't fancy keeping me company, do you?"

She snatched her arm away. "I most certainly do not!"

He laughed. "I was only jesting with you!" Then he lay back down and closed his eyes, and it seemed within seconds, he was back dozing once more as if she'd never disturbed him at all.

The following morning, she was awakened by a cock crowing loudly somewhere outside. The morning sun was already beginning to filter in through the bedroom window. She sat up in her comfy bed and looked around the room. It was a nice pleasant bedroom, painted yellow walls with a couple of small paintings of the countryside, hung here and there. She straightened the colourful quilt on the bed and drew back the curtains. Who needed paintings when you had that wonderful view outside? It seemed to be miles and miles of patchwork green fields of different shades, and some a glimmering gold, corn she guessed. And in the distance a fine sliver of aqua marine. The sea.

She looked down at the courtyard outside and noticed Jake Morgan walking with a black and white sheepdog at his heels. As if realising he was being watched, he stopped, turned and stared up at her bedroom window, causing her to back away. A shiver ran down her spine. She was going to make sure no harm came to Mrs Owen. She didn't trust that young man one inch.

Once she had washed and dressed, she roused Hannah and aided her to wash and dress too, helping her on with her pretty blue-flowered gown. She brushed Hannah's long chestnut-brown hair, then piled it up on top of her head, securing it with some hair grips.

Hannah looked at her enquiringly. "Do you know where we are?" Rebecca asked.

Hannah shook her head. "No. Where are we?"

"We're at your aunt and uncle's farm in Cardigan."

"Auntie Mable?" Hannah's eyes sparkled with life.

"Yes."

She was obviously happy about that, having previously forgotten she'd encountered her last night. As they walked downstairs together, the smell of bacon cooking permeated Rebecca's nostrils. Mable had laid the large pine table in the kitchen. Already seated there, was a ruddy-complexioned, middle-aged man. He looked up and smiled, already halfway through devouring a plate of bacon and eggs. Beside him, sat Jake Morgan, chomping on a hunk of bread.

"Well come on you two," Mable greeted. "We're up at the crack of dawn in the country. Please seat yourselves."

"Good morning!" Rebecca greeted, and the middle-aged man nodded in return.

"Good morning to you, Miss. I'm Rhys Watkins I help on the farm and this 'ere beside me is Jake."

"Yes, we have already met," Rebecca said bluntly, staring as hard as she could at Jake. But he kept his eyes averted.

Mrs Evans placed a plate each of bacon and eggs in front of the women. Rebecca gazed in horror as Hannah began to eat with her hands. Picking up a knife and fork she placed them in Hannah's hands. "Now, Hannah, you know how to use a knife and fork, that's what you do at home."

Hannah smiled and nodded, then began to eat her food as a young child might with cutlery, awkward but able. But at least she was trying.

Jake looked up and smirked. Rebecca noticed Rhys kick him with his boot under the table. Jake immediately rubbed his ankle. "What did you do that for?" he glowered.

Rhys ignored him, and turning towards Rebecca said, "So you're from the notorious Merthyr Tydfil then, Miss?"

She blinked several times. "Yes I am. Notorious? What do you hear of the place?"

Rhys dunked his bread in the runny yellow of his egg and took a bite. "Oh just that there's some horrible things there. You know filthy air belched out from the ironworks. Thieves and vagabonds, ladies of ill repute, that sort of thing."

Jake sniggered, and then, as if expecting Rhys to boot him again, stood to leave the room.

"Next time make sure you excuse yourself, my lad," Mable said flipping him around the head. "Especially when there's ladies present."

He rubbed his ear. "Well I don't see no ladies!" he shouted, and left the kitchen slamming the door behind him.

"I'll swing for that lad, you see if I don't!" Mable muttered.

Turning her attention back to Rhys, Rebecca replied. "Yes, Merthyr Tydfil does have all of those things as would most places I would imagine, except for the ironworks. The place is overcrowded mind, and we see a lot of cases of injury as a result at the hospital."

"You're a nurse, are you?" Rhys asked, his eyebrows lifting with surprise.

"You seem staggered," she laughed.

"Well maybe I am. I just had you down as a companion for Mrs Owen. You must be clever to be a nurse."

Rebecca's cheeks flushed. "Oh I wouldn't say that." Turning her attention to Hannah she scolded, "Remember your knife and fork?"

Hannah nodded and picked them up again. It was like dealing with a toddler sometimes. She sighed and carried on eating her own breakfast.

***

Rebecca helped Mrs Evans with the washing up of the dishes following breakfast and then later, they were taken on a tour of the farm. Mr. Evans was still attending to the sick dairy cow who now appeared to have perked up.

Hannah broke away and ran into her uncle's arms. "Well if it isn't my favourite niece!" he exclaimed. "How are you *bach*?"

She laughed coquettishly and ran off with her uncle in pursuit. It was hard for people to understand Hannah's behaviour if they did not know of her or the situation.

Hannah's laughter echoed around the old barn, only occasionally muffled by the sounds of the cattle lowing.

Mable's forehead creased into a frown. "It's hard to see her this way," she said. "The last time I saw her was at her wedding to the good Doctor. She seemed a picture of health then, and a fine woman. Now she seems more like a child."

Rebecca put her hand on the old woman's shoulder and looking into her eyes said, "Hopefully, this break will do her good. Or at least Doctor Owen seems to think so."

Mable quirked a brow of derision. "I seriously doubt it, my dear. It might do her good to come here yes, the fresh country air, but I don't think she'll ever be the same again. It was childbirth that did this to her. I'm sure of it. It happened to an aunt of mine years ago, she was the same after the birth of her child."

"What happened to her?"

"She died unfortunately. She couldn't be left alone and one night she wandered out when all were asleep and was found face down in the duck pool at the bottom of the garden. Bless her soul. I think Hannah might have inherited her madness from that side of the family."

Rebecca had no doubts that Mable was probably right.

***

They spent the rest of the day walking and picking flowers from a nearby field. Rebecca thought it would do Hannah some good to relax and even thought that maybe some painting would be beneficial for her.

As they were heading back to the farmhouse she noticed a figure behind a tree and she narrowed her gaze to see who it might be. Straining her eyes, she recognised the youthful, muscular figure of Jake. Why was he staring at them? It made her feel most uncomfortable. She didn't much fancy him joining them for a meal at the table again, but she needn't have worried as when they were heading for their evening meal, Mable announced that he had gone to help Mr. Evans herd up the sheep in one of the nearby fields. Breathing a sigh of relief, Rebecca sat down to enjoy a hearty meal of beef pie and vegetables. It was one of the best she'd ever eaten, even better than when Daniel had taken her to dine at the Bentley's Hotel in Merthyr.

Daniel! She didn't want to think of him but she couldn't help feeling bitter toward him and Jane. Pushing the thought away, she concentrated on the remainder of her meal which wasn't hard to do.

***

The following day a letter arrived from Doctor Owen.
Dear Rebecca,

I trust this letter finds you well and that my wife is not too much of a handful for you. If you find this to be so, then you must send me a telegram immediately and I will send Mr. Cookson with the carriage to collect you and bring you home.

I have managed to procure another nurse to cover your duties at the hospital, though she is not as efficient as yourself. Rest assured this is none of your concern. All I am bothered about at the moment is that my wife gets plenty of peace and fresh air.

Please do not hesitate to contact me if there is a problem.

My sincerest good wishes,

Mansell Owen.

Folding the letter, she placed it in her dress pocket. She was beginning to develop feelings that she knew were ungodly, and experienced a pang of guilt that she should do so while Doctor Owen's wife was in her charge.

"A letter from home was it, *cariad?*" Mable appeared behind her. Rebecca was so absorbed in her thoughts that she had not even heard her approach.

"Yes it is. It's from Doctor Owen enquiring about his wife's welfare." She experienced a rush of blood to her cheeks and hoped it would not show.

"There's good that man is to Hannah. It's a pity she can no longer be a proper wife to him."

Rebecca nodded, knowing full well that Mrs Evans was speaking in a carnal sense and it scared her that she felt she, herself, could be the one to give love to what she saw as a very lonely man.

As soon as they returned to Merthyr she decided it would be best to avoid Doctor Mansell Owen as much as possible.

Chapter Six

The following day, Mrs Evans suggested they call to the village to sell her homemade buttermilk and cheese, baked goods, and Gwyn's vegetables to the local shop. Rhys brought around the horse and cart and the four of them, including Hannah and Mrs Evans, went into the village of Llanbadarn Fawr.

It was a beautiful morning with the sun filtering through the branches of the trees and glistening off the sea in the far distance. From where they sat on the cart as it trundled along the country rickety road, they could see the spire of a church, indicating the direction of the village.

Rebecca gasped in awe at the pretty little village with its quaint thatched roofs and little shops here and there. It was nothing like the heaving metropolis of grey old Merthyr Tydfil back home. The pace of life seemed different here as if people were more concerned with living off the land rather than from some heavy industrial machine, spewing out clouds of smoke, dust and fire.

It was a welcome respite from the upheaval back home and she could well understand why the Doctor chose to send his wife here. She had written him a letter; Mable told her to post it at the village post office which was run by a lovely married couple who spoke only in the Welsh language, but Rebecca managed to convey her wishes to them.

She hadn't quite known what to write last night, but when the household was asleep, she had sat down at the dressing table and penned a letter beneath the light of an oil lamp.

She'd written the words;

Dear Doctor Owen,

You will be pleased to know that Hannah is settling well here and loves being at the home of her aunt and uncle. Yesterday we went for a lovely walk and picked the wild flowers, tomorrow we are going to the village in order for Mrs Evans to sell goods from the farm.

I, myself, am more than happy here for time being. So rest assured that if there is a problem I will contact you.

Yours Sincerely,

Rebecca.

There was far more she would have liked to have said and of a less formal nature, but it didn't seem appropriate somehow.

Rhys helped the ladies down from the cart and Mable gave them all something to carry. She handed Hannah a wicker basket of various cheeses to carry. The rounds of cheese were wrapped in muslin cloths. Rebecca carried two baskets: one of cauliflower and cabbage, the other potatoes. Mrs Evans herself carried a basket of rosy red apples. Rhys had the heaviest job of all carrying a large silver churn of buttermilk.

The village shop was more than happy to purchase Mrs Evans's wares. Indeed it appeared that a deal had already been struck so that constant supplies of her goods were sold there. As Mrs Evans explained later to Rebecca, she also baked and sold her wares too, which were in high demand. Villagers loved her *Bara Brith*, *Teisen Lap*, Welsh cakes and crusty bread.

Mrs Evans worked so hard though. Rebecca could see that. She was up at the crack of dawn to help her husband, Gwyn, with the milking, then there were the chickens and goats to feed, and then breakfast for everyone. There were fresh eggs daily from her favourite laying hens.

Following breakfast, she cleared up and washed and scrubbed the flagstone floors, and then set about the task of washing everyone's clothes in her wooden tub, with a dolly-peg to swish the clothes back and forth in hot soapy water. Then she used a mangle to feed the clothes through so they were as rinsed out as much as possible before pegging them on the clothes line.

They flapped about in the breeze until dry enough to bring in for her to iron and air. She did this all on a daily basis, and when the weather was poor, dried the clothes on a big clothes rack that stretched over part of the kitchen in front of a roaring fire, then it was hoisted above their heads. By hook or by crook, every piece of clothing was washed when necessary and dried and ironed within the same day. She didn't hold with the 'Monday Wash Day' rule.

When she had been paid a pretty piece for her goods, Mrs Evans took them all to a small tea room in the village run by a Mrs Clancy, who served such dainties as miniature sandwiches, jam and cream scones, and other baked goods, some of which she purchased readily from Mrs Evans. A deal was struck once again and the two women shook hands. Rhys refused to join them there, claiming it was unmanly to be seen in such an establishment only frequented by dandies and ladies, so he went for a pint of ale at The Black Lion instead.

Hannah was remarkably well behaved, and for once, did not show them up with her unladylike behaviour. Rebecca had also noticed a faint blush to the woman's cheeks and a sparkle in her eyes. The country air was definitely doing her some good.

When they got back to the farm, Rebecca helped Mrs Evans bring in the washing from the line outside as the cows were lying down in the field. Mable had told them that was a sure sign of rain. Rebecca noticed a lot of country sayings had an element of truth to them.

Hannah was sent to bed for an afternoon nap while the women set about the mammoth task of ironing the clothes and putting them to air in front of the fire before being put away.

An hour or so later, Rebecca went to check on Hannah, but there was no sign of her in her room, just the imprint of where her body had lain on top of the bed. Feeling alarmed, she looked out the window and could see the woman heading for one of the fields with Jake in hot pursuit.

Mouth dry, she ran downstairs and out through the kitchen door without even a word to Mrs Evans, who stood there open-mouthed.

Gasping for breath, she ran to catch up with them, just as Hannah appeared to be adjusting her skirts.

"What's going on here?" she demanded, glaring at Jake.

"Just been having a bit o' fun that's all!" he smirked.

"What exactly have you been doing to Mrs Owen?" her voice now trembled with emotion.

"Nothing. Just playing a game of hide and seek with her that's all. She was fed up staying in that room."

Somehow Rebecca did not believe his explanation. "Are you feeling all right, Hannah?" she asked.

Hannah nodded and ran off back towards the farmhouse.

"I am telling you now," Rebecca said firmly, "if I catch you anywhere near my charge again, you'll have me to deal with. I can assure you if you harm a hair on Hannah's head you'll lose your job on this farm. Understood?"

He nodded, then turned in the direction of the barn, and walked away with his hands dug deep in his pockets.

***

"Did that man hurt you, Hannah?" Rebecca was in Hannah's bedroom as the woman lay prostrate, face down in the bed with her head buried in the pillow.

When no answer came save for a muffled sound, Rebecca walked around the bed so she could make eye contact with her charge. A lone tear coursed down her cheek as she nodded and then wept pitifully.

Rebecca encouraged Hannah to sit up and held her in her arms, gently stroking her hair. "Please can you tell me what Jake did to you?"

"He...he..."

"Pardon?"

"He untied my ribbon and ran away with it, Miss."

Hannah could never remember Rebecca's name. Rebecca heaved a sigh of relief, noticing for the first time that the lilac bow she had tied in Hannah's long hair was missing. "So he was just teasing you, and that's all?"

She nodded. "I didn't find out until I came back into Auntie's house."

It was a relief to know the lad hadn't interfered with Hannah in a carnal sense, but it concerned her that she thought he had. "Come along now and wash your face, it will be high tea time soon. Auntie has been baking today and she wants us to try out her batch of scones."

Hannah's face lit up as she beamed at the mere thought of it.

Rebecca poured a jug of water into the flowered basin and helped Hannah wash her hands and face, then she brushed her hair and applied a new bow to it. "Now," she said firmly, turning Hannah around to face her head on, "you must promise me that you will tell me or your aunt or uncle, if Jake makes any approaches to you when none of us are around. Do you understand me?"

Hannah lowered her gaze and nodded shyly. "Yes, Miss."

"Then all is well and we shall take tea with your auntie downstairs. Then afterwards we can do some painting if you like?"

Hannah nodded enthusiastically, then ran off as if without a care in the world. Rebecca hoped she wouldn't forget her warning.

The following days passed in a blur and Rebecca was beginning to miss home. Jake had thankfully kept his distance. She hadn't bothered to ask him for Hannah's ribbon to be returned for fear of antagonising him. Hannah had plenty of pretty ribbons in the drawer in any case.

Auntie Mable seemed to be slowing down and this concerned Rebecca with her nurse training. Her legs and ankles were swollen and she was becoming short of breath. "You must rest more Mrs Evans, you are doing too much for a woman of your age..." Rebecca scolded good-naturedly.

Mable nodded. "Aye, you are right, *bach*. But who will do all this work if not me? Gwyn is too busy on the farm; we should have had some daughters. Hannah is the closest thing to a daughter for me, but of course, she is now more childlike than ever."

Rebecca had to agree. "Well, promise me one thing, you will see a doctor, Mrs Evans, just to check all is well."

Mable nodded. "Very well, but I haven't seen one for years, fit as an ox, I was."

"Yes *were*," reminded Rebecca.

Something outside the kitchen window caught her eye, two silhouetted shadows in the courtyard were in some sort of heated discussion. Fists began flying and Rebecca ran for the door in time to see one run off in the distance and the other rolled up in agony on the floor, clutching his stomach.

As Rebecca drew close she could see it was Rhys. "Are you all right?"

He groaned and held his head. "It was that rum young 'un, Jake. He stole something from the house, I couldn't tell what it was, but I chased the scoundrel and tried to get him on the ground but he whacked me a solid punch in the head which floored me, and then one in the stomach. I'm still seeing stars, Miss."

"You take your time and stay where you are, Rhys. I'll go back to the house and fetch a blanket to cover you up."

He nodded gratefully. She returned within minutes with Mrs Evans's best Welsh Woollen blanket from the couch and a pillow to rest his head.

"Thank you. You're an angel of mercy. I can tell you're a good nurse," he muttered.

She was just about to say something when he took hold her of hand and kissed it, and then in a low husky voice, said, "You know you'd make someone a good wife you would, Rebecca."

Immediately she withdrew her hand for fear he should have designs upon her, and putting on her best ward sister's voice, she cleared her throat and said, "Well I'll be telling Mr. and Mrs Evans about this in the morning and I think we should contact the local constabulary too."

Rhys groaned. "No, Miss. There's ways and means I'm telling you. By all means tell Mrs and Mrs Evans about the theft so they can check to see what it is that's missing, but I'll deal with that rap scallion myself!" Hearing the tone of his voice, she had no doubts about that. It sounded as if he had taken that punch when off guard as he was quite a hefty chap.

"Do you know which room he took whatever it was he stole from?"

"Aye, it was the parlour. Mrs Evans got some nice stuff in there see, best bone china, ornaments and knick knacks, all sorts..."

She stayed with Rhys until he had stopped seeing stars and helped him to his feet. "You could do with a nice cup of tea..." she offered, draping the blanket around his shoulders to keep out the chilly night air.

"I could do with more than that..." he laughed as she helped him inside the farm house.

"I'll see what I can do," she promised. "A tot of whiskey or brandy wouldn't harm, I'll be bound. Particularly as you tried to stop a theft tonight."

He nodded gratefully as she helped him to a chair and turning towards the window, she wondered where Jake had escaped to under the cover of darkness.

***

Once Rebecca had given Rhys a tot of whiskey and left him warming himself by the fireside, she went to have a word with Mable about the incident.

The woman looked up from the embroidery she was in the middle of working on.

"But Jake wouldn't do that to me, he's been a son to me!" Mable protested.

"I'm afraid he has stolen from you, Mrs Evans."

Mable laid down her embroidery. "But how do you know in any case?" she stared deep into Rebecca's eyes.

Rebecca hated telling the woman the truth, but it had to be done. "Because..."

Rhys, who had quietly approached, and was now standing behind her, spoke, "Because I saw him do it!" Rhys finished her sentence for her. "He was creeping out of the parlour and I saw him stuff some things into his pockets, Mrs Evans. When I accused him, his face went right red like, and then he hit out at me when I gave chase."

"I've given Rhys a tot of whiskey to calm his nerves," Rebecca explained.

Mable shook her head. "It's a very sad day that I can no longer trust young Jake."

"There's something else you both should know..." Rebecca hesitated as she chewed her lip. "The night we arrived here from Merthyr...our carriage was held up by two men. They demanded money. One of them was Jake!"

Mable's hands flew to her mouth. "Oh, please, this is all too much to take in." She began to breathe erratically.

"Quick!" Rebecca shouted to Rhys, "Go and fetch Mrs Evans a glass of water."

Rebecca knelt near the woman, and taking her pallid hand, advised, "Try to relax your breathing, Mable..."

The woman's breaths were short and shallow and her complexion now took on a blueish hue. She nodded and eventually, her breathing came back under control. Rebecca realised it had been a huge trauma for her.

Rhys returned. "Sorry, I couldn't find any glasses, a cup will have to do."

Rebecca nodded and took the cup to Mable's lips. "Now sip that slowly," she advised.

Mable's colour eventually returned. "I'm sorry. This happens to me now and again if I get upset about something," she puffed.

Rebecca took her wrist and checked her pulse, which was erratic. "Have you ever seen a doctor about this?"

Mable shook her head. "No, and please don't go telling my husband either. He's got enough to worry about."

"Well I won't say anything for now," Rebecca said, "but I think you need to see a doctor. Who is he?"

"Doctor Montgomery, he has a house in the town of

Aberystwyth."

"Aye, I know it," Rhys nodded. "I'll go and fetch him right away."

"No, you will not!" Rebecca said firmly. "You can ask one of the farm hands to do it. You've had a nasty shock yourself. In fact, it would be a good idea if whilst the doctor was here, he checked you over too."

"But I need to find out what was stolen first!" Mable protested.

"All in good time, let's see what the doctor has to say first," Rebecca advised.

***

After the doctor had examined Mable Evans, he took Rebecca to one side. "So you're a nurse, you say, Miss Jenkin?"

She nodded. "Yes, I work at the General Hospital in the town of Merthyr Tydfil."

"I know of the town, though have not heard of that hospital. Anyhow, it's my feeling that Mrs Evans is seriously ill. Her symptoms of breathlessness and fatigue make me think so. I've also had a look at her limbs and they're very swollen. Another sign, I'm afraid."

Rebecca blinked. "Is there anything you can give her, Doctor?"

"Due to her advanced age and condition, all I can prescribe for now is a tonic..." he reached into his leather bag and handed her a brown bottle with a cork stopper. "It's as good as anything, oh and plenty of rest. Ensure she gets that."

Rebecca shook her head. Wasn't there anything else that could be done for the poor woman? "But Doctor, surely there's some physician somewhere who could help Mrs Evans."

"It's all a question of money..." he said grimly, as he put his bowler hat on his head. "The best heart physicians are in London and it would cost a great deal for her to even be examined by one of those fellows." He patted Becca's hand and added thoughtfully, "She's so lucky to have a nurse like you staying here, Miss Jenkin."

He lifted his bag and left the room unable to hear Becca whisper, "But I won't be here forever."

***

Rebecca went in search of Rhys. "Did the doctor examine you on his way out of here?" she asked, when she found him seated at the kitchen table.

84

"Aye, he had a quick look at my head and said as long as I wasn't getting any headaches, dizzy spells or bouts of vomiting, I should be all right, lass."

Rebecca frowned. What was the matter with these countrified quacks? The doctors in Merthyr Tydfil seemed far more in touch with modern medicine. She thought of Daniel and his recent visit to St. Barts in London, then she gritted her teeth. Well some doctors in Merthyr were good men, but not all.

***

When Mrs Evans had rested and taken her tonic, she insisted on checking on what had been stolen from the parlour. She heaved her heavy frame out of the armchair by the fireside in the kitchen and made her way to the room, closely followed by Rebecca and Rhys, whilst Hannah was out with her uncle checking on the cows in the barn.

After a few minutes of searching the room, Mable turned to the duo and declared, "Well, I can't see anything missing at all? Maybe I was right and you've both falsely accused the lad."

Rhys looked at Rebecca and shook his head, sadly.

Rebecca touched the woman's shoulder. "Take your time now Mable, are you quite sure nothing is missing? Maybe you put something in this room that wouldn't normally be in here."

Mable's hands flew to her face. "You're quite right Rebecca. I just remembered, my little jewellery box was in here. I was getting ready for chapel the other day and wanted to fix my best brooch to my blouse. Oh, where is it?"

They glanced around the room, and then, Rhys knelt down and looked under the table. He rifled beneath the long chenille cloth and brought out a small wooden box.

"Yes, that's it!" Mable exclaimed delightedly, as he handed it to her.

She lifted the lid, her bottom lip trembling. "My jewellery—it's all gone!"

Rebecca put her arm around the women as she wept. "Please try not to upset yourself, Mrs Evans. It will put a strain on your heart. What was in the box?"

"My best brooch, my mother gave me when I was twenty one, it came all the way from London...a bracelet, oh and no...the string of pearls Gwyn bought for me when we married..."

Rebecca helped the woman to sit down. This was simply awful. Poor Mable's life had changed in just a day, not only now being informed how seriously ill she was, but her most treasured possessions had disappeared into the bargain.

Rebecca watched as Rhys pursed his lips in anger. "I'm going out!" he declared, making for the door.

Rebecca spoke, "But where to?"

"The Black Lion to find that thief, Jake, before he tries selling any of that stuff!"

She pulled him back by the arm. "But you've had a bad blow to the head. It would be foolhardy to go out now and maybe get clobbered by someone so much..."

"Younger? You mean Rebecca. Aye, well he might be younger, but I have so much anger in me right now that a herd of wild horses couldn't stop me." He strode off towards the door.

"Wait!" Rebecca shouted after him. "I'm coming with you!"

***

Rebecca raced after Rhys, trying to catch her breath. Hearing her footsteps he turned. "Look, The Black Lion is no place for a lady, Miss Jenkin!" he said firmly.

"That maybe so," she puffed out plumes of steam into the cold night air, "but you've had a nasty head injury, and as a nurse, I feel duty bound to see to your welfare."

He let out a sigh. "Very well, but return to the house and fetch a shawl, the air is bitterly cold tonight. I'll go and get the horse and cart and wait in the courtyard for you."

She smiled to herself as she headed back to the kitchen to retrieve her shawl, realising that Rhys would do anything for her.

"I won't be long, Mable!" Rebecca shouted. "I can see Gwyn and Hannah are on their way back from the barn."

She closed the door and made her way to the horse and cart.

***

When they pulled up outside the Black Lion, the crowds of revellers were spilling out onto the street, tankards in hand. The smell of ale almost made Rebecca retch, giving her second thoughts about entering the establishment, until she remembered Rhys's blow to the head and Mable's missing jewellery.

"What's going on here then?" she whispered to Rhys.

"I dunno, but I intend finding out..."

Rhys pushed his way past the horde and into the noisy tavern with Rebecca tentatively walking behind him.

It was noisy inside the inn as men crowded around the bar area. Rhys tapped one man on the shoulder, who was gaily relating some tale to his circle of onlookers.

"What's going on here tonight, Dylan?"

Dylan turned. "Haven't you heard? There's a big ship washed up on the shore at Aberystwyth. The men are saying there's rich pickings to be had. It's thought to have come from the West Indies. We're going to get together and make our way there first light."

Rhys harrumphed loudly and looking at Rebecca, said, "Keep an eye out for that rascal, Jake. It's a shame there's so many men out of a night as it will make it harder to find him."

She nodded. "And what of that shipwreck, might he be there?"

Rhys shrugged. "I've heard these tall tales before, the men add yards on. Last time that happened, the big ship wreck turned out to be a little fishing vessel that had overturned. But still, maybe you have a point; he might be looking for rich pickings himself and might go with the men in the morning." He rubbed his chin thoughtfully.

"It's worth a thought." She patted him on the shoulder.

"'Ere, Ieuan," Rhys said, turning to the small bald-headed man next to him, "do you think there's any truth this time about this shipwreck business?"

"Not sure really, but there's been talk that there may be rum aboard, so worth looking into I reckon!" He smiled heartily, raising his pewter tankard, to reveal a missing tooth. A red spotted scarf was tied jauntily around his neck, and it was a long time since his white shirt had seen hide nor hair of a bar of soap beneath his leather gillet, but Rebecca reckoned this was more than worth a thought. Even if there turned out to be no bounty on board or washed up on the shore, the mere pull of the thought of barrels of rum, was enough to make a highway man get on his horse and head for the shoreline—that much she was certain of.

"What time are the men meeting in the morning?" she demanded, wiping the smile from Ieuan's face.

"Hey, we don't want no women folk tagging along, it's not for the likes of a lady!" His eyes narrowed.

"I don't intend going myself," she explained in a more gentle tone. "It's for Rhys to know what time to set off, so he can clear it with his employers."

"About 5.30 maybe. We're meeting outside this pub, and the men will bring their horses and carts. You can bring yours, can't you, Rhys?"

Rhys nodded and then glared at Rebecca. "I think, it's about time, we got you back to the farm," he said, taking her by the elbow and guiding her through the swollen throng.

Once outside the pub, she turned to him. "What's the matter with you?"

"I'll tell you what's the matter, shall I? It was daft of you in there announcing I was going to join the men in search of the shipwreck. Now someone's bound to mention it and Jake Morgan will be one step ahead of the game!"

Rebecca shook her head sadly, realising that Rhys was right. "I'm sorry, Rhys, I didn't think..."

For a moment he softened his stance and lowered his voice. "I know you meant well, Rebecca, but please, I've had so many run ins with Jake Morgan, I just want to nail the bastard! Sorry for my language, but Mrs Evans isn't the first he's robbed blind."

She nodded. "Yes, I know, remember, he tried to rob our carriage when we arrived?"

"Sorry, I was forgetting..."

"Who else has he robbed?"

"Well, talk is he goes for the vulnerable and the weak, often targeting the elderly. Promises them he will work labouring, but he's crafty, he gets them to pay up front, just does a little work without finishing and also makes off with their valuables. I warned Mr. and Mrs Evans about him, but they refused to accept he had a bad bone in his body!"

Rebecca could weep for those poor, trusting people he'd conned out of their hard-earned pennies, she hated injustice of any kind. "And what of the villagers? Don't they do anything about this?"

"Well no, some are scared of him and he tends in general to rob from neighbouring villages, but now he's messing on his own doorstep as it were, it just has to stop."

"I agree, but what of his background?"

Rhys appeared to be about to reply when a man dressed in top hat and long coat, brushed past them. His clothing at one time might have been elegant, but now on inspection, had seen better days. As he entered the Black Lion, she heard a cheer go up amongst the men.

"Who's he?" she asked, looking directly at Rhys.

"Cled Morgan. Jake's father...that's what I was about to tell you. The lad has some protection as people fear his father. He owns a lot of land around here and loans out money to the villagers. All very well of course, but if they can't repay, he sends around his thugs to demand it from them and then puts up his prices. So those poor folk indebted to him, just can't win."

Rebecca was beginning to get the picture. "Like father like son..." she mumbled.

Rhys furrowed his brow. "What was that?"

"Just thinking how alike those two men are, they both take from the vulnerable and needy. They're a pair of bullies!"

"Sssh," Rhys warned. "You never know who's listening. Walls have ears!"

Rebecca nodded. "Very well, the situation just makes me so angry, though!" she huffed.

Rhys guided her back to the cart, and once they were on board said, "Yes, you and me both..."

***

By the time Rebecca rose the following morning, there was no sign of Rhys at the breakfast table and neither did Mable Evans speak about him, nor last night's incident with Jake. She just had a sad, despondent, look in her eyes. Rebecca tried to help as best as she could. "It might be an idea if you employed a young girl to help you with the chores, Mrs Evans," she advised, as she finished the remainder of the breakfast dishes, rinsing the final plate, she set it down and dried her hands on her pinafore. "Now, how about a nice cup of tea in the parlour?"

Mable nodded, then Rebecca followed the elderly woman into the room where she settled her down by the fire, already lit by Gwyn.

She left her to doze in the armchair whilst she made the tea. "Now Hannah, you go and find your uncle while I talk to your auntie, do you understand?"

Hannah nodded eagerly and ran off in the direction of the barn where Gwyn was busy collecting eggs in a basket.

Mable's eyes flicked open as Rebecca handed her a cup of tea. "I must have dropped off there for a moment," she apologised.

Rebecca smiled. "Needed the rest I expect." She took her own seat opposite the woman, so both sat either side of the fireplace. "I meant what I said, please think about getting a young girl in to help you with the chores, Mrs Evans."

Mable nodded wearily. "Yes, I know you're right, *cariad*. Maybe you could ask around the village for me later today? She'll need to be strong mind you, it's back breaking work here and I can provide her with a room once..."

"Once we've left you mean," Rebecca butted in, not minding at all. It was inevitable they would be leaving soon. She missed home in any case and couldn't bear being away from her own family for much longer. Also there was the worry of leaving her position of ward sister for so long. Although the good Doctor was paying her handsomely to be nurse maid to his wife, she longed to get back on the ward to work. There, she would be so busy she wouldn't even have time to think about Daniel anymore or how he had treated her.

Mam had sent a short letter yesterday, telling her she was doing well and the twins had a healthy pair of lungs on them. Bill next door, had taken them all out for the day for a picnic in Ponsarn. Rebecca had smiled to herself, they were becoming quite a little family. And what of her father? What was he doing right now? She wondered.

The remainder of the day went by in a blur of activity as Rebecca divided her time between helping Mrs Evans with the chores and keeping an eye on her charge. It was like coping with a young child caring for Hannah as she had no boundaries of decency or decorum.

By eventide, there was still no sign of Rhys, and Rebecca found herself pacing the floorboards. Who could she speak to about this matter? She couldn't discuss it with Hannah and didn't want to worry her hosts.

At supper, Mr. and Mrs Evans asked why he hadn't returned, they'd allowed him leave for the day, but obviously hadn't questioned why. Rebecca was about to say something when the kitchen door opened and Rhys stood there grinning from ear-to-ear.

"Well, I didn't have any luck catching the lad, but look what I've got for us!"

Rebecca stood and drew closer, then hearing voices, she watched as Rhys and his friends rolled in several wooden barrels in through the kitchen door, making a racket as they manoeuvred them across the flagstone floor.

"Good heavens!" exclaimed Gwyn. "Are they what I think they are?"

Rhys chuckled. "Yes, Gwyn. We're in for a good night and possibly a good few months on this stuff. It'll do Mrs Evans the world of good to have a sup of that. Might even sell some to the Black Lion and if I do, Mrs Evans, I'm going to buy you a new brooch and pearl necklace. Won't replace what you had before, but I feel as you've been so good to me, I'd like to do that for you. And Mr. Evans, I'm sure you won't mind a glass of rum?"

Gwyn rubbed his calloused hands together, then patted Rhys affectionately on his back, "I don't mind if I do!"

Rhys smiled nervously at Mrs Evans. "Come on then, sit by the table everyone, we could all do with a little drink this evening!"

Even the men who helped Rhys, joined them, and the atmosphere was one of conviviality, where they could forget their problems for one evening. Hannah was already tucked up safely in bed.

Rebecca wondered what tomorrow might bring?

Chapter Seven

Rebecca had worried about the rum being taken from the shipwreck, but as Rhys had explained, it got washed up on the shore, and all the crew feared drowned. It was viewed by the people of the area as 'fair pickings'. Even the local constabulary had removed a few barrels which Rhys reckoned were for their own consumption, so there would be no come backs, which was a relief. Rebecca had high moral standards, higher than some maybe, but she well understood the reasons folk went in search of their bounty.

Next morning, she approached Rhys in the courtyard. "So did you find Jake Morgan on your travels yesterday?"

He shook his head and patted his brow with his 'kerchief, it was quite warm in the sun and he'd undertaken some back breaking work, chopping up sticks for the fire. "Unfortunately, no. But I overheard one of the men mention that he'd gone to work on another farm in the area, belonging to the Williams family. He'll make trouble there and rob them blind, I'll be bound, unless..."

"Unless, what?"

He frowned. "Unless I put a stop to it."

She touched his arm gently. "Just be careful, Rhys. I wouldn't want to see you getting hurt..."

He smiled at her, and for a few seconds their eyes locked, then the moment was broken as Mrs Evans came out of the farmhouse to ask if they were ready for breakfast.

"We'll be right with you, Mrs Evans!" Rebecca called. She'd need to get a shift on to wake the sleeping Hannah; Mansell Owen had been right, the country air was doing his wife the power of good.

Rebecca entered the bedroom, surprised to find Hannah already up and awake, she'd even managed to get her dress on herself, which Rebecca buttoned up at the back. "Have you been to pass water, this morning?" she asked gently.

Hannah nodded, but before Rebecca could finish her task in hand, Hannah swiped at the glass vase on the windowsill, which contained large dog daisies, yanking them out, then poured the water into the porcelain wash bowl.

"No, Hannah!" Rebecca said firmly. "We can't use that water to wash your face and hands." She'd rather have given her a full wash down before the woman got dressed but realised it might be more work to undress and redress her, so a cat's lick would have to do for now. Finally, she got her charge ready and seated at the kitchen table.

Rhys smiled at Rebecca from across the table, he had a mischievous twinkle in his pewter eyes.

When breakfast was over and Rebecca had sent Hannah to help Mr. Evans in the field, Rhys took Rebecca to one side. "Do you have a moment, Miss Jenkin?" he asked.

Rebecca found his formal approach quite endearing. "Yes, but then I must do the washing up to help Mable, she needs to rest as she's been up since the crack of dawn."

"Aye. I know that. What I need to ask you is, if you would have an afternoon free to spend with me? I thought maybe we could go into that fancy cake shop in the village for a tea time treat."

"And there's me thinking you'd never step foot in one of those, Rhys Watkins! You told me they were only for dandies and ladies!"

"Yes, and maybe they are. Haven't changed my opinion about that, but I would like to take you out some time."

"You mean as in courting?" She blinked several times.

"Aye, and why ever not!" he exclaimed loudly. She quite liked this forthright side of him she was seeing. "Why shouldn't two people who are unattached not spend time in one another's company?"

Rebecca paused for a moment. Rhys was right, what was stopping them? "Yes," she said eventually, "I would very much like to go to the tea room with you. How about tomorrow afternoon if they can spare you from the farm, Rhys? We can also ask around to see if we can get a young girl to help Mrs Evans at the farm then."

"Grand idea!" Rhys enthused, then he flicked his rolled up cap open and replaced it on his head, before going outside to help in the field. "I'll pick you with the horse and cart about 2 0'clock!"

Rebecca wondered what she had let herself in for, then went off to wash the dishes.

***

The following afternoon, Rhys turned up on time and drove them in the horse and cart into the village of Llanbadarn Fawr as promised to Mrs Clancy's tea room. He was well spruced up in a clean white shirt, smart trousers, tweed jacket and brown tie. Instead of his usual flat cap, he wore a brown bowler hat and looked quite the gent. It was obvious he'd gone to a lot of effort.

Rebecca wore her cornflower blue floral tea gown with puffed sleeves and plain matching coloured jacket that complimented the dress. Pinned to the neck of the gown, she wore a Cameo brooch, and carried a sun parasol under her arm. On her hands, she wore white lace gloves. If Rhys was quite the gent, then she felt quite the part of a lady this afternoon.

When they arrived, he helped her down from the cart and held the shop door open for her. Making quite a fuss as they were shown to their table, he drew out a chair for her to sit down. Although a mere land worker, his manners were impeccable compared to Daniel's. She shuddered when she thought of how he had treated her, having pulled the wool over her eyes.

They spent a pleasant hour or so eating a selection of Mrs Clancy's small neat sandwiches and fondant dainties. She poured the pair Earl Grey tea in a proper china tea pot with cups and saucers to match. Everything was just perfect. Rhys was an attentive suitor who she liked immensely. She was aware that he was besotted with her, whilst if she were being honest, although she had fallen for Doctor Daniel, it was Doctor Mansell she really felt something for, but being a married man, he wasn't available to her. Could it be true these feelings she had for the man? Did he feel them too? Or was she just imagining things?

"A penny for them?" Rhys asked.

Her cheeks seared hot with blood as she realised she was blushing at the thoughts she'd been having about Mansell. She didn't want Rhys to realise she was thinking so strongly about another man, so she replied, "I was just feeling a little hot that's all and wondered whether to go outside for some fresh air."

"Oh, it has been a lovely day for this time of the year. I'll just settle the bill with Mrs Clancy and then we can take a stroll around the village and enquire about employing a young lady to help Mrs Evans with the chores at the farm."

Now she felt a pang of guilt as Rhys was just so nice to her. She didn't deserve so much attention when she was thinking of another man, yet she couldn't get Mansell Owen out of her mind, no matter what she did. She hadn't heard from him since that letter last week and hoped he wasn't worrying too much about his wife.

They left the tea room and walked around the village, arm-in-arm, with Rebecca putting up her parasol to shield her fair complexion from the sun. When they approached the Black Lion pub, she glanced at the church beside it, shrouded by trees, it stood majestically as a beacon of hope for the village. Although she had noticed it the other night in the dark, now in the daylight it looked much more impressive.

"What is the name of the church?" she asked.

"St. Padarn's. It's been in the village for many a year. Since Medieval days in fact. At one time there were monks living in it. They were from the Gloucester area, but the Welsh drove them away!"

Rebecca found this information from Rhys quite surprising. "And how do you know of this?"

"I might not be well educated, but I can and do read a lot of books, Miss Rebecca. I'm interested in that sort of thing, history and such. Didn't have much schooling as a lad as I worked on my uncle's farm, but my aunt taught me to read and write. It was she who introduced me to all the great classics, Dickens, Chaucer, Defoe, the lot!"

She smiled and nodded, then pausing asked, "Where do you think are the best places to ask about employing a young girl to help at the farm?"

"Well I suppose the pub is where we'd get best response, but I think we should ask around the small shops first, we might have asked in the tea room before we'd left."

Eventually, Rhys encountered a friend outside the pub, who was unloading wooden kegs from the back of a cart and rolling them towards the landlord. Rebecca wondered if they were the same kegs from the shipwreck, but said nothing. The man smiled heartily when he saw Rhys. They shook hands. Rebecca kept her distance as they talked men's talk with one another. Then finally, Rhys said they were looking for a young girl to help Mrs Evans at the farmhouse. The man told the pair that his eldest daughter, Sarah, could do the job. She was seventeen-years-old and could live in at the farm with Mr. and Mrs Evans.

"Send her around to the farm first thing in the morning!" Rhys shouted as they walked away.

"Are you sure you've done the right thing?" Rebecca asked. "Do you know the girl?"

"Rest assured, I know the Griffiths family well. She's a lovely young lady. Honest and reliable in every way. They're overcrowded in Tom's house as it is, and his wife is having another baby. It's the answer to that man's prayers!"

Rebecca guessed that for the family, having another wage would be a Godsend, and give them a bit more space at home.

Rebecca nodded. It wasn't that she doubted Rhys's good judgement, more that she wanted to employ someone for Mable who was worthy of working at the farm. After what happened with Jake, she realised what the importance of engaging a trustworthy person was.

***

The following morning, Sarah turned up early at the farm, she looked clean and well dressed and had impeccable manners. Rebecca was relieved to see that Mable remembered her from being a young child.

Sarah set to work immediately, rolling up her sleeves and donning an apron to wash up the breakfast dishes. Rebecca admired her spirit and wished that some of the nurses she worked with were so keen to undertake their tasks first thing in the morning.

Now Rebecca could concentrate more on Hannah rather than worry about Mrs Evans. The woman's movements had slowed down a lot since Rebecca had arrived at the farm and it concerned her greatly. Rebecca decided to send a telegram to Doctor Owen to see if he would consider coming to the farm to check on his wife's aunt.

She was a little upset when she'd received no reply, but a few days later, there was the sound of horses's hooves approaching in the courtyard. Hannah ran to the window to look outside. "A carriage!" she exclaimed excitedly. "There's a man getting out and coming here!" Her voice sounded apprehensive and childlike.

Rebecca went to look for herself, lifting the curtain to get a better view, in time to see Doctor Owen alighting from the carriage just as Hannah ran out of the room. It saddened her to realise that Hannah no longer recognised her own husband and seemed to fear him as a stranger. Rebecca rushed to the door, eager to allow the Doctor access.

"I got your telegram a few days late, I do apologise," he said, removing his top hat to enter the low beamed farmhouse. "I was in London on business."

Rebecca smiled, feeling the tension that had been building up, slowly begin to ebb away. "You're here now and that's all that matters. Would you like some refreshment after your long journey? Sarah has made some lemonade."

The Doctor nodded. "That would be lovely. And who is Sarah, might I ask?"

Rebecca let out a long breath. "A young girl from the village we've taken on to help Mable with the chores."

The Doctor seated himself at the polished pine table and Rebecca went to fetch him the pitcher of lemonade and two glasses, it had been keeping cool in the pantry for the past few hours. She poured them both a drink.

"Thank you," he said, lifting his glass and taking a sip. "Obviously you couldn't tell me too much in the telegram, due to the cost, but I gather it's rather serious about Mrs Evans?"

"Yes, I'm afraid so. We got the doctor out to see her, but he says there's nothing he can do, and just suggested a tonic which he sold to me. It sounds like congestive cardiac disease to me."

Doctor Mansell stroked his chin thoughtfully. "The best physicians are in London and would cost a fortune. So that's just not practical. I can examine her myself and maybe get her to Merthyr where medical advances are further forward than in this back water!"

Rebecca nodded. "That would be a good idea. I know Daniel Evans has had experience of heart conditions when he studied at Barts Hospital." Although she didn't care to say the man's name, but she knew he was the best for the job.

"Can I examine her right now?" Mansell asked.

"She's sleeping presently, I'll wake her soon. Meanwhile it would be nice if you could see your wife."

Mansell's face clouded over. It upset Rebecca that he hadn't even asked about his wife's welfare and she, herself, had ran to her bedroom as soon as he entered the room as if fearful of his approach.

"I garnered the impression she was frightened when I entered," he said. "I thought it best for her to get used to seeing me around here as I will need to stay a day or two. I should hate it if she fell into a bout of hysteria, which she is prone to do."

Rebecca guessed that Mansell was speaking sense, and brightened at the thought of the good Doctor staying under the same roof as herself. They got on really well as they chatted away with ease, so much so that she'd almost forgotten why he was here in the first place. That was until Rhys burst into the kitchen, out of breath. "Miss Rebecc—" he began, but on seeing the pair at the table, his face clouded over. "And who might this be?" he glowered.

"Rhys, this is Doctor Mansell Owen. Hannah's husband."

As soon as she said the words, Rhys's features softened and he smiled, then he went over to the table to speak to the Doctor, pumping his hand with delight at meeting him at long last. "I've heard a lot about you, Doctor. I assume you're here to see Mrs Evans?"

Mansell nodded. "Yes, I intend taking her to see a physician in Merthyr, and maybe, if Rebecca doesn't mind, take her and Hannah back to Merthyr at the same time."

Rhys's features fell. "Oh," he said, and lowering his head, mumbled something unintelligible.

Rebecca stood in front of him. "But you knew I was only here for a short while," she explained.

He nodded. "Aye. It's just I thought you'd be here a while longer yet."

She gently touched his shoulder, then he excused himself and left the room. It surprised her how upset he seemed to be about the situation.

"I think you've got an admirer there, Rebecca," Mansell said, then added, "and who could blame him, you are a beautiful person both inside and out."

Rebecca's heart thudded as he said the words, he drew closer and looking into her eyes, lifted her chin and planted a kiss on her lips, making her heady with desire for him. Then as if remembering where he was, Mansell drew away, just as Sarah burst into the kitchen.

"I've put Hannah to bed, Miss," she said. "She seemed to be in a strange mood."

"That's fine," Rebecca said. She had earlier explained to Sarah the situation with the Doctor and his wife.

As if to change the subject, Mansell asked, "Where is that tonic you mentioned earlier, I should like to take a look at it, please?"

Rebecca went to the kitchen cupboard and removed a brown bottle which read, *Healthy Heart Tonic! A spoonful a day keeps the doctor away!*

Mansell studied the bottle carefully. "Quacks!" he exclaimed angrily. "This kind of stuff is nonsense. He uncorked it and sniffed, then tasted it with a spoon. "I'm afraid to say it's as I suspected, just sugared water, nothing more. At most it will rot the teeth, at best it might provide a placebo effect, but will do no real good. At least I don't think it contains arsenic like some of these compounds can. That doctor, whoever he is, is a charlatan! He's probably getting someone to bottle this stuff and selling it off to patients. No wonder he made out there was no more he could do. The man is a fraud, a shyster!" Rebecca had never seen the Doctor look so angry before. As if realising, he turned to her. "Sorry. It just makes my blood boil that a member of my profession can do this kind of thing, and to vulnerable patients too! If it were not for the fact you are a nurse and staying here, Rebecca, it's possible that my wife's aunt would die from lack of good care and living off sugar water! If I could get my hands on that man I'd knock his block off!" Sarah, who had been standing close by, made to leave the room. "I'm sorry young lady, but who is the doctor around these parts?"

"Doctor Mongomery from Aberystwyth, Sir..."

"And is he a good doctor, this fellow?"

"I don't know to be honest with you. All I know of him is he sells bottles of his cure alls from the back of a cart in the weekly fair at Aberystwyth. People come from miles to buy bottles of it!"

Doctor Owen tutted. "When's the next one going to be held?"

"Tomorrow, Sir," Sarah replied.

"Right, thank you, Sarah. You can go about your business now. Please keep an eye on my wife, Hannah, for me, whilst Rebecca takes me to examine Mrs Evans." When the girl was out of earshot, the Doctor took Rebecca to one side. "Tomorrow, I'd like you to attend the weekly fair with me, Rebecca, if you don't mind?"

She nodded, worrying as to what the Doctor had in mind.

Rebecca gently roused Mrs Evans who looked surprised to hear that Doctor Owen had come all the way from Merthyr Tydfil.

When Rebecca had got the woman dressed and looking presentable, she sent Sarah to make tea whilst she was examined. Afterwards, Mansell spoke outside the bedroom to Rebecca. "Yes, you are correct, nurse, it looks like dropsy, fluid in the legs, pitting oedema. When I pressed her lower limbs with my thumbs, the indentation remained for some time. I am afraid that the build up of fluid could eventually kill her if it collects around the heart. I'd like you to restrict fluids for time being. Keep her mainly to water. She can have that cup of tea for now, but after that strictly water only, until she is seen at Merthyr."

***

That evening with Rebecca's assistance, Sarah made a tasty rabbit stew with dumplings and they all sat at the table to dine, including Mr. and Mrs Evans, Hannah and Rhys also. Hannah kept glancing shyly at her husband and putting her head down. Mansell's eyes had began to well up and Rebecca feared he was near tears. Once the meal was over, Rebecca decided to move into Hannah's room so that the Doctor could get a good rest in a room, on his own. That night, she was aware that he slept only inches away from her in the room next door and wondered what he might be thinking right now.

She couldn't sleep because of it and brought her shawl to wrap around herself when she went downstairs to drink a glass of milk, and afterwards wandered out into the courtyard and sat on a felled tree trunk gazing up at the stars. Hearing the kitchen door slam shut, she startled to see Mansell walking towards her.

"Mind if I join you?" he asked. He was dressed in an embossed dressing gown and slippers, which seemed strange to see the man who usually dressed so elegantly in well tailored outfits, in casual garb.

"Not at all..."

He sat beside her on the tree trunk. "Rebecca..." he began.

"There's no need for words, Mansell. It's just impossible..."

"How did you know what I was about to say?"

"Because I feel I know your thoughts. It's almost as though we are so in tune with one another, we can speak without words."

He took her hand in quiet reassurance. "How right you are. I just wish sometimes..."

She turned to face him and placing a finger on his lips, said, "Please don't. You mustn't say it, you have a wife."

"But she is dead to me, can't you see, my Hannah has gone for good."

Rebecca shook her head. "You don't know that, you must get her to see a specialist, Mansell."

"Don't you think I've tried, Rebecca? That evening you dined at my house we had returned from seeing a psychiatrist in Cardiff, who diagnosed her with Melancholia of Childbirth. He said my wife was fraught with her nerves and had somehow regressed back to childhood, he couldn't be sure if she would ever be the same again."

Rebecca squeezed his hand and allowed him to cry silently, for now it was all she could do.

***

The following day after breakfast, Rebecca accompanied the Doctor to the weekly fair at Aberystwyth. He was that intent on speaking to Doctor Montgomery, like a man on a mission, she had never seen him so angry before. Hannah had been left in Sarah's charge for the day.

As the carriage approached the outdoor market which was set up in some fields, Rebecca noticed the crowds gathering all around as farmers and traders sold their wares of: cheeses, various meats, fruit and vegetables, bread and cakes, jams, wooden toys, knitted garments, even clothing.

In one corner of the field was a Punch and Judy show where children sat watching the hook-nosed puppet shout in a high-pitched voice, "That's the way to do it!" How they laughed uproariously. In another corner was a boxing booth where a man in a bowler hat shouted, "Who dares fight the fittest man in Cardigan? If you last the round—I'll pay you a shiny sovereign!" Several men were already removing their jackets to queue up to take on the man, as their wives watched on anxiously. In the third corner, was a gypsy caravan where you could get your fortune told for a farthing, and finally, in the fourth corner, a man stood on a wooden platform extolling the virtues of a 'Doctor's Cure All' in a brown corked bottle, as another man passed them to him from the back of a cart.

As they approached, Rebecca noticed that all the bottles looked exactly the same except for having different labels which said, "Healthy Heart Tonic!" or "Rejuvenating Liver Tonic!" People were queuing in their droves to purchase bottles and bought not just one bottle, but two or three at a time. Some people in the crowd appeared sick, one elderly lady with a hacking cough, tightly wrapped her shawl around her shoulders. Another man, who limped badly, held up his hand to ask for a bottle. It appeared that these people had come far and wide seeking a cure for their ailments. And all the while, Doctor Montgomery acted the showman as people cheered and praised him.

"The bloody scoundrel!" Mansell shouted, so that several people turned to glare at him.

"Sssh!" Rebecca warned, but Mansell continued to shout until he caught the attention of the quack.

Montgomery glanced up and laughed nervously. "Would you like a good tonic, Sir? Sounds like you might have a sore throat with all that shouting you're doing!"

Mansell beat a path through with his cane. Then turning to the crowd shouted, "This man is nothing but a charlatan. He calls himself a doctor, but he recently visited a family member who has congestive cardiac failure and just gave her one of his tonics. It's just sugared water I tell you, fit for no purpose except rotting your teeth!"

People in the crowd began to murmur and one man shouted. "How do we know you're telling the truth, Sir?"

"Because..." Rebecca butted in, "this man is a well respected doctor in Merthyr Tydfil. His name is Doctor Mansell Owen and he works at the General Hospital in the town. I, myself, am a ward sister and I can vouch for his good character!"

The people in the crowd looked at the pair dubiously.

"Well I'm still buying the tonic!" a woman shouted, and others nodded in agreement, meanwhile Montgomery was packing his wares away in a suitcase.

"Look he's leaving!" a large woman shouted. "It must be true what that doctor from Merthyr said!"

The crowd rushed forward and reaching into their bags and baskets, began to pelt Doctor Montgomery with all sorts, tomatoes, eggs, apples, anything they could lay their hands on, until the doctor was forced to drop his suitcase and make off on the back of the cart with the other man who'd been helping to steer the horse.

When the crowd had quietened down, people gathered around to shake Doctor Owen's hand. "I never realised until now, Doctor, that the man was a fake!" Shrieked one elderly lady.

Mansell shook his head. "Why would you?" he said sadly.

"One thing's for certain..." a young man bellowed, "he won't be back here again in a hurry!" And the crowd began to disperse.

Mansell took Rebecca by the arm and led her to a stall selling toffee apples. "Fancy one?" he asked. She nodded politely. "I don't usually make it a habit to eat such sweet confectionary but something like this now and again, won't harm. That tonic on the other hand, if it were taken several times a day, could lose a man or woman his teeth!"

He purchased two toffee apples and they strolled to a nearby mound beneath an oak tree, where they enjoyed the sweet treat, easy in one another's company. The sunlight through the leaves of the tree produced a dappled effect in early September, the warmth comforting her.

"You should make more of an effort though, Mansell, to speak to Hannah. You hardly spoke to her at the breakfast table this morning," Rebecca said.

"It's not that I didn't want to speak to her, it's just I don't know how to anymore."

Rebecca rubbed his back as a term of affection, she really felt for the man sat beside her.

"Well why don't we both take her somewhere tomorrow?"

He nodded. "Maybe, but I did plan visiting a hospital in Carmarthen tomorrow."

"Oh? Is that to do with your work?"

"No. Actually it's an asylum for people like Hannah. The psychiatrist in Cardiff told me about it."

"But surely if you have to put her in one of those places, it should be a little nearer to home?"

"I was just thinking this might be best all around."

"Better for whom?" she asked indignantly. "Better for you, isn't it?"

"I was thinking of the children really, I want to protect them and I thought as she has family in the area..."

"Well I'm not convinced. Mable is very sick as you know, and Gwyn is so busy on the farm, and in any case it's not that near here. We passed through on the way, it's miles away. But I expect you already knew that. You just want to lock your wife away and forget all about her, don't you?"

She stood and brushed down the skirts of her dress and headed back towards the carriage.

"Wait!" Mansell shouted after her.

Rebecca just couldn't believe the Doctor was willing to leave his wife behind and so far away from home.

If Tobias Cookson, the carriage driver, was surprised when she got back into the cab, he wasn't saying so, he discretely opened the door and helped her inside. Mansell arrived a couple of minutes later out of breath and they drove back in silence to the farm.

***

When they returned to the farm it was as if all hell had broken loose, Gwyn and Sarah were calling out Hannah's name and Rhys was jumping on his horse and cart.

"What's going on?" Rebecca asked a weary looking Gwyn.

He mopped his brow with a handkerchief. "Hannah wasn't in her room earlier like we all thought, she must have gone out wandering..."

"Oh no, this is all my fault for leaving her to go to the market. I should have realised Sarah wouldn't have enough time to keep an eye on her."

"Don't blame yourself. It's odd, as one moment she was having a lie down and the next she was missing, she was checked on moments before that."

Mansell stood staring at them all. "Come on, we must find her, she's a danger to herself!" he said firmly. "Sarah and Gwyn, you search the barns and sheds, and Rebecca and I will search the fields. Where has Rhys gone to?"

"He's gone to ask at neighbouring farms if they've seen her." Gwyn rubbed his eyes as if worn out by it all.

Mansell nodded. "Good idea. And what about Mrs Evans?"

"She said she'll stay at the house in case Hannah returns, she can't go far in any case her legs are badly swollen this morning," Sarah chipped in.

Rebecca had a bad feeling about this and now the earlier sunshine had gone all together as grey clouds gathered overhead. Gwyn had said he thought a storm was brewing last night, but she hadn't believed it when the sun had emerged early that morning. Yet, country folk seemed to sense these things.

She wracked her brain to think where Hannah might have gone to, she tended to stay close to everyone, the only time she'd wandered off previously, was when Jake had been at the farm that time he'd enticed her. A sudden chill filled her veins. She grabbed Mansell's arm.

"Oh no! I have a fear that a young farmhand might have her, called, Jake Morgan!"

Mansell studied her eyes. "Why do you say this?"

"He worked at the farm here but has since left, he stole some of Mrs Evans's jewellery. The first night we arrived he tried to hold up the carriage!"

Tobias Cookson, who had been standing close by, nodded.

Mansell's eyes grew wide. "But why did neither of you tell me of this?"

"We didn't want to worry you," Rebecca replied. "There's something else too..."

"What?"

"One day, Jake pulled a ribbon from Hannah's hair, teasing her so she chased after him, they were not gone long, but I saw her adjusting her skirts. She swore he hadn't touched her."

Mansell's lips were now set in a firm line, he could hardly bear to look at Rebecca.

"I wish you'd both have told me what you knew!" he cried angrily.

"But then, what would you have done, Mansell? Neither you nor Hannah's own mother were in a position to care for her. Her mother has the children to tend to and you have your work at the hospital."

He shook his head. "If anything happens to her, I'll never forgive myself..."

Nor me, either, Rebecca thought to herself.

They searched until it got dark but still there was no sign of Hannah. Finally, Rhys returned, saying that he'd gone to the Williams farm that Jake was working at, but the owner had seen neither hide nor hair of him for the past few days. "I told him to check none of his valuables was missing!" he laughed ironically.

This was no laughing matter however, what could they do now?

There was a long silence until Rhys suggested going to the Black Lion to ask people there.

Mansell seemed to think that a good idea and went with him, but for now, there was nothing they could do until resuming the search at first light.

***

After keeping an all night vigil, Rhys and Mansell returned at first light to say the men from the pub would be helping in the search for Hannah. Mable's eyes were full of tears. Rebecca feared for the woman's health as she had slowed down drastically this past couple of weeks.

"Hannah's been like a daughter to me..." she explained. "Her mother's been bringing her to the farm a couple of times a year ever since she was a baby. We spent many a happy time here, Christmases too." She sobbed into the frills of her apron as she sat in the armchair. No one had slept that night. A lantern had been left to burn bright in the window, while Rhys and Mansell asked at the pub, Gwyn had taken the sheepdogs out to see if they could find her overnight. Sarah had kept everyone going with refreshments and Rebecca had thought and thought where might Hannah have gone and she hoped for the young woman's sake she wouldn't have gone anywhere near Jake Morgan.

"Tell the men they're welcome to come back here for refreshments!" Mable called weakly after Rhys and Mansell as they departed from the kitchen. Mansell turned and nodded, unable to utter a word and Rebecca's heart went out to him.

"Take the two dogs," Gwyn suggested.

"I've got an idea," Rebecca suggested, "take an item of Hannah's clothing as the dogs might connect the smell of that with her."

"Grand idea," Rhys spoke for the first time and smiled at Rebecca, almost as though he understood what she might be going through.

She ran upstairs to the bedroom and took Hannah's night gown from her bed, for the first time, she noticed a book about flowers on the bedside table, she took it with her.

"I don't know if this is of any help," she addressed Mansell, "but I found this book on the bed, it's about wildflowers and it was open as if she had been looking at the pictures!"

"That's the book I gave her when she arrived..." Mable said. "You're right Rebecca, she loved looking at those beautiful illustrations..."

Mansell took the book from Rebecca and flipped through it. "A lot of these are flowers that grow in woodland," he said thoughtfully. "Like foxgloves and bluebells...I think it might be a start if we search any wooded areas..."

"Good idea," Rhys agreed.

It gave Rebecca some comfort to think that was where her charge might have been headed and not gone off with Jake Morgan. She'd noticed that whilst the woman seemed to have lost passion for the things she loved previously when she was well, she still liked flowers a lot.

"Well let's hope that she's found soon," Mable said, as cheerfully as she could. "Although it was raining last night, it wasn't that cold outside and it was only a drizzle of sorts."

Rebecca nodded. She hoped wherever Hannah was she was safe from harm.

Chapter Eight

Rhys and Mansell returned later that day without any success from either themselves or the search party. They were all about to call it another night for the search as darkness descended, when they heard a tap on the kitchen window.

Rebecca dashed out to the courtyard to see Sarah flailing her arms wildly.

"What's the matter?" she asked.

"Sssh! We mustn't frighten her," Sarah said. "I've found Hannah, she's in the old barn sleeping on some hay."

As Rebecca walked with Sarah, a sense of relief flooded through her as she realised all was well, but knew they mustn't scare the woman. So quietly she went into the barn and followed Sarah up the wooden ladder into the hay loft, where they found Hannah still asleep; her chestnut hair spread out on the straw, a look of pure innocence about her. In her hand, she still clutched some wild flowers she must have picked earlier that day.

"Well thank goodness for that..." Rebecca whispered. "But I thought you and Gwyn checked here yesterday?"

Sarah shrugged. "We did, but I suppose she could easily have hidden amongst the hay or been elsewhere and then afterwards came here to sleep."

Rebecca gently roused the sleeping woman, who looked none the worse for wear. By her side were some apples she must have taken from the windfall in the field, and there was a trough of water down below, she had neither starved nor gone thirsty, thankfully.

Hannah smiled when she saw Rebecca, wrapping her arms around her neck as an infant might do when she saw her mother. Rebecca's heart went out to both the woman and her husband, who she could see now truly did care for his wife's welfare.

***

Following a good night's rest, it was decided the following day, that Rebecca and Hannah would return to Merthyr, where the Doctor said he had plans to convert the attic of the house for his wife and bring in a live-in nurse, so Rebecca could return to work at the hospital. She had mixed feelings about returning home as she was leaving Mable and Gwyn behind, but now at least, they had Sarah to help with the chores. Mansell said he would also fix it soon for Mable to come to Merthyr to be examined by Daniel Evans.

When they were packed up and about to leave, Rebecca looked around for Rhys to say goodbye, but he was nowhere to be seen. Well, she guessed she wouldn't be seeing him again and maybe it would be painful for him to say farewell to her in any case. A large lump of disappointment rose in her throat which she swallowed down.

What did she know about him anyhow? Only that he was one of the kindest men she had ever known and she didn't doubt for a second that one day he would get to grips with Jake Morgan and get him to recompense for what he'd done to Mrs Evans. At least she knew he was around too, to keep an eye on the elderly couple.

Taking one last look around, she stooped to kiss Mable on the cheek and shook hands with Gwyn, thanking them both for their hospitality. "Make sure you take care of Mrs Evans, young Sarah," she advised the girl. Sarah nodded. "And please ensure she gets plenty of rest. Goodbye, everyone!" She waved her hand and climbed into the carriage, opposite Mansell and Hannah.

The Doctor held his wife's hand on the journey home. Hannah now appeared to be more subdued than usual, it was evident how precious she was to him and how close he'd come to losing her.

***

Life back in Merthyr took some getting used to once more. Rebecca returned to helping Mam and the twins in between her shifts at the hospital. Her path hadn't crossed with Daniel Evans since that night he'd ended their relationship in such a cruel, offhand manner, but she heard he was due to examine Mable the following week and she was glad of that.

She received a letter from Sarah telling her all was well at the farm, but there was no mention of Rhys whatsoever, and she wondered about him. What was he doing right now? Did he still think of her?

Days turned into weeks and weeks into months, and before long, it was almost Christmas. The ward had been decorated with paper lanterns and a real Christmas tree installed at one end of the ward in front of the window. Silver bells, candles, and little ornaments, adorning it, and a candle was lit each Sunday of Advent.

She continued to work with Mansell Owen, but something was amiss, the light had appeared to have gone from his eyes. One evening at the end of her shift, she called him into her office.

"Please sit down," she beckoned. He did as asked, removed his glasses and rubbed his eyes. "Now what's wrong, Mansell?"

He looked at her with glassy eyes. "It's Hannah."

"Has she become agitated again?"

"No, this time it's the opposite, she doesn't want to get out of bed and the nurse told me she vomited last night, yet I can't really see anything wrong with her physically. It's so strange."

Rebecca's blood ran cold and the hairs on her neck stood on end. "She couldn't possibly be pregnant could she, Mansell?"

He shook his head. "No, of course not, we haven't had any marital relations since before the birth of our last child. It wouldn't be right in her condition. It would be like taking advantage of her. What's wrong? You look pale, Rebecca?"

"I was just thinking that night she went missing, no one knew the whereabouts of Jake Morgan, could he have interfered with her?"

"I bloody hope not! Sorry Rebecca, I mustn't swear in front of a lady."

"Don't worry about that, you've every right to be angry. Mansell, you must examine her to see if she's pregnant, just in case. If you don't feel right doing it, then please allow Daniel Evans to do so."

As much as she disliked Daniel, she knew that he would be the right person to examine the Doctor's wife if Mansell couldn't do it, due to circumstance of a possible conception.

"Look at me, I'm supposed to be a good physician and I can't recognise whether my own wife is pregnant or not. That honestly hadn't occurred to me."

"It's too close to home that's why. But if she is pregnant, then it's a despicable thing to have done to her. How has she been since we returned from the farm?"

"Quiet, very quiet. Not herself at all, but then she hasn't been herself for a long time. Since we made the attic into quarter for her, she dislikes coming down into the rest of the house, but I encourage the nursemaid to take her into the garden every day."

"That's good, she needs fresh air. And the children?"

"My mother-in law-has done a fine job with those, but I fear they are getting too much for her. She should be resting not running

110

around after young children. If only my wife were well just as she should be."

"And Mable, did Daniel Evans examine her?" Rebecca asked tentatively.

"Yes, a few weeks ago. Unfortunately, although he medicated her with Digoxin, which is made from the foxglove for her condition, he fears it is only a question of time."

"Did he tell her that?"

"I'm afraid so. She begged him to tell her the truth."

"So she knows and understands she is in her final days?"

"Yes, my mother-in-law plans to visit her later this week to say her goodbyes. It will be hard though, as I don't think the nurse can manage the children as well as Hannah."

"How about I step in to help you whilst she's away? If only for a couple of days? I have leave due from the hospital."

The Doctor shook his head. "Oh, I couldn't expect you to do that for me, Rebecca."

"You can and you will. You have been good to me Mansell, helping to supply extra nurses for the ward to lighten the load."

He nodded. "Very well, but first please come to my house after your shift while I examine my wife as I fear she'll become upset if I do that alone, she trusts you, Rebecca. Although the nurse, Maria, is good with her, Hannah hasn't bonded as well with her as she did with you."

Rebecca nodded, fully understanding and appreciating his dilemma.

***

Rebecca accompanied Mansell following her shift, with a view to reassuring the woman. Hannah smiled when she saw Rebecca and ran toward her like a young child.

"That's the most animated I've seen my wife since we returned from Llanbadarn Fawr!" Mansell exclaimed, with a smile on his face.

It was so good to see.

"So, she's been subdued since she got back to Merthyr?" Rebecca asked.

"I'm afraid so." He shook his head and sighed heavily.

The nursemaid in attendance, interjected. "Excuse me, Doctor, but there's something else too..."

"Go ahead, Maria," the Doctor instructed.

"It's just that sometimes I've caught her rocking back and forth like as if it's a form of comfort to her. Then other times hitting her head against the wall. Extremely emotional."

Mansell nodded and stroked his chin as if deep in thought.

This wasn't the Hannah that Rebecca had come to know. Although the other was in some way in another place mentally, she wasn't in turmoil, she'd seemed happy enough in her own world.

After a great deal of coaxing and soothing, the Doctor examined his wife's abdomen as she reclined on the bed with Rebecca holding her hand and singing gently to her.

After readjusting Hannah's clothing and Maria taking her out to the garden, so they were left to speak in confidence, Mansell gravelly said, "From my palpations of the abdomen, it feels as though the womb has moved up to indicate the baby is of 3 or 4 months gestation, which would tie in with the time my wife was in Cardigan with you."

"So, it has to be Jake Morgan's child she's bearing!" Rebecca exclaimed.

He shook his head. "Not necessarily – how about that Rhys fellow at the farm? He would have had the opportunity? Look at the way he went off in the horse and cart to search at the neighbouring farms when she went missing! Maybe he wanted to find her before she told us what might have happened!"

Rebecca frowned. "Oh no, Mansell! You mustn't think that way at all. Rhys was the one searching for Jake that time he stole Mrs Evans's jewellery. He's a fine and honest man!"

Mansell stared into the flames of the fire. "Well, whoever it was, will be horse whipped if I ever find them!"

She gently laid her hand on his shoulder. "And what will you do now about the situation?" she enquired.

He turned, and drawing a breath said, "I'll bring up the baby as my own, even though it will be a bastard, no one need know the truth. It will be better for the child as if this were discovered, it would have that stigma over its head all its life."

"But people will then think it bad of you fathering a child to a vulnerable woman, they will assume that of course believing you've somehow coerced your wife."

"Let them assume what they wish. Though not that many around here know of the truth of the situation of Hannah's mental illness as she remains locked away from society."

"You'd be surprised Mansell how gossip gets around the village..."

Rebecca was thinking of what her mother had told her about a woman who'd once lived in the village of Abercanaid called, Maggie Shanklin. The woman had been jealous as hell of her mother, Kathleen. Both were Irish by birth, but Maggie saw a lot of her own lost youth in Kathleen and had taken every opportunity to gossip and cause trouble whenever possible.

Mansell grimaced. "Yes, but what else can I do? I don't want everyone to know what's happened to my wife, they might think she's been loose with her morals."

Rebecca let out a long breath. "Well, maybe you could give the baby away to a childless couple, put him or her up for adoption, or make them a ward of the Parish..."

"I don't know, I shall have to think about it. If I make the infant a ward of the Parish, the child will end up in the workhouse like Dickens', Oliver Twist. I wouldn't wish that on any child." He shook his head vigorously as if the mere suggestion were abhorrent to him.

"Well, don't think too long about it. The pregnancy will be evident soon enough," Rebecca said gently.

"For time being at least Hannah is confined to the home." He rubbed his chin thoughtfully. "You might be correct about giving the baby to a childless couple being the better option. My sister, who lives in Aberdare, and her husband, have been trying for a baby for years, she has reached the age of thirty five and fears she is now barren. I could ask them. Also if the baby goes to live at their home at least he or she will be out of this valley."

"I think it could prove to be the best option for all concerned, Mansell," Rebecca whispered.

"But I fear for my wife's mental state as the birth approaches. I need to take advice from the psychiatrist at Cardiff. He'll know what to do, this could though, tip her over the edge. She acts like a child, so will not understand what's happening to her."

Rebecca tried to smile in reassurance, but failing dismally, just nodded.

***

The following day, Rebecca called around to her mother's home to tell her that she wouldn't be able to help out with the twins as Mansell's mother-in-law would be away visiting her ailing sister in Cardigan and she was needed to help with his children.

Her mother just smiled. "Not to worry, although the boys are growing up and into mischief, Bill next door helps me out. He took them out on his horse and trap the other day."

"Oh goodness, how could he look after them on his own whilst steering that contraption?" Rebecca couldn't believe her ears.

"He has a niece and nephew, Sam and Diana, they're almost grown themselves now, they sat on the back with them. He took them all for a ride to Morlais Castle and back. By the time they'd returned, they were all but worn out and ready for bed. It gave me a couple of hours peace, I can tell you. A chance to put my feet up for once."

"Glad to hear it, you ought to rest more, Mam. Have you heard anything from Utah lately?"

She shook her head. "I never thought I'd hear myself say this but your father must be all consumed by that Mormon religion of his. When my own family converted to the faith, I wasn't too sure about it. That's partly why I was happy to run way with your Dad. Oh, I loved him of course I did, but I'd been raised as a Catholic. In fact, I've started to go to mass at St Mary's regularly now when James or Bill can mind the boys for me. In time I'll take them along too."

Rebecca had noticed a change for the better in her mother and put it down either to the Church or the presence of Bill next door, however, she understood her mother could never marry Bill whilst her father was still alive as it went against Church teachings. Divorce was a dirty word to Kathleen Jenkin.

How she pined for her father though, there were times when she longed to speak to him, she missed not having that fatherly presence around, and if she were being honest with herself, she realised that her relationship with Mansell Owen was very patronly. He being a good deal older than herself by as much as fifteen years or so, she guessed. How sad it was though that a man like him, at the pinnacle of his career, should lose his wife for it was almost as if she had died or gone someplace else, and Rebecca couldn't see any remedy to the situation.

Her thoughts were disturbed as James came in through the back door as she was chatting with her mother, whilst the twins were sleeping upstairs.

"Hello, Becca!" he said, looking surprised to see her. "Nice to see you!"

She rose to her feet and gave him a hug. "It's good to see you, too!" How her brother had grown into quite the young man, looking so handsome in his new twill suit. "How are you getting on at work, enjoying it?"

He beamed. "Yes, I am actually. The partners have been giving me extra responsibility and suggested that I eventually train as a solicitor, but I'm not sure about that..."

"Oh James, but what an opportunity for you! They must surely see something in you to say that. I hope they are paying you extra for all that responsibility, mind?"

He shook his head. "No, not really, but they are good to me and would pay for any training I choose to undertake. Mr. Goldstein presented me with this!" He put his hand in his pocket and extracted a small oblong-shaped wooden box, opening it to reveal a silver fountain pen.

"That does look expensive, James," Rebecca enthused.

"Yes, he told me to take care of it and I do. I don't leave it hanging around anywhere, it's the nicest thing I've ever owned, apart from that wooden train I used to have as a child of course!" he said, gazing at his mother, who smiled on proudly.

"Yes, your father insisted on buying you that, James," she said. "'Twas in the window of a toy shop in Merthyr High Street just before Christmas one year, beside it was the most beautiful porcelain doll I'd ever seen, dressed in all green velvet. He bought it for you Rebecca, because in a funny way the doll reminded him of me when we first met. I had a best dress that was green velvet..." she looked away wistfully.

Rebecca held her hand. "Oh Mam, I still have that doll upstairs, don't I? I'm a bit old for dolls now but I'll never part with it. You miss Dad, don't you?"

Her mother brushed away a tear with the back of her hand. "Of course I do, Becca. He's my husband and even now I still care about him. You know what I think we should do, is all write him a letter telling him what's going on here in our lives back in Merthyr Tydfil, telling him about the funny things the twins have got up to, and their progress too. How they're both walking and talking. How you went to Llanbadarn Fawr for a few weeks, Becca, how you're doing at work, James..."

James scowled. "You two can write one if you wish, but I'm not going to. He left us all here in the lurch without a thought for any of us! I'm going upstairs to change out of my suit!" He left the kitchen slamming the door behind him. How he reminded Rebecca of her father when he behaved like that. Her mother was about to go after him, when she held her back.

"Don't Mam, please. Leave him be for now, he's entitled to be upset. We all are, particularly you..."

Her mother smiled. "I know. But I'm no longer upset. I still love your father of course I do, but he's made his decision to leave and that's that."

Rebecca didn't really believe what her mother said, even if she believed it herself.

***

That weekend, Rebecca helped at Mansell's home. The children were lively and the eldest, Thomas, kept asking about his mother, who appeared to be kept well away from them all. He was only seven years of age and she didn't quite know how to explain things to him.

He tugged at her skirts, "When can my Mama come to play in the garden with me again, Miss Becca?"

She knelt down to his level. "Oh Thomas, your mother is not well at the moment, darling," she ruffled his hair. The boy looked up at her with huge china blue eyes through thick fringed lashes. Eyes that seemed to question so much but expected so little in return, all he wanted right now was his mother. As the eldest he was trying desperately to be the 'man of the house' when his father was away, but he was too young to take on that task.

Although Hannah had been mentally unstable, she had still played with her children up until now, yet it was more as if she were a child herself. They enjoyed her playful childlike behaviour and hadn't questioned it until now.

"Mama spends a lot of time sleeping..." Charlotte, who was six-years-old, and almost as tall as her brother, pouted.

"She needs plenty of rest right now," Rebecca explained. Oh dear, this was going to be difficult for their father to explain to them about the baby. Maybe it would be best if Hannah could go to live with her brother and sister-in-law until the baby was born, as her own children wouldn't know about the child then and neither would the villagers.

She deliberated later when she had a break as the nursemaid relieved her of her duties for an hour whilst Hannah was asleep, so Rebecca called to see her Aunt Lily who lived nearby. Rebecca knew that her Aunt Lily and Uncle Evan would say nothing of her concerns to anyone as they were used to members of the chapel congregation confiding in them. Evan was well respected in the community as a minister, and Lily too, as she had once opened a school there for the children.

So she sat facing her aunt at the kitchen table of her cosy home. "Yes, I agree, it might be best that Hannah be sent to Aberdare to have the baby, but I feel those little ones might suffer so in any case. In a sense they've already lost the mother they knew and loved. I had a friend once, called, Elsa Morgan. She lived in the village and was a lot older than myself. We became firm friends; she ran the village shop and helped me at the school. She took on a young child called, Betty. Betty had been abandoned by her family, who left her behind to fend for herself. That little girl was mute and in a terrible state, but with the love and care of Mr. and Mrs Morgan, she came on leaps and bounds and began to speak once more..."

"What happened to Mrs Morgan, Auntie?"

Lily's eyes filled with tears. "She passed away many years ago, and her husband died not long afterwards. Some say he died of a broken heart..."

"And what became of Betty?"

"She still lives in the village. She's married now with children of her own, thanks to the start Mrs Morgan gave her. I suppose what

I'm trying to say is that children are adaptable and with plenty of love and care, they'll nourish and grow."

It gladdened Rebecca's heart to hear her aunt say that.

"Rest assured that Evan and I will pray for Hannah and the new baby, though the circumstances are awful. She must either have been coerced into having sex with someone, or otherwise raped...which doesn't bear thinking about. I don't know if the villagers are gossiping about this or not to be honest, we've heard nothing in this house, so let's hope no one knows about it."

Rebecca breathed a sigh of relief, the last thing the Doctor and his family needed was to be the subject of idle gossip.

Feeling a lot better after leaving her aunt's home, she returned to the Doctor's house. His horse and carriage had been stabled outside and she went inside the house to find evidence that Tobias Cookson had left his boots in the middle of the kitchen floor. His long black coat he wore as coachman, strewn across a chair. Thankfully, the Doctor wasn't in as he would have frowned at such slovenly behaviour. She tutted and moved the boots near the back door to avoid anyone tripping over them.

There was no sign of the nursemaid, so she guessed she'd taken the children out for some fresh air. So she decided to check on Hannah in the attic bedroom. She wasn't very happy that the woman had been left alone, but maybe if she was asleep, it would do no harm. As she got to the foot of the stairs, muffled voices emanated from above, which disturbed her.

Something was wrong.

Removing her shoes so she should not be heard, she stealth fully climbed the wooden attic steps. Hannah's bedroom door was ajar as she approached. Heart pounding and mouth dry, she saw Tobias Cookson stood close to the bed, staring at Hannah. Slowly, she placed her hand on the door knob and pushed it so the door opened further.

"Come on... you know you want to!" he said playfully, unaware of any observer.

At first she wondered what he was up to, until his tone and manner changed, he had a lustful look in his eyes, so much so, he hadn't even noticed Rebecca stood near the door.

"Come on, Hannah!" he said, more forcefully this time. "Give a man a bit o' pleasure, we can play our game together."

Hannah began to shriek with fear as Tobias drew near and began to fumble with the belt of his trousers. She wrapped the bed cover tightly around her as if it would somehow magically protect her from the man.

"No!" Hannah shouted, as Rebecca remained rooted to the spot, but imminent danger for her charge spurred her on, and she burst her way into the bedroom.

"What on earth is going on here, Mr. Cookson?" she accused, raising her voice to a level she rarely used.

Cookson turned to face Rebecca. A deep flush appearing from his neck up, he loosened his shirt collar with his finger, almost as though he were suffocated by the sudden intrusion. "Nothing," he muttered. "Nothing at all!"

"Then why is your belt undone and why is Hannah so upset?" She moved to comfort Hannah and cuddled her in her arms on the bed, softly stroking her hair as the woman sobbed.

"We were just playing a game that's all. You like a bit o' fun, don't you gal?" his laugh sounded hollow.

"I think you had better go right now!" Rebecca instructed.

Cookson buckled up his belt, then she heard him run down the stairs. He was barefooted, so she guessed he had removed his leather boots so that neither Hannah nor anyone else, should hear his footsteps going to the attic. It made her blood run cold realising this might have been going on for a long time. How many visits had he made to Hannah's bedroom? She shuddered to think. So maybe he was the one who had got Hannah pregnant and not Jake Morgan. It was difficult to tell though as maybe both had taken advantage of a vulnerable woman.

Just as Rebecca was about to question Hannah about the matter, she heard the front door slam as the Doctor returned and an altercation in the hallway took place.

"What on earth is going on?" The Doctor accused Cookson.

Cookson didn't appear to answer, so Rebecca ran to the foot of the stairs. "Stop him at once, Mansell!" she exclaimed. "I think it was Tobias who got your wife pregnant!"

The Doctor fought to contain the man, who was quite strong and fit. "I ain't got no one pregnant, don't believe her, Doctor! I only went to your wife's room as she had been left in the house on her own!"

The Doctor, who had the coachman in a bear hug, let go of him and glared at Rebecca, who by now, was at the foot of the stairs, inches away from both men.

"Is this true, what this man says?" The Doctor accused.

Rebecca nodded. "About your wife being on her own, yes. The nursemaid was taking care of the children whilst Hannah slept for me to have a break, but when I returned they'd all left the house..."

Mansell's face reddened. "I can't believe that my wife was left here alone, and you, Sir," he said, referring to Cookson, "shall be horsewhipped if it's true you interfered with my wife in any way!"

Cookson paled. "I...I...I'm telling you the truth, Doctor Owen. I just went to check on the welfare of your wife."

"Then why were your boots and coat left in the kitchen?" Rebecca demanded.

Doctor Owen glared at Cookson.

"Because my boots were muddy and I thought if I left my coat behind it would not scare her. She doesn't seem to like my black coat, maybe it makes her think of death or summat like that."

Rebecca shook her head. "I very much hope you're not going to fall for that one, Mansell," she said firmly.

"I really don't know what to think!" The Doctor narrowed his gaze as he stroked chin, as if trying to make sense of the situation.

"Well get yourself up to your wife's bedroom and you'll see just how distressed she really is!" Rebecca shouted.

"I haven't finished with you!" the Doctor said, referring to Cookson. He took the steps to the bedroom with Rebecca following behind, she could still hear Hannah sobs as Mansell gently cradled his wife in his arms on the bed.

As Rebecca entered the room, she could tell by the way Mansell looked at her, the sadness in his eyes, that he realised she'd been telling the truth. At that point they heard the front door slam shut and realised Cookson had left the house.

"I thought you'd want to horsewhip the brute!" Rebecca shouted, her anger taking over.

Mansell shook his head. "No, not right now, my wife needs me. The police shall deal with this..."

"Very well. I shall send someone to ask one of them to call here later. She knew most of the officers at the police station as they'd been her father's former colleagues. They would not make light of this situation.

Sadly, she descended the stairs and opened the door to see if Cookson was still around, but of course there was no sign of him, just the nursemaid coming up the hill with the children in tow. She sent the children to play in the garden as she confronted the woman.

"Maria, why did you leave Mrs Owen alone in the house?" Rebecca accused.

Maria shook her head. "It was only for a short while, look we're all back home now!" The nursemaid's eyes shone and her demeanour was one of cheerfulness, which added to the annoyance Rebecca now felt, thinking the woman had enjoyed a nice time, while the mistress of the house, a pregnant woman, was almost raped by a brute in her very own bed.

Rebecca lowered her voice, "That might be the case but whilst you were away, Tobias Cookson entered her bedroom and was about to force himself upon Mrs Owen."

Maria laughed nervously. "No, this is just a joke, please tell me that it is?"

"It's no joke. Please believe me I would not joke about such matters in any case! It makes me wonder now if Cookson was responsible for Hannah's pregnancy. How often would she have been left alone for in the past?"

Maria shook her head. "Well not at all really. This is the first time I've ever left her alone as I knew you weren't far away at your aunt's house and would return shortly, she was fast asleep when I left. The children were playing me up, so I took them out. I'm sorry for going even though we all had a lovely time. So he didn't actually touch her then?"

"No, not as such this time, but when I approached he was unbuckling his belt and his tone and manner implied he wanted carnal knowledge of her. He mentioned something about 'playing their little game', which led me to believe this has happened before now."

"The only thing I can think of is maybe he has gone to her bedroom at night then. I sleep in the bedroom just below and Mary

Jacob's room, their grandmother's, is next to my own. She sleeps well though, so maybe she wouldn't hear anything. I haven't heard anything myself during the night. Though he went to Llanbadarn Fawr when you were staying there. Might it have happened then?"

"I've no idea. I did suspect someone else of interfering with her, but now I'm not so sure. There's no real harm done this time, Maria. But from now on, please ensure that Mrs Owen is not left in this house unattended, understood?"

Maria nodded. "You have my word on that. Sorry, it was foolhardy of me to have left her this afternoon."

"Don't worry too much about it, what's done is done, and you might have done us all a favour as else we shouldn't have known Mr. Cookson was up to anything at all."

Chapter Nine

The police Inspector, Ieuan Griffiths, called that evening to the house, he was an associate of the Doctor's, knowing one another from the Cambrian Lodge meetings.

He took matters very gravely and insisted his men would be on the lookout for Tobias Cookson, there had been no other complaints about the man as far as they were aware, but in the Inspector's words, "No woman is safe in a community with that sort around!"

When he'd left and Maria had settled Hannah for the night after Mansell had prescribed a strong sedative for his wife, both Rebecca and Mansell took a glass of sherry together in the drawing room. The children were fast asleep, so they were all alone downstairs.

Mansell cleared his throat. "I'm so glad you saw what that man tried to do today, Rebecca. And I'm really regretful that I trusted him too much."

"Well to be honest, I can see why you trusted him, Mansell. He did his job well. I can't take that away from him and he did once save us from those highwaymen, but I'm a bit annoyed with myself really..."

He gazed at her intently. The room was dim and she could see the reflection of the flickering flames of the fire in his eyes. "Oh, why is that?"

"The night we arrived at Llanbadarn Fawr, Tobias was a bit forward with me. He was sleeping downstairs when I approached him, speaking to him about a matter of concern, he joked, asking if I wanted to join him. I was quite affronted at the time, but he made out he was only jesting with me, now though, I'm not so sure."

"Maybe he wasn't. You are an attractive woman after all."

Rebecca felt her face flush. She changed the subject. "So, you're going to have to look for a new carriage driver?"

"I'm afraid so. I need to employ one so I can get to the hospital quickly if necessary, and sometimes I need to go farther afield."

Rebecca suddenly had a good idea. "I think I know someone who might be perfect for the job. He's not quite as young as Cookson, mind you."

"And who might that be?"

"It's our neighbour back home, Bill. He already has a pony and trap, so is used to horses and I expect he could do with the money."

Mansell smiled. "Splendid idea. So this chap is trustworthy?"

"Oh absolutely! I can vouch for him. He helps my mother out a lot. He's been so kind to her since my father absconded."

There was a long silence as if the news was unexpected to the Doctor's ears. Then he spoke softly. "Oh, I had no idea your father had left, Rebecca. That must be hard on the family as don't you have a younger brother?"

"Three actually, my mother gave birth to twin boys last year. They're walking and talking now and are a pair of mischievous scallywags."

He threw back his head and laughed. "So your mother has her hands full then and I'm taking you away to care for my brood here?"

"Well it's only temporary of course, until you find someone. But yes, she does have a lot on her plate right now."

Doctor Owen looked thoughtful for a moment, "So she could do with a bit of peace and quiet sometimes, I'll be bound?"

Rebecca nodded, wondering what was going through the good Doctor's mind. "And of course, if Bill were to come and work for me, she would have even less help."

"Yes, maybe you should think then of employing someone else, someone younger, it was only a thought..."

He drummed his fingers on his chin. "I think I might be able to help you, maybe employ someone to help your mother even, if it's just twice a week to help care for the twins so your mother has some time to herself, and maybe assist around the home. What do you say, Rebecca?"

She blinked several times. "That would be marvellous, Mansell, but we could never afford something like that."

"Just accept it as payment for all the extra work you've put in helping my wife and children. It is a small price for me to pay." He smiled broadly, and she could have hugged him, but felt it wasn't the proper thing to do under the circumstances.

And so it was arranged that a young girl would be employed to help Kathleen Jenkin at her home twice a week, causing much amusement amongst the neighbours who thought it high and mighty of her to have a 'servant of her own' as the gossips referred to young Polly.

Over the following weeks, Rebecca watched her mother put on a little weight, her cheeks regaining their former colourful bloom, her eyes shining once more. Kathleen Jenkin became more the mother she had always known before her father had done a bad thing.

Now her mother wasn't worn out all the time and had even made enquiries about singing on stage again, this time at the Theatre Royal at Pontmorlais. The theatre manager was pleased to take her on, and although she would never be that big singing sensation she once was, as she didn't have the time to commit to her singing career anymore and her waning youth had become evident, she was happiest on stage singing. She'd got her passion back for life once again.

***

And so Hannah was sent to live in Aberdare with her brother and sister-in-law, George and Bella Morris, who both welcomed her with open arms. The good part about it was she already knew them really well and was comfortable with both. Being childless, the couple had time to devote to their new charge. Hannah looked happier than she had in a long while. Mansell and Rebecca visited her regularly, but she was kept well away from Abercanaid, so the pregnancy would not be known about.

It was around this time that a telegram arrived at the Doctor's house informing him that Mable Evans had passed away. Arrangements were made for him to attend the funeral with Rebecca, his mother-in-law, Mary, being still at the farm house.

When they arrived after a long journey, Sarah welcomed them by the door. She was dressed all in black as were all the other mourners. The farmhouse was packed out with people, mainly appearing as though they were farming folk. Mary presided over the affair with Mable's husband, Gwyn, by her side. Gwyn appeared fragile, but nodded at them as they entered the house.

In the parlour, a table had been laid full of sandwiches, fruit cakes, a side of ham, apple tarts, pitchers of lemonade and glasses. A matching set of china tea cups and saucers were employed in preparation for the funeral tea. Mary instructed Sarah to cover the food with a clean linen table cloth so it should keep fresh whilst the men were away for the burial.

A minister arrived at the home with a funeral director, who had his horse-drawn hearse parked outside in the courtyard. The glass-cased vehicle sent a shudder down Rebecca's spine. It was attached to two white horses that wore black plumage on their heads. It was hard to believe that Mable had passed away, though Mansell had said it was a blessing as she would suffer no more.

The Minister took a short service in the house in Welsh:

"Ein Tad, yr hwn yn y nefoedd..."

The Lord's Prayer translated as, "Our Father, who art in heaven..."

The mood in the house was sombre as they all bowed their heads in reverence. Rebecca sneaked a peek out of the corner of her eye to see if she could spot Rhys, but there was no sign of him and she found herself feeling disappointed that he wasn't around. Where on earth was he? He thought a lot of Mr. and Mrs Evans, it seemed unlike him to miss this event. It would have been too much for Hannah to have attended as she wouldn't have understood what was going on, and in her condition, she might have got herself upset.

The Minister, Dewi Morgan Jones, spoke about Mrs Evans's life, how as a young girl her family had moved into Llanbadarn Fawr from a neighbouring area and how they'd worked the land. Both her parents had died young, but Mary her elder sister, had managed to help her keep the farm running with the assistance of their brother, Tom. Tom and Mary had moved to Merthyr Tydfil seeking work in later years, but Mable had met Gwyn and married and kept Crugmor Farm, the family home, running.

"She was a hard working woman, who will be missed by all..." the minister continued in Welsh. Rebecca was so glad she could understand the language as many in her town were now losing their native tongue in preference of the English language. "Particularly her Husband, Gwynfor..." he continued in a booming, resinous voice.

Someone sobbed loudly and Rebecca turned her head to see it was Gwyn himself who was patting his eyes with a handkerchief. They were a very close couple and it was hard to see how he could now go on without his beloved wife.

The door opened quietly and Rebecca noticed Rhys slip into the room, looking smart all dressed in black and wearing a crisp white shirt. She wondered where he'd been to.

"And now..." finished the minister, "we'll take the short journey to the chapel, where Mrs Evans shall be laid to rest."

People looked at one another with tears in their eyes, there was a lot of mumbling as the men left the house, until all that remained were herself, Mary, Sarah and a couple of Mable's friends and family. The ladies set about making tea and sat to eat the food whilst telling tales of what a lovely person Mable had been and how she'd be missed.

It was a long time until the men returned and even then they were fewer in number.

"Where are they all?" Mary asked, with some concern.

"They've gone to the Black Lion for a jar or two..." Mansell explained. "Don't look so cross, Mary. You know full well it's traditional for the men to go to the pub after a funeral."

She shrugged. "Well I do know that of course, but I thought maybe they'd have come back for a bite to eat first and then gone for a drink." She sighed heavily.

Mansell draped his arm around his mother-in-law's shoulder. "My that fruit cake looks delicious..." she immediately smiled and perked up. The good Doctor certainly had a way with him.

Rebecca guided Gwyn to a chair and asked him if he was all right. He nodded blankly, so she brought him a cup of tea and a Welsh cake.

"He's in shock," Mansell explained. "At one point at the burial I feared he'd throw himself in the grave with his wife, that bereft he appeared."

She nodded. "What happened to Rhys?"

"I think he went to the Black Lion with the rest of the men. Only four of us came back here I'm afraid. You can't blame them though, it's how we men cope with grief, we're not as strong as you ladies are."

She couldn't disagree with that. It was true, women spoke about their concerns, whereas most of the men she knew, especially her father, buried their heads in the bottom of a tankard of ale.

They'd both arranged to spend the night at the farmhouse before setting off back to Merthyr the following day. Bill was by now working as a coach driver for the Doctor. He got to sleep on the horsehair sofa downstairs whilst Rebecca slept in the same room as Mary. The Doctor got his adjoining room next door. By the time

Rebecca was ready for bed, sitting by the kitchen table sipping a glass of milk, the kitchen door burst open and there stood Rhys.

"I'm so pleased to have caught you before you leave, Rebecca..." he said. She was pleased to see he wasn't inebriated. "My apologies, I didn't have much time to talk to you earlier." She could see he was now in his work clothes.

"What happened then?"

"Earlier I missed the funeral service at the house as I'd been helping with one of the cows giving birth in the barn. Got myself cleaned up afterwards as quick as I could and ran hot foot over here to see you. I intended coming back to the house after the burial, but something cropped up at home then I went to the pub for just the one drink, but I'm here now."

She smiled. "And I'm very glad you are."

"Where's Doctor Owen?" he frowned.

"Upstairs sleeping. He's really tired. All this business with his wife has taken it out of the poor soul."

"And you, Rebecca...how has it affected you?"

"Oh, I'm all right, Rhys. Really I am. Just a little tired sometimes between working shifts at the hospital and helping my mother and Doctor Owen."

"No time for yourself then?" He gazed into her eyes. "Come and live here...I could provide for you, we could help Gwyn on the farm, you'd love it and I'd love it if you would be my wife..."

She averted her eyes. "Oh Rhys, I just don't know what to say, I like you a lot and I admit to missing you, it's just that..."

"That you don't love me...?"

She nodded. "I am extremely fond of you."

"Well that's a start and that's enough for me, maybe in time you'd grow to love me?"

They heard a noise and startled, turned to see Doctor Owen entering the kitchen still in his funeral garb.

"I thought you'd gone to bed, Mansell?" Rebecca said.

"No, I went for a walk as I knew I wouldn't be able to sleep."

"I've got just the thing for it, a tot of rum! We had some from the old shipwreck a couple of months back!" Rhys declared loudly.

Surprisingly to Rebecca, the Doctor nodded. "That would be fine."

"Well, I'm off to my bed," she said, seeing as how the two men intended drinking and she did not. She left them to it, but it was a long time before she fell asleep and then she was dreaming about both and wondering which one she would like to spend the rest of her life with.

Chapter Ten

The very next day after breakfast Rebecca, the Doctor, and Mary Jacobs, left the farm for Merthyr Tydfil. Bill was doing well with his duties as coachman. Rebecca had got to say goodbye to Rhys as they spent a while walking around the field together. He'd asked her to think about the matter he'd mentioned previously, she agreed and said she would write to him the following week.

In fact she thought about little else, so much so that one day her mother interrupted her thoughts whilst she was visiting her family home.

"What's going on, Bec?" she asked.

"Nothing really, Mam."

Her mother exhaled loudly. "Come on, this is me, your mother you're talking to. I know when you've got something on your mind!"

She explained to her mother about her feelings for both men and what Rhys had suggested to her.

"Well I don't know this Rhys man, but he sounds a good sort to me. Not every day a lady gets a proposal of marriage, is it, Rebecca?"

Rebecca's cheeks seared with heat. "I suppose not..." she said thoughtfully.

"Now about the Doctor...'tis another matter entirely. The Doctor's wife is clearly insane to the point of madness, but just because 'tis so and he also has feelings for you, doesn't make it right. Far from it my girl. 'T'would do you good to distance yourself from the man."

"But I can't do that, Mam. I work with him at the hospital!" She raised her voice a notch, her mother's suggestion were as if a bucket of cold water had drenched her, washing away her hopes and dreams.

"Yes, you can, and you will. It's not right and deep down you know it isn't, Rebecca. In fact, if you continue to work for him at home, people will begin to talk, especially as his wife is away and sometimes you spend time under his roof helping out with the children."

"But Mary Jacobs, his mother-in-law, has returned home." She held up the palms of both hands as if in defence.

"That maybe so, but that won't stop any gossip. Believe me, Becca, I've been the subject of gossip in my time and it isn't very nice. Either move hospitals or marry Rhys, that's my advice!"

Tears filled Rebecca's eyes and she ran to her old bedroom realising it was definitely Mansell she loved as it hurt at the thought of being parted from him. It would tear her in two. Although she missed Rhys, that didn't hurt in quite the same way.

Her mother followed after her and after allowing her daughter to cry, took her in her arms and said, "No listen to me, where has love ever got anyone? I ask you that? Look what happened to me and your father. Marry Rhys, but get to know him a little better first so you know he really is the character he portrays. 'T'wouldn't be the end of the world, you won't be that far away, we can always come to visit you. I think it would be lovely for your little brothers to visit a farm! Think of all that fresh air they'd get into their little lungs."

Rebecca nodded through glistening tears. Her mother was probably right. She should just leave Mansell to get on with his life, he had the money to employ someone else to help at the house, and now his wife was being cared for in Aberdare, it should make things a whole lot easier. One thing she didn't want to do though was to transfer back to the General Hospital as Daniel was there. She was beginning to consider marrying Rhys might be a good option.

***

Over the following few days, Rebecca made a concerted effort to keep away from Mansell, so much so, that he accosted her in the hospital corridor and ushered her into her own office.

"What's going on?" he demanded.

She froze for a moment. "I've just got a busy shift Doctor, I...I need to get on with my duties."

He tried to make eye contact with her, but she averted her gaze. "Tell me the truth, Rebecca," he asserted.

She let out a long breath before replying, "Very well. Rhys has asked me to marry him and I plan on leaving here soon."

He grabbed her arm roughly, then closed the space between them so she was forced to look into his eyes. "No, you can't do that...I need you here..." She could feel his warm breath on her face and her heart raced accordingly.

"In the hospital you mean to run this ward? Or to help with the children at your home?"

"No, no...that's not what I meant at all. I would miss you so very much Rebecca. I think I'm in love with you." He pulled her toward him and then his lips were on hers, consuming her with so much passion her head started to spin.

She came to her senses and pulled away with her mother's words ringing in her ears. "We can't do this Mansell. I feel the same way about you, but we can't hurt your wife. It wouldn't be fair."

"But how will she be hurt? She no longer recognises me as her husband and can no longer be a wife to me..."

"Nevertheless, it is wrong in the eyes of the Lord. You made certain vows to her. No, this has convinced me I'm doing the right thing by marrying Rhys."

He lowered his voice, "So you'd rather marry a man you don't love than find some love and comfort with me?"

Her eyes began to well up with tears, and a lump had risen in her throat. "Yes, that's just about the sum of it..." She pulled herself out of his embrace and began to walk away without turning back, her footsteps echoing down the corridor.

By that afternoon, she had informed Matron she would be leaving the following month and would serve her notice, then she wrote to Rhys to say she would be paying him a visit soon.

"You've done the right thing, Bec," her mother said later that evening when she told her. "Soon you'll forget all about Mansell Owen, you'll see if you don't." But she knew she would never forget him and she didn't want to either.

***

The Doctor was kind enough to allow his carriage to be used to take Rebecca to visit Rhys for a few days at Llanbadarn Fawr. Rebecca thought under the circumstances it was most kind of him, as inside he must have been hurting very much. She reassured herself she was doing the right thing. Indeed, what if Hannah one day got well again and found her husband was in love with another woman? She just could not bear to think of that.

As the coach trundled along the country lanes of Cardigan, she thought back to a few months ago when they'd first come to this place, a lot had happened since then. Hannah was now pregnant and living in Aberdare, Mable Evans had passed away, and now she was to be the wife of Rhys Watkins. It made her feel all funny inside just thinking about it. It wasn't only Rhys though she was coming to see, she wanted to see how Gwyn and Sarah were coping too. It must have been so hard for them without Mable around. Mable had been the heart and soul of Crugmor farm.

It was decided that Rebecca would return to Merthyr, the day before Christmas Eve, as she wanted to spend Christmas with her own family. There was a lot to do, shopping in preparation for the big day: a goose from the poulterer, fruit and vegetables from the market, presents for the boys. She wanted to get something special for those and some small gifts for Mansell's children too. She had toyed with buying Mansell a present but thought it might give him the wrong idea, so decided to just purchase for the children instead. She sighed thinking how hard it must be for them all.

When they arrived at Crugmor Farm early evening, Rhys was there to greet her. He took her in his arms and was about to plant a kiss on her cheek, when she turned her head in the direction of Bill, the carriage driver. "Better leave it for now..." she whispered.

He nodded. "I was just pleased to see you, that's all. I want to kiss you so much!" He laughed heartily. Whilst it did not repulse her, after the kiss she'd shared with Doctor Owen, it was difficult for her to think of anything else, but she knew she had to.

"Leave it until later," she advised.

He took her hand as they walked. "Did you have a safe journey?"

"Yes, all went well. I spent a lot of the time reading a good book."

"Which one was that?"

"Little Women by Louisa May Alcott..."

Rhys nodded, then smiled broadly. "I know it well, my aunt loved that book."

In truth she hadn't read all that much at all, although she'd tried to read the book, she'd found herself reading the same words over and over as she lost concentration as Mansell's face appeared between the pages. Her feelings ran so deep for him. She inhaled a composing breath and brought herself back to the present moment. "I think Bill could do with a tot of rum and something to eat after driving the carriage all that way!" she laughed, looking over at him, he'd just dismounted and nodded eagerly.

"Aye, my stomach's growling with hunger!" he said, as he followed behind them. He was a good man who still took care of her mother and the boys, if only things were different for both her and her mother, then they would both be with the men they wanted to be with in life, but circumstances dictated otherwise.

After Sarah had dished up a bowl of cawl with crusty bread for them all, Rebecca went in search of Gwyn and found him in the field with the dogs rounding up the sheep. He had one hand over his eyes as if straining to see where the rest of the sheep had gone. He smiled when he saw her and put down his wooden walking stick.

"How are you, Mr. Evans?" she asked gently.

"I'm doing all right, don't you be worrying about me, young Rebecca..." His dark rheumy eyes had a faraway look about them, as though he were some place else, which she could identify with as that's how she felt these days too.

"Are you managing on the farm? To run things?"

He nodded. "Yes, Rhys has put in lots more time in working here and brought his nephew, Emlyn, to work with him some days. He's been a Godsend that man. And I hear you're both to be wed to one another?"

Rebecca's blood chilled her to the bone. "He told you about that?"

"Aye, and I'm glad he did too. He wanted to know if you could both move in to the old cottage on the farmland. It hasn't been used for years, mind you. Mable's brother, Tom, lived there for years until he moved to Merthyr. Then after that it was used if we had visitors sometimes, but it's been uninhabited for about ten years. It's not in bad condition mind, just needs a bit of cleaning up and a lick of paint. Just been using it for a bit of storage lately, but we can soon clear that out."

Rebecca nodded, trance-like. Things now seemed to be happening beyond her control but it did seem to give Gwyn something to look forward to. Somehow realising she must seem ungrateful, she thanked Gwyn for his very kind offer of the cottage. "Well then," she said, "if we are to move in there, then I shall repay you by helping around the farm, cooking, baking, cleaning and what have you. Is that acceptable to you, Mr. Evans?"

He nodded, a big beaming smile on his face. At least once she moved in, she could make sure he was well cared for. Sarah was a good help to him but she was still young and might not understand how lonely the man felt without his wife by his side.

A chill wind blew, forcing her to wrap her woollen shawl tightly around her body. In the far distance, behind the dry stone wall, she spotted the cottage Gwyn had spoken of. It looked small but she could make it cosy enough. She had a wedding to prepare for.

"Don't stay out here too long, Mr. Evans," she advised, "it's a cold wind this evening, come back to the house and have a nice bowl of warming cawl."

He nodded and lifted his hand as if to say, "May be later." She left him to his thoughts in the field and headed back to the farmhouse. It would be good to sit by the fireside and relax, though it wouldn't be quite the same without Mable there.

***

The following day, Rhys took her on the horse and cart into the village and they visited Mrs Clancy's tea room.

"I'm thinking we could make it a January wedding..." Rhys enthused as he took her hand across the table.

Rebecca quickly withdrew her hand. She didn't want anyone to witness their intimacy with one another, not yet, until she felt more comfortable about the situation. Her heart pulsed strongly. "Oh, I didn't think you'd want to wed so quickly...I was thinking maybe the spring time? The weather will be better then."

"I think January would be best, why wait? Are you church or chapel?"

"Chapel...I used to go three times a day at one time, but being a nurse now, I sometimes work on the Lord's day, so just attend when able. What about you, Rhys?"

"I'm church myself. I'd love it if we could wed at St. Padarn's Church, it's where the Watkins family have worshipped for many generations. Would you mind if we married there? We'd have to have the banns read out of course, which would mean us visiting together on three consecutive Sundays in a row..."

She smiled, it was evident how much this all meant to him. "I don't mind. It's a pretty church and if it means a lot to you and your family, then it's all right by me..."

"And of course, we could have our children christened there too!" he said excitedly.

This was all moving too quickly for her, but she realised that as Rhys was a lot older, he probably felt as though time were running out for him.

To change the subject, she asked, "Have you heard any more about the whereabouts of Jake Morgan?"

"Aye, the rascal went off to make his fortune in London, believes the streets are paved with gold."

"How long since?"

"Well word has it that it was the time he left the neighbouring farm..."

"So he couldn't have interfered with Hannah that time she went missing then..." she said to herself, "so the baby must be Tobias Cookson's!"

"Pardon?" he frowned.

"I was just thinking aloud, I hadn't told you but Hannah is pregnant!"

"But I don't understand, I thought she was mentally unbalanced."

"She is...but when we returned to Merthyr the Doctor noticed his wife had become unwell, vomiting, feeling tired, I suggested it could be pregnancy and so he examined her and it was."

"But surely he wouldn't allow his wife to become pregnant by him, that's not right in her state!"

"No, you've got it wrong. It's not his baby. One day I found the coachman, Tobias Cookson, trying to interfere with her and she was shrieking as if scared of him. "I believe it's his, he must have been visiting her room at night."

"That's terrible. I remember that man now—he slept at the farmhouse after bringing you here, a couple of times I seem to recall. He should be made to pay for it!" The knuckles on Rhys's hands whitened as he clenched his fists and his mouth set in a grim line. She had no doubt if he caught up with Tobias Cookson, he'd pulverise him, especially as he hadn't had chance to get to Jake Morgan for stealing Mable's valuables. 'An eye for an eye...' was Rhys's favourite saying, he was far more old testament, than new.

***

By the end of her stay in Llanbadarn Fawr, Rebecca was beginning to get used to Rhys's ways and had reassured herself she was doing

136

the right thing in marrying him. They visited St. Padarns and booked the wedding for the end of February, compromising with one another as it was in between January and the beginning of spring.

When Rebecca arrived back in Merthyr Tydfil, her mother was nowhere to be seen. Polly, the home help, was looking after her brothers, who were playing in the back garden.

"Where's my mother?" she asked.

Polly smiled. "She's involved in a rehearsal for a special Christmas concert tomorrow evening at the theatre. She's getting us all complimentary tickets. James has offered to look after the boys as he's already seen the show in an earlier rehearsal this week, so you and I, and Bill next door, will be going. Oh, and I think your aunt and uncle from Abercanaid also!"

Rebecca clasped her hands with delight. "Oh, that sounds wonderful. I can't wait to hear Mam sing on stage once again."

Polly blinked several times. "How long ago was the last occasion?"

"I think I would have been about ten-years-old. It was at the Temperance Hall where she sang, 'Myfanwy' in front of its composer, Doctor Joseph Parry!"

Polly shrieked with delight. "I didn't realise your Mam was so accomplished until one of the neighbours told me. Mrs Warren said your mother once sang on the London stage!"

Rebecca nodded proudly. Then her younger brothers saw her and came running towards her, with toothy, dribbling grins. She stooped down and gave them both a big hug as they squealed with delight.

Christmas was going to be great this year.

***

Following Kathleen's wonderful performance at the Theatre Royal, they all went back to the family home for a meal. It was later than planned as her mother had taken several curtain calls, as many people had remembered her from the early days of her singing career and gathered around the stage door after the performance to speak to her, which Kathleen had relished, treating each one as if they were very special indeed.

Polly had already prepared a nourishing potato and leek soup with crusty homemade bread, this was followed up with a large side of boiled ham with seasonal vegetables. Lily had brought along some mince pies she'd baked that morning.

Afterwards, Rebecca told her aunt and uncle of her plans to wed Rhys Watkins. Evan raised a questioning brow, but wisely kept his opinions to himself, but her Aunt Lily, led her into the kitchen where they would not be disturbed while the others chatted away merrily in the parlour. If the twins were not asleep then James would have played some Christmas carols on the piano, he was becoming an accomplished pianist, and most days his mother practised singing her scales alongside him, while he tinkled the ivories.

"Are you sure about marrying this man?" Lily whispered.

Rebecca shrugged. "My head tells me I should..."

"But your heart dictates otherwise!"

She nodded. "It's a complicated affair..."

"In what sense might I ask?"

Rebecca lowered her voice. "I'm in love with someone else, Aunt Lily, and he's in love with me, but circumstance prevents us from being together."

Lily's eyes widened. "Are you telling me this man is married, Rebecca?"

"I'm afraid, I am. But it's not as it sounds. We have neither of us done any wrong except for one shared kiss."

Lily draped her arm around her niece's shoulder. "Love is never clear cut, my dear. You can't tell your heart how it should feel, but what you can do is keep well away from any danger it might get itself in to. Tell me, am I correct in thinking it is Doctor Owen you're in love with?"

"Yes, it is..." Rebecca chewed her bottom lip.

"Well, just because you feel in love with him doesn't mean you should act upon those feelings. On the other hand, I'm not so sure you ought to marry a man you do not love either..." She fell silent for a moment then carried on. "You see, it happened to me once upon a time." Her aunt's eyes took on a wistful look.

Rebecca blinked. "What happened, Aunt Lily?"

"It was after your Uncle Evan suffered that blow to his head and lost his memory. He seemed to have forgotten at the time just what I meant to him. Meanwhile, whilst I was in Utah, your Uncle Delwyn found another Saint who was seeking a wife. He was a lot older than myself, and recently widowed. He was such a good man too..."

"Had Mollie been born by then?"

"Yes, she was quite young but he was prepared to take her on as his own child. That's the sort he was. Prosperous too. He owned his own store at Great Salt Lake. I could have had it all Rebecca."

"So, what happened?"

She let out a long breath before replying. "Your uncle's memory returned and he recalled all that I'd meant to him, so he came in search of his wife and child. I'm afraid to say I broke the man's heart when I broke off the engagement to return to my husband."

Rebecca shook her head sadly and touched her aunt's shoulder, it seemed they both had a lot in common, she hadn't realised what the woman had been through.

"I suppose what I'm trying to tell you is..." her aunt continued, "if you marry someone for convenience sake, it might not be fair on him. He could get badly hurt if it's really someone else you yearn for."

Rebecca knew her aunt spoke a lot of sense but at the same time, wasn't it better to make Rhys's life a little happier? He had enough love for the both of them. It would also stop her pining for Mansell Owen, a love she could never receive.

"I see what you're saying, but I feel the need to leave Merthyr to put Mansell out of my mind."

Aunt Lily lowered her voice to barely a whisper. "Rebecca, there are other ways of doing that without marrying a man you don't love. You could find work as a nurse in another town maybe? Or switch wards."

"I should not wish to work there anymore anyhow!" she replied rather too vehemently.

"Ssh!" Lily said, "Keep your voice down, we might be overheard." Her aunt frowned.

"It's awkward for me working at the hospital anyhow as it is, due to a young doctor called, Daniel Evans. I really liked him a lot when we were courting, but when I got the chance to better myself with the position of ward sister on the Isolation Ward, he took it as an opportunity to find someone else. I was dropped without as much as a 'bye as you leave!'"

Aunt Lily's features softened. "Oh *cariad*, I remember you were seeing him for a while. I wondered what happened between you both. You have been wronged that is for sure, cads like that aren't even worth your time let alone thinking about. Go back there to work, but just ensure you're positioned somewhere where you don't have to work with either one another. And if you do encounter Doctor Evans, just paste a smile upon your face and say, 'Good day!' and walk on your way. That way he will see what a good life you are living without him!"

"Oh Aunt Lily, you are so wise!" She hugged her aunt warmly.

"Thanks for saying so, Rebecca, but it's years of experience that have made me this way. Now let's return to the party before they miss us!"

Rebecca smiled and followed her aunt to the parlour.

Chapter Eleven

The following day, Christmas day, the family were up early for a service at the nearby chapel where the minister spoke about finding hope at the foot of the cross and how love came down to earth in the form of Baby Jesus. It was a moving service, and a stirring rendition by the congregation of 'Oh Come Emmanuel', sent a tingle down Rebecca's spine. Her mother had attended an early morning mass at the nearby Catholic Church, but still came along to the chapel service. Though Rebecca wondered for how much longer she'd attend as the Catholic faith was becoming more important to her mother every day, and it all seemed to coincide with the departure of her father. But if it brought her mother comfort, then it was a good thing in Rebecca's book.

After speaking with other members of the chapel, as several elderly women 'oohed and ahhed' over the twins, Rebecca managed to slip away and return to the house to help Polly with the Christmas dinner. The young woman had already plucked the goose and put it in the oven to roast before the service. Rebecca had peeled the vegetables the night before, so they only needed boiling and the table set for dinner. Her Aunt and Uncle had returned to Abercanaid late last night, as Evan had a chapel of his own to run. If they were living nearer, Rebecca surmised they would most probably attend services at the same chapel instead. As Rebecca covered the table with a pristine white table cloth and set the cutlery, she wondered what Mansell Owen and his family were doing right now and she could have wept for them all.

***

With a new year on the way and the celebrations finally over and done with, Rebecca returned to Llanbadarn Fawr to help at the farm after giving in her notice at the hospital. Gwyn and Sarah were so pleased to see her and they all set about sprucing up the little cottage for her impending wedding to Rhys. Rhys, himself, had renovated some old furniture for the place, an old Welsh dresser with intricate woodcarving on its doors and a solid pine table and chairs. Gwyn had given them the feather bed from one of his spare bedrooms as a wedding present and a colourful hand embroidered quilt Mable had sewn before she'd passed away, that brought a lump to Rebecca's throat.

And so it was arranged that Rebecca and Rhys were due to marry on the last Saturday of the month of February. Mam and the boys were going to stay at the farmhouse with Gwyn and Sarah. Aunt Lily and Uncle Evan made arrangements to travel to the village too, especially for the wedding. Evan ensuring he had another minister to cover at the chapel for them for a few days. They were to be put up at Rhys's family home nearby.

Mrs Clancy from the tea rooms baked a special fruit cake for the occasion, she iced it too. Rebecca and Sarah, set about preparing a sumptuous feast afterwards as many of Rhys's friends and family would be joining in the celebrations. Mrs Clancy had a friend, who was a dressmaker, who made a dress of the finest ivory satins and silks for Rebecca, embroidered with seed pearls and miniature ribbons. It nipped her in at the waist and had leg-o-mutton sleeves and a bustle at the back, overlaid with delicate lace. She felt beautiful in it. Sarah was good with hairstyles, so on the morning of the wedding pinned up Rebecca's hair in an elegant chignon knot, which left small tendrils of hair to frame her face.

"Oh Becca, you look so beautiful!" her mother enthused. She entered the bedroom as Rebecca gazed at herself in the long mirror. Sarah stepped aside and looking at Rebecca for confirmation she was happy with her hair, made to leave the room.

"Mam, am I doing the right thing marrying Rhys?" she said, turning around to face her mother.

Her mother's eyes filled with tears. "Yes, I think you are, Rebecca, for you must think about the present and at this moment in time, you and the good Doctor cannot be together, he has a duty toward his wife."

Rebecca hung her head in shame for asking such a question but Aunt Lily's words kept going through her mind. She took a deep breath of composure.

Her mother handed her the small bouquet of white roses and green trailing ivy. "My favourite bloom..." she said wistfully, her eyes now too, filling with tears. "Your father gave me a huge bouquet of white roses when I performed on the London stage and then years later, when I performed in front of Doctor Joseph Parry at the Temperance Hall in Merthyr."

Rebecca squeezed her mother's hand in reassurance, realising for the first time how this wedding would bring memories to the surface as she thought of her own marriage to Dafydd Jenkin. That had not been so grand of course as they had fled America for Wales and got married in haste in Cardiff. Maybe it really was a case of, 'Marry in haste repent at leisure...'' there. Yet, it couldn't really be so could it? Over the years Rebecca had witnessed the love both parents had for one another, it was only in recent times that their marriage had fallen apart.

"Come along then, Mam..." she said firmly. "Let's find James as he's to give me away at the ceremony. Even though Dad's not here, James has turned into quite the young man and I will be proud to be on his arm."

Her mother smiled then dabbed at her own eyes with a lace handkerchief. Then she fumbled in her reticule and brought out a blue ribbon. "Here place that in amongst your bouquet as it's blue, it will bring you good luck. Now you have something old, don't you?"

Rebecca nodded and fingered the silver locket around her neck. That had come all the way from Ireland and was one of her mother's treasured possessions. "Yes, I do."

"And something new is your dress, how about something borrowed?"

"Well Sarah gave me her pearl hair pins, which I shall be returning to her, so yes."

"And I've given you the blue, so we are set to go!"

Rebecca's stomach lurched. It was too late now, the wheels were in motion and she was about to marry one of the kindest, hardworking men she had ever met in her life. So for time being she quashed all thoughts of Mansell Owen.

***

Gwyn drove Rebecca and James into the village on the back of his horse and cart which was decorated with garlands of flowers. Rebecca's mother, brothers, and aunt and uncle, were in front in another carriage loaned by Mrs Clancy for the occasion. She was an astute thrifty, business woman, as she'd said on more than one occasion, "Take care of the pence, and the pounds will take care of themselves!" She also owned properties in the area, and although now widowed, there was no pulling the wool over her eyes.

The cart bounced along the country lanes as Rebecca thanked her lucky stars the day had kept dry for the wedding, even though there was a chill in the air. James looked at her and smiled. "You do look beautiful, our Becca..." he said.

"Well in all my born days, I never thought I'd get to hear you pay me a compliment!" she teased.

James grinned broadly. "It's true though and it sounds as if Rhys is a good man."

"Aye he is!" Gwyn chipped in. "He was a Godsend to me and my late wife. He'll make a fine husband for Rebecca!" He paused. "By the way, any news about the Doctor's wife?"

Rebecca shook her head, not wishing to be reminded of the situation, but poor Gwyn of course, had no idea of her feelings for the man. "No, I haven't heard from the family for some time..." she said, which in essence, was the truth. When she'd been home for Christmas she'd made a conscious effort not to contact the Doctor. She wondered though if the police had ever caught Tobias Cookson and taken him to task for what he did to Hannah.

Bill, was still working as a carriage driver for the Doctor, so her mother had got news second hand from him, but she suspected that her mother had withheld certain information from her to protect her.

As they approached the village, she noticed the spire of St. Padarn's Church nestled amongst the trees, and her heart skipped a beat. Rhys was there right now waiting for her arrival. Her mind still flipped back and forth between doing the right and wrong thing. One moment she thought it ill-considered to go ahead with the wedding, and the next, it felt the absolute appropriate thing to do. She had never been in such a quandary in all her born days.

James took her hand. "Try to think nice thoughts, Becca..." he advised, as Gwyn pulled the cart up outside the entrance of the church. Was it that obvious to her brother how nervous she felt? She nodded, and he helped her down from the back of the cart. Gwyn dismounted and tethered the horse to the church railings.

Rebecca silently prayed and then looked up at the darkening clouds above, it was as if they reflected back to her what her heart experienced inside.

Then quite suddenly, the clouds parted and a beam of sunshine filtered through, and then they parted even more to reveal bright azure blue skies. It was almost as though the heavens were clearing just for her, for today, for her marriage to Rhys. Now, finally, she felt as though she were doing the right thing. The wedding party ascended the steps and stood at the door to the church where a signal was given to the organist to commence. The sound of Mendelssohn's, 'Wedding March' was played, and as she walked down the aisle with James at her side, she became aware of the place filled with people. Heads turned as she passed by. Colourful bows and flowers were attached to the end of the pews and there was a large floral arrangement either end of the pulpit. Flickering flames of candlelight gave the whole place an ethereal feel. God was in his heaven and all was well with the world. As she reached the pulpit where Rhys stood, with his friend beside him as best man, he turned to look at her with so much love in his eyes, it affirmed inside her she was doing the right thing.

Afterwards, the church bells rang resounding all over Llanbadarn Fawr and beyond, drifting towards Cardigan Bay. The married couple stood outside the church as people threw rice and wished them well and when everyone had departed to make their way to Crugmor Farm for the wedding feast, Rebecca and Rhys remained a while as if they realised it would be many hours before they would be alone again that day.

"I love you, Rebecca," Rhys said, gazing into her eyes. She looked into his and allowed herself to accept his love and return it to him. "Come on then Mrs Watkins, Gwyn is waiting for us with the horse and cart, we'd better go as we don't want to keep our guests waiting too long."

She smiled and allowed him to take her left hand, where her gold wedding band shone and shimmered on her finger, a token of their new life together.

***

They spent the afternoon of the wedding feast back at Crugmor farm, where food was a plentiful and the drink flowed freely. Gwyn and Rhys still had a couple of barrels of rum salvaged from the ship wreck to use up. Though most guests either drank raspberry cordial, lemonade or else supped tea. Only a few of the rougher men from the village drank the rum. Rebecca wondered what her aunt and uncle would say as they were both teetotallers and full supporters of the Temperance Movement that had taken Merthyr Tydfil by storm.

Too many men, and sometimes women, in the town had succumbed to the evils of the demon drink.

But Rebecca needn't have worried, Uncle Evan reminded her that this was a wedding celebration and even Jesus had turned water into wine at the wedding feast at Cana. It was all about moderation, he said.

Rebecca caught Aunt Lily and her mother whispering in the corner of the kitchen and she wondered what they were up to.

"What's going on here?" she asked.

The women just smiled and her mother put her finger to her lips. "Ssssh!" she said. "Come with us, Rebecca."

She followed them out into the courtyard. By now the sun had set, leaving behind gold and scarlet flames of fire in the sky, and as was usual during late February, the nights were long, so it would get dark soon. She lifted her dress to avoid the hem from dragging in any muck, and followed them both to the cottage where she and Rhys would make their new home.

Aunt Lily opened the door, and there inside, flickered a log fire, bathing the cosy living room in a golden glow, the room warm and inviting.

"That's so kind of you to heat up the cottage up for us!" Rebecca exclaimed.

"That's not all..." said her mother. "She led her to the pantry which was full to over flowing with lots of fruit, vegetables, preservatives of all kinds in jars, labelled with the words, 'Strawberry Jam', 'Pickled Onions', 'Chutney', and 'Beetroot'. There were various cakes and breads and a large pat of butter.

"Oh my goodness!" Rebecca's hands flew to her mouth. She'd never seen so much good food in all her life.

"We'll send over a side of ham from the farmhouse later, we just need to see if there's enough left first from the wedding party..." Aunt Lily said, "But there should be as we boiled two."

There was more whispering. "What else is going on?" Rebecca wanted to know.

"Go up to your bedroom!" Her mother said.

They all climbed the winding stone stairs to the only bedroom in the cottage. There, Mable's handmade patchwork quilt was laid out on the bed in colours of lilac, lemon and white, and new cotton embroidered pillow cases set it off. On closer inspection, Rebecca could see her name sewn into the corner of one side of each case with Rhys's name on the other, attached to one another by embroidered red roses.

"Oh, that's so beautiful!" she gasped, and then turning, saw the new white lace curtains on the windows. An oil lamp burnt brightly in the corner of the room.

"Look behind you!" her mother said.

Rebecca turned to see the most beautiful night gown hanging on the back of the bedroom door. It was absolutely exquisite. Drawing up close to the garment, she could see it was apricot silk, encrusted with seed pearls and ribbons with an appliqué of two butterflies on the pockets.

"But how?" she asked, looking at her aunt and mother for explanation.

"The food in the pantry is a gift from me and your Uncle Evan," Lily explained. "The pillowcases, curtains and nightgown are from your mother as a wedding present to you."

"Oh thank you so much!" Rebecca wiped away a tear of happiness. She hugged both women.

"You like them then?" her mother asked.

"I love all of it! I am so blessed! Thank you both!"

***

That night when all the wedding guests had departed and everyone was asleep in the farmhouse, Rebecca and Rhys sat in front of the fire drinking cups of cocoa in one another's arms, and when they departed to go to bed, it felt like the most natural thing in the world as he led her upstairs to the bedroom.

Rhys removed his clothing and slipped into bed as she undressed behind a screen. She hung her wedding dress on the back of the door, removing her new night gown and placing her dress on the hanger instead. Then she draped her undergarments over the screen and slipped the new gown over her head. It fitted beautifully, skimming her curves beneath. Her heart beat wildly, she had never known a man intimately before, save for a few kisses from Daniel Evans and that passionate one from Mansell Owen.

She really didn't know quite what was expected of her. As she approached the bed, Rhys looked at her with longing in his eyes as he drew the bedcovers back for her to join him.

147

"Oh Rebecca, how beautiful you are...I am a very lucky man..."

She slipped under the covers beside him, trembling. He leaned over and drew her towards him, his breaths short and shallow as he swooped, his lips crashing down on hers in a clumsy fashion. She wondered if he'd been with a woman before as he was a bachelor but the way his hands began to run pillage over her body, she knew that he had and wondered how many women there had been in his life.

Before she knew it he was squeezing her breasts so hard, her nipples hurt, she winced and let out a little yelp of pain, but this seemed to arouse him even more. Then quite suddenly his hands yanked on the hem of her nightdress, dragging it over her head, even before she'd had chance to relish wearing the beautiful garment, making her feel vulnerable as she was entirely naked as the day that she was born, a feeling she wasn't used to.

He pushed her roughly back down on the bed and his hands roamed up her thighs until they found her vagina. He probed with his fingers and let out a low moan of desire and even before she had a chance to realise what was happening, he was on top of her prising her legs apart, heavy and rampant, trying to enter her, his hardness evident of just aroused he was.

This wasn't how things were supposed to be, was it? Was this what marriage was all about? Her instincts were to push him off her, but she knew that the marriage night was hard for a lot of women to endure. So instead, she gritted her teeth and prayed it would come to an end soon, that he'd have his release and roll over and go to sleep.

"For goodness sakes' relax, Rebecca, or it will never get in there!" he commanded.

His hardness was against her, trying to penetrate her but she felt dry and clenched inside. She tried to relax by breathing deeply.

No one told her it would hurt this much and when he finally entered her, seeming very satisfied that she'd been a virgin, a tear coursed down her cheek as silently she sobbed inside.

"Come on girl, don't just lie there, buck those hips!" He said. "It'll give me more pleasure... You're like a bloody plank of wood underneath me!"

She felt like yelling at him to get off her and leave her alone, but he kept rhythmically moving above her, plunging away, a man intent on his mission. Even if she wanted to she couldn't get him off her petite frame, not just because he was so much bigger than she, but because he was fully focused on his own wanton desire.

She was so sore inside, although this was obviously a pleasure for him for her it meant pain.

Fully sated, Rhys growled as he released his warm ejaculation inside her, it was a guttural sound she had never heard before, seeming to arouse from the pit of his stomach, but he seemed pent of his passion and she was so thankful for that. Rebecca let out a sigh of relief, which Rhys seemed unaware of. He kissed her firmly on the mouth, telling her what a wonderful experience it had been as she was nice and tight inside, not like some of the tarts he'd been with over the years, and that in time, she would come to love carnal relations, too. Then he rolled off her, and turned over in the bed, with his back toward her. Before too long, she could hear his heavy rhythmic breathing beside of her.

Sore between her legs, she heaved herself out of the bed, her breaths short and shallow at the shock of what had just happened. Then she noticed her nightgown still in the bed where he'd roughly removed it. She was dismayed to find the garment sodden with blood, it must have been beneath her the whole time, then gazing down she felt a trickle of warm blood running down the inside of her thighs. She had heard of this happening to virgins before now and realised it was because it was her first time, but it didn't happen to everyone. Maybe it was because Rhys had been quite rough with her, seeming only to care for his own pleasure. She quickly mopped between her legs with an old towel and threw on a day dress while she set about boiling pans of hot water to fill a cast iron tub. Then she ripped off the dress and sat inside the bath, fiercely cleansing herself of her husband's ejaculation and the blood seeping from within. She closed her eyes and tried to relax, hopefully it wouldn't be like this every time they engaged in marital relations. She feared the beautiful new gown would be ruined, but after drying herself and putting on a fresh night gown, she left the soiled one to soak in a pail of cold soapy water overnight. If it wasn't that her mother had spent so much time painstakingly making that garment, she would have set fire to it, not ever wanting to see it again as it would forever be a reminder of her husband's defilement of her once pure body.

When she awoke next morning, Rhys's side of the bed was already empty and with some relief she realised he'd gone off to work at the farm at first light, milking the cows in the barn.

She was relieved to find the blood had soaked out of the night gown and gave it a good wash in warm soapy water and hung it on the line to dry. It saddened her though to think that the beautiful gown her mother had made with care, had been ripped off her quivering body without any thought and doused in her own blood by such a violation. By the time Rhys returned mid morning for a rest and a bite to eat, she had done all the washing, cleaned and tidied the small cottage from top to bottom, and had a plate of ham, cheese and pickle with crusty bread to serve to him. Nervously, she turned as he entered the kitchen.

"You're looking glowing this morning, *cariad*," he greeted, bending down to kiss her cheek, then he took her in his arms with her back facing his front so she felt his erection press up against her leg. He began to lift her skirts, fearing he was about to enter her or take her to the bedroom again, she pulled away, brushing down her garments.

"Sit down, I've got breakfast here for you..."

He smiled and sat himself at the table. "More of the same tonight? I hope?" He winked at her, slapping her hard on the bottom, and she turned away, her face searing hot and heart racing.

She nodded, and placed the plate of food in front of him, he grabbed her hand, pulling her towards him. "You are happy and glad you've married me, Rebecca? Aren't you?"

"Yes, of course I am." For some reason her left eyelid twitched, something that seemed to happen if she felt a little nervous.

"That's a relief, as I want us to try for a baby as soon as possible while you're still in full fettle!"

She realised he wasn't a bad man, and maybe no different to a lot of men who had been brought up to believe that the pleasures of the bedroom were just for them and them alone, save for a few bad ladies who also enjoyed it and got paid for it too. It's just she felt there should have been more to it than that. That he ought to have taken his time. But who could she speak to about such matters? It would not be appropriate to speak to her mother, maybe Aunt Lily would give good advice, she'd try to meet with her before she left for Merthyr.

150

After her husband had eaten his fill and she'd rejected his attempt for them to go back upstairs, with excuses of having to help Sarah at the farmhouse, he kissed her saying there would be plenty of time for fun later, and made his way back to the fields.

She quickly washed the dishes, tidied herself up and found her cape and bonnet and went in search of her aunt who was staying with Rhys's mother. Her mother-in-law was a very small lady, who spoke mostly the Welsh language. She was inoffensive enough and quite welcoming towards Rebecca. She'd seemed to have enjoyed herself at the wedding yesterday and allowed Rebecca into her home to meet with her aunt. Feeling uncomfortable about talking about such matters in her husband's former home, Rebecca suggested they go for a stroll to Mrs Clancy's tea room. If her aunt was puzzled she didn't show it, she explained things to Evan, who was busy writing his Sunday sermon for the following week and well supplied with homemade offerings of tea and fruit cake from Mrs Watkins.

As they strolled into the village, her aunt suddenly caught Rebecca's arm. "Our Becca, what is troubling you, child?"

It wasn't often that her aunt referred to her in that sense, so it took her entirely by surprise. "Is it that obvious, Auntie?"

"I'm afraid it is." Aunt Lily's eyes were full of concern for her niece.

Rebecca chewed on her bottom lip, not knowing quite what to say. "Last night...last night wasn't what I was expecting it to be."

"Oh?"

"Yes, it hurt a lot and I bled too."

"Well that's to be expected for some ladies as it was your first time."

"I know, but my husband was quite rough with me, so much so I cried afterwards." Tears welled up once more at the thought of her memory of the previous night.

"And did he comfort you afterwards?"

Rebecca swallowed the lump in her throat. "No, he fell asleep. To tell the truth, he didn't know about that, he seemed oblivious to it."

"Then I tell you what you need to do is tell him like you told me. It's a fair bet he doesn't even realise this, Rebecca."

"I suppose you're right, but I don't wish to hurt his feelings and didn't know quite what to expect."

"Listen to me...I can tell you this woman to woman, it does get easier with time. Don't hesitate though from telling him how you felt, I'm sure he'll understand."

She nodded. "I hope so."

Her Aunt patted her niece's hand. "Come on, let's go the tea room and try a selection of fancies and a pot of tea, it shall make you feel a lot better."

On the way, they passed the church Rebecca had married in just yesterday, but it felt like a lifetime ago.

***

That evening when Rhys returned from his work, Rebecca had a beef stew and dumplings waiting for him on the table, so hot it was steaming, sending a delicious odour wafting throughout the cottage.

His eyes gleamed when he saw his plate. "My goodness, there's a great asset to me you are as a wife, Rebecca Watkins!" He sat down to devour it and afterwards she gave him some apple pie she passed off as her own, but really she'd bought it from Mrs Clancy's tea room and didn't want to show she'd been there with her aunt for fear he would ask questions.

When he was full up with food, and sitting in front of the fire with his boots off relaxing, she broached the subject of the bedroom.

"Rhys, you enjoyed our first night together, didn't you?"

He smiled, "Aye it was a great day and particularly afterwards..."

She chose her words carefully not to upset him. "As I was a virgin it was a slightly uncomfortable experience for me," she looked away, somehow she couldn't show him just how painful it had been for her.

He looked into her eyes. "I'm sorry Rebecca, you should have said so. I got carried away see, been a long while since I lay with any womenfolk and even then, none were virgins like you, they were well-experienced women of the world."

She held his hand. "I know, but I was frightened. It was my first time with a man."

Gently he touched the side of her face as the tears fell from it. "Well it shall not happen again. Tonight I'll be very careful with you, *cariad*, and we shall stop if you want to, that's a promise."

Relief flooded through her. Her Aunt had been right. Rhys was as good as his word that night as when they went to bed, he held her for the longest time and slowly, on this occasion, took his time to touch

152

and caress her, something she found quite exciting as he slowly circled his fingers between her legs making her feel moist. This time when he penetrated her, although initially she winced with anticipation, it felt a lot better, so much so, she took the initiative to respond to his fervent kisses.

And when it was over and he'd found his release, she lay back in his arms, she hadn't reached the skies with her own pleasure yet, and realised many women didn't ever do that, but it was a start and whatever she thought, she realised her husband loved her very much indeed.

Chapter Twelve

When her family returned to Merthyr, Rebecca finally settled down into country life and being Rhys's wife. Early mornings she began to get up at first light, set the fire and see her husband off to work, then went about her daily chores of washing and cleaning both her home and the farmhouse.

At midday, she was always around to feed Rhys, usually a fry up of farm cured bacon, sausage and eggs. Then afterwards, she went to help Sarah at the farm, usually this involved, baking, a little light housework and ironing. By the time she arrived back at the cottage, there was a bare amount of time for her to put her feet up with a cup of tea before Rhys returned home. She'd get his meal ready on the table, the dishes washed, they'd spent a little time either just talking or reading to one another, and then it was off to bed. Now, she no longer feared going to bed in the evenings with him, in fact, she looked forward to those evenings when he wasn't too tired, but month after month, when she hoped she'd become pregnant, it never happened. Rhys would tell her not to worry as he didn't mind if she could never have children, but in her heart it was all she was beginning to yearn for.

It was one day during the hot summer that year, when she received a letter from her mother. She hadn't seen her family since the wedding but they wrote to one another regularly. The tone of her mother's letter sounded alarming.

Dear Rebecca,

I've received word from Utah that your father is on his way back to Merthyr and he wishes to claim the twins and take them back with him. I am so worried, beyond belief. I cannot allow him to take away two children that he's never known and as I won't fall in with his plans of going with them, I am going to have to fight him for custody. I really do not know what to do.

Rebecca felt the warmth drain from her body as her veins turned to ice. Surely he couldn't do that, could he? As much as she missed her father, she'd never thought he'd be as cruel as to do that to her mother, but then again, he had left her in the first place to fend for herself. Would the law be on her father's side or her mother's

154

though? She would have to ask James about that, Mr. Goldstein could tell him.

She discussed it later with Rhys, who suggested that maybe it would be a good idea for her mother and the young boys to stay with them at Llanbadarn Fawr for a while. James, though, as his job was in Merthyr, would remain behind and keep an eye on the house. Whilst Rebecca thought it a good idea, she didn't like the idea of leaving James alone.

"He's a grown man now, Bec," Rhys said firmly. "He's already of marriageable age, anyhow."

She hadn't thought of it that way before. "I suppose you are right. I don't even know if he has a girlfriend. I should ask him next time we meet. I'll write back then and offer Mam and the twins the chance to stay here for a while, where they shall be safe."

Her husband touched her gently on the shoulder in reassurance. "The last thing I want is for you to feel unsafe, *cariad*," he said, lowering his head to kiss her cheek. How she wished she could give him a child of his own.

***

Once receiving the letter of invitation from Rebecca, her mother wasted no time in arranging transport to Llanbadarn Fawr. Bill asked Doctor Owen's permission to drive them to the village. Mansell Owen was very amenable and sent a message of best wishes to the married couple and a beautiful painting of Cyfarthfa Castle that he'd had specially commissioned by a local artist. Rebecca was thrilled when she opened the gift, which was wrapped in thick brown paper and tied with string. She asked Rhys to hang it over the fire place, although a little grand for their tiny cottage, it was a reminder of home and the good Doctor himself.

Her mother and the boys were settled at the farmhouse. The boys loved it on the farm seeing all that open space and adored helping Gwyn on the farm, though at their ages they didn't do much more than run around and play with the sheep dogs. Rhys loved having them around too and would hoist one or another on his shoulders as he set out to the fields. Mam assisted at the farm when she was able, baking and cleaning, and Sarah welcomed the extra help she received. Gwyn, too, seemed to enjoy Kathleen's company of an evening when he'd finished work for the day, though he still seemed slightly morose and lost at times.

The only cloud now on the horizon was her father's return as she feared he'd snatch her brothers and head back to America. She blamed that new religion of his and cursed at the thought of how he had divided his family and ruined what he already had. Rebecca decided to put it all out of her mind and concentrate on her new life, after all, he could hardly find them in Llanbadarn Fawr. She decided to write to Aunt Lily and Uncle Evan to warn them about the situation, although her father was Lily's brother, she'd had more than her fair share of grief herself with him over the years.

A couple of weeks later, she was pleased to receive a reply saying that if and when they encountered her father, due to the given circumstances, they would not give the address away. So with much relief, Rebecca carried on with married life.

***

Christmas was fast approaching, there were red berries on the holly leaves that year, which country folk said indicated a bad winter ahead. It was certainly cold enough and everyone made sure they donned more clothing than usual. Rhys wore two pairs of combinations beneath his clothing. Kathleen had knitted him and Gwyn some thick working socks, gloves and scarves which both men were grateful for. Rebecca always made sure her husband had a hot meal awaiting him whether he arrived home for a main meal or just a light bite to eat.

The first fall of snow had arrived in Cardigan late November, and the twins loved it, playing snowball fights with one of the farmhands or sledging with Sarah. Rhys even took them to see how frozen the pond was at the edge of the field. In summer, it was lovely as there were fish and frogs, dragonflies, and all kinds of birds there. She once saw a beautiful Kingfisher in all its azure blue and flame-chested glory. It dipped its beak into the pond to find a fish and made off with it in one fell swoop, much to her amazement. She'd had to call Rhys to ask him what kind of bird it was as she'd never seen one before. Now though, the pond was iced over and the surrounding trees layered with snow, it was beautiful in both summer and winter.

Bill called to see her mother and the boys once a month when Doctor Owen allowed him a couple of days leave and personal use of the carriage. Unfortunately, when he last arrived he had bad news. Hannah, who had given birth to her child a couple of month's previously, had become more distraught than ever when the child was handed over to her sister and brother-in-law. She'd returned to Abercanaid and now wasn't uttering even a word. All day and night she remained in the attic room of the Doctor's house just humming an unrecognisable but haunting tune. Bill said he found it most eerie.

Today was his last day of leave to spend with Kathleen and the boys and he was making the most of it. He helped them to build a large snowman in the field and Gwyn kindly donated some of his old tattered clothing for them to use along with an old bowler hat, with a carrot as a nose. They were all having a delightful time, so much so, that Rebecca asked Gwyn and Rhys if she might invite him for Christmas dinner, which they heartily agreed to.

So all the family were gathered together on Christmas Eve, apart from Lily and Evan, who remained in Merthyr for the chapel Christmas services. Rebecca had sent their presents by post. A book of poems for her aunt and a new fountain pen for her uncle to write his sermons, they had both been so kind to her. The Doctor had allowed Bill three days leave over the holiday period and loan once more of his carriage.

Fleetingly from time-to-time, Rebecca thought of Mansell, seeing his face dance before her, his kind eyes twinkling at her, then she'd dismiss the thought and the image would disappear once more.

"Penny for them, Becca?" Rhys asked, as they strolled through the field together to check on the cows.

"Oh I don't know if they're worth that!"

"Oh sure they are..." he took her by the hand. "Any thoughts you have are precious, *cariad*. You know if anything's troubling you..."

Deciding to be truthful she said, "I do worry about Hannah. Bill tells me she's now not speaking at all to anyone."

Rhys stopped a while, removed his cap and scratched his head. "Yes, it's a mystery that. No doubt that Tobias Cookson's actions might have made her mute, I'll be bound!" he raised his fist in anger.

"Possibly, but I got the impression it happened after her baby was taken away and handed over to her in-laws. Although she has the mind of a child, who knows what she's feeling inside."

"Aye, it might well have reminded her of when the other children were born, triggered something off, like."

"No doubt."

They carried on walking, the snow so cold beneath her feet that Rebecca felt it transfer up her body. Her nose was as frozen as her toes. She shivered and wrapped her two woollen shawls tightly around her shoulders. She had lots of layers of clothing on underneath, it seemed to get very cold here in winter as it was near Cardigan bay, but equally, hotter than Merthyr in the summertime.

Rhys hugged her to him. "Feel any warmer now?" he asked, puffing out plumes of steam.

She nodded.

"Good, we'll soon be in the barn where it will be a bit warmer with all those bales of hay and the cattle breathing their warm breath!" he laughed.

When they arrived, he lit several lanterns and hung them on hooks from the wooden rafters.

After checking the animals were all right, Rhys went over to see to Daisy, who was reputed to be the best milker of the herd. He patted her and she eyed him up and down beneath her thick lashes, she appeared to be feeding well though. Thankfully it wasn't calving season or it might have been dangerous for them to draw up close. The rules of the countryside had to be respected, they were disrespected at someone's peril. Satisfied, all was well, Rhys finally extinguished the lanterns and they both left the barn to return to the cottage for their supper.

"I'm starving," he said, patting his belly.

Rebbeca smiled, she loved feeding up her husband. In the distance, she saw smoke curling from the chimney of the farmhouse and Sarah busy at the kitchen window. She wondered what her mother and the boys were doing right now, guessing her mother probably would have bathed, changed, and put them to bed for the evening.

That night following supper, Rebecca slept soundly, until suddenly she was awoken by both sheep dogs barking in their kennels outside. Startled, she sat up in bed, her heart thudding wildly. She roused her husband who was sleeping soundly beside her.

"Wassa matter?" he mumbled, evidently at that point between dream and waking time.

"Rhys...there's something wrong—the dogs are barking frantically!"

He pulled himself up on his haunches, and then after digesting her words, shot out of bed and went to the window. He peered outside and then shouted, "It's the big barn, it's on fire! Quick, I'll see what I can do, you wake Gwyn and Sarah! He quickly pulled on his trousers and shirt, then ran outside shouting, "Fire!" to rouse everyone.

By the time Rebecca had pulled a shawl around her shoulders and tugged on a pair of boots, Gwyn had appeared at the farmhouse door.

"It's the barn, Gwyn, it's alight!" she shouted, then pushed past him to rouse Sarah and her mother inside the house.

Thick smoke was emanating from the wooden building, and the scary sounds of spits and crackles could be heard.

"It'll go up like a tinder box in there!" Gwyn shouted. "All the wood and hay..."

The cows were beginning to show signs of distress as they mooed deeply.

Rebecca and Sarah filled a couple of metal pails with water from the trough outside the barn. Rhys and Gwyn took the pails and entered the barn to dampen the flames, whilst Rebecca's mother soothed and quieted both boys, who'd awoken to all the shouts.

"Be careful both of you..." Rebecca warned the men as they desperately fought to douse the flames.

Minutes later, after throwing several buckets of water over the bales of hay, the fire was extinguished. Rhys held a lantern in his hand. "That was fortunate!" he exclaimed. "It must have only just started, good job the dogs barked. I must have forgotten to put out one of the lanterns earlier. It must have fallen from the rafter onto a bale of hay, fortunately the bales must have been a bit damp. No real damage done except a couple of burnt bales, the livestock are fine."

"I'm not so sure that it was your fault," Rebecca said, "I watched you put out all the lanterns earlier."

"Are you sure?" He blinked several times.

"I'm positive as I am concerned about that kind of thing. I'm just the same when I work at the hospital—safety first!"

"Well that can only mean one thing," Gwyn declared loudly, "someone has deliberately set fire to this barn!"

A shiver coursed Rebecca's spine.

After ensuring all the cattle had settled down, and by now the dogs had ceased barking, Rhys secured the barn for the night.

"I'm going to keep a vigil!" he shouted.

"Yes, we can take it in turns!" Gwyn offered.

"Oh no, Mr. Evans, we can't have you staying up half the night—" Rebecca intervened, "we'll send word to a couple of the farmhands and it would be best to get in touch with the local police, too!"

"Pah!" Rhys scoffed. "They're not much good around these parts, a bunch of clowns, they are! I'll put word out at the Black Lion. Someone wishes to see this farm go under!"

Gwyn nodded sagely. "I can't afford to lose any livestock. This is my livelihood—I've been farming since I was a lad."

"Well hopefully it won't come to that." Rhys shook his head.

They left Rhys keeping watch at the barn, while Sarah went in search of the farmhands. Usually the young lads either kipped on the old horsehair sofa downstairs where they could keep warm by the fire or out in one of the barns in warmer weather. What if it had been one of those who had started the fire by accident? Or even worse, what if they'd been asleep in the barn when the fire started and got injured or died because of it?

Rebecca worried that somehow Rhys might whip together some sort of vigilante group from the village to track down the culprit and bring him to justice.

***

The following day Rebecca was speaking to her mother in the farmhouse kitchen.

"But who would do such a thing, Bec?" her mother asked with a worried frown on her face.

"Rhys thinks maybe it's the work of a neighbouring farmer, Jack Wilkes, who Gwyn fell into dispute with last year over a boundary issue between both farms. The farmer in question, claims that Gwyn stole part of his land. Gwyn says differently mind, he says the land has always belonged to Mable's family. The dispute only came about when Rhys erected a fence between the two properties."

"Hmmm some folk are strange like that. Odd though it was never an issue beforehand, but to try to burn someone's livestock and barn is dreadful! I wouldn't have thought a farmer capable of it!"

"I would!" Rhys had just entered the kitchen.

"Any news?" Rebecca blinked.

"Aye, there is and all. Been down to the Black Lion this afternoon, that's where I just came from. The men are talking about storming Jack Wilkes's property and stringing him up from a tree!"

"Oh no, I don't want that!" Rebecca said. "Anyhow, we don't know whether he's at fault, do we?"

"Maybe not, but it'll get him to talk if necessary. He'll be squealing like one of his pigs before too long!"

Rebecca could see just how serious Rhys was being. An ice-cold chill ran through her veins.

***

Rebecca was washing dishes in a tin bowl at the cottage, when the hairs on the back of her neck bristled. Someone was watching her, she was sure of it. By now it was dark and Rhys hadn't as yet returned from work. She drew the curtains and locked the door.

Ten minutes later, Rhys arrived home from work, "Why's the door locked?" He asked, when she'd allowed him entry after he'd had to knock.

"I don't know if I'm being foolish Rhys, but I felt that someone was watching me at the window, so I locked the door, did you see anyone on your way back here or hanging around outside?"

"No, I haven't, we're going around first light to get to the bottom of the business with Jack Wilkes. So if it's him, I'll find out."

News of this made her feel worse, she was hoping the men wouldn't go through with their plan, but then again, if it was him who started the fire in the barn then it needed sorting out before anyone was injured.

Her husband removed his jacket and washed his hands at the stone bosh, then sat at the kitchen table where she dished up a roast chicken dinner with vegetables. At least food was plentiful living on the farm at the moment, but if Gwyn and Rhys lost their livelihoods, what then? Would they be forced like many from farming backgrounds in West Wales to relocate in Merthyr Tydfil and work in the ironworks? She hoped not. She didn't mind going back home to live but didn't want that kind of work for her husband. Many of the ironworkers worked long hours for little pay and there was always the risk of injury from burns and by other means. At the General Hospital she'd seen burns, crush injuries and even loss of eyes and limbs.

Rhys ate his food and then looked at her, "Come here, Bec!" he beckoned.

She did as asked, then he drew her to him and sat her on his lap. "Do not fear, *cariad*. All will be well..." when he said those words she felt reassured. Then he nuzzled her neck and kissed her passionately, removing the pins from her hair, so her hair cascaded upon her shoulders. They stood and made their way to the bedroom, at least if she became pregnant it would give her something to focus on other than her worries about the farm.

***

The following afternoon, a couple of constables appeared on the farm. Apparently a gang of men had entered the property of one Jack Wilkes, neighbouring farmer, and dragged him from his bed, hung him from a tree upside down and whipped his hide. The man did not confess to anything but was badly injured. Did anyone at Crugmor Farm know anything about this matter?

Rebecca shook her head and hoped the constables would not ask after the whereabouts of her husband.

"So you didn't hear or see anything then, Madam?" the elder of the two with the bushy moustache asked, gazing intently into her eyes as if trying to catch her out.

"No, I did not." They were standing just outside the farmhouse door where Rebecca had been helping Sarah with the washing and ironing. She wiped her damp hands on her pinafore.

"Anyone else at home?" The younger, clean-shaven constable, peered behind her at the open door.

"Only Sarah the help, my mother, and my twin brothers," she replied truthfully.

"Well might we have a word with your brothers then?" the elder constable asked.

Rebecca smirked to herself. "Yes, very well..."

The constables looked at one another as if to say, "Perhaps we're on to something here."

A moment later, Rebecca returned with one brother in her arms and the other by her side.

The elder constable snorted loudly, turned on his heel and left without saying anything, with the younger policeman in hot pursuit behind him.

When they'd departed for their carriage, Benjamin asked, "Who the funny men, Becs?"

"They're police constables, Ben," Rebecca replied.

"Why they come here?" Daniel asked.

"They just called to see if we had any news for them..." Rebecca replied.

Daniel nodded, but she knew he didn't understand at his tender young age, and she hoped neither twin would ask any more questions.

Rhys turned up at lunchtime. "I heard what happened," she told him. "The police called here earlier."

He frowned. "Well we didn't get anything out of him, he swore he was innocent."

"So, all of that was for nothing!" She threw up her arms in mid air.

"Not really, Wilkes now says he's happy to say the land belongs to Gwyn, so we got something out of it!"

"At what cost though, Rhys?"

Her husband just shrugged, then changing the subject asked, "Anything here to eat before I get back to work..."

Somehow she was finding it difficult to get used to the ways of country folk and their forms of justice. It was all very well though now Gwyn could say the land was his, but it still meant one thing, there was still someone out there who had set fire to that barn and no one knew who that person was.

***

Rebecca decided to put things out of her mind as Christmas approached. She'd knitted a new shawl for her mother, Rhys had crafted two wooden trains with wheels for Ben and Daniel. One was painted blue, the other red. She wondered what she could get for Rhys himself that would be befitting for him. Although he did hard manual graft with his hands, he was also an intellectual sort, so she decided to get him a copy of 'A Tale of Two Cities' by Charles

Dickens. There was a small shop in the village that sold all sorts of curiosities, it was there she found a pipe and tobacco for Gwyn, and the green covered book, heavily etched in gold lettering on the cover. There was just one gift remaining and that was for Bill, who would be arriving on Christmas Eve. He had been a good friend to her mother and almost a father substitute for the twins, so she wanted to buy him something extra special, so at the same shop she purchased a carved wooden walking cane made from white oak.

She'd noticed him limping slightly at times which he put down to old age and creaking bones, so she guessed it would be useful, even though he was not yet sixty years of age, not old at all really. She appreciated though that people who'd worked hard all their lives in some of the occupations in Merthyr Tydfil, aged more quickly than the rest of the population. Bill had once been a miner like her father, until an injury had caused him to leave his job. She guessed that was the real cause of his limp, but he was too proud to admit it.

She would have liked to have bought something for Mansell but it was too late to post a gift to him anyhow, she had sent the ones destined for Merthyr a couple of weeks previously, and in any case, it might not have been appropriate to do so under the circumstances. She still wondered from time-to-time how he was.

On Christmas Eve afternoon, the women folk settled down for a break as they'd spent all morning baking mince pies and bread, icing the Christmas cake, and now a large ham was cooking on the stove. So they sat at the table, her mother had a small smile on her face which she guessed was due to Bill's impending arrival later. Sarah stopped to wrap presents for the boys. She'd spent her hard earned money on a sailing boat for them, which Rhys had said he'd take them to the pond to sail when it had thawed out and quite understandably, Sarah was keen to go along too.

They were just about to rise from the table and begin work once more when Rhys burst in through the farmhouse kitchen door dragging a large Spruce tree behind him. "See what you can do with this!" he exclaimed. Sarah clapped her hands together in joy.

"It looks like a big one, I've never seen a tree that size before except at chapel!" said Rebecca.

"I just chopped it down from the wooded area on Gwyn's land, he gave me permission. He's coming behind with some holly branches and mistletoe."

At the mention of mistletoe, Sarah's cheeks flushed. Rebecca wondered if she was seeing someone and wanted a sprig.

Rebecca noticed Rhys winking at the girl, causing her to turn away. It was almost as though they shared some sort of secret she wasn't privy to and it made her uneasy inside.

There was an air of conviviality at the farmhouse the rest of the afternoon, and a flourish of expectation. Then there was a clattering sound and Sarah rushed to the window. "A carriage has pulled up!" she exclaimed.

"Oh, it's Bill!" Her mother patted her air.

Rebecca smiled and went to allow him access.

He dismounted from the carriage, but his face appeared clouded over.

"What's the matter?" Rebecca asked. "Is anything wrong with my brother?"

"No, he's fine, he's inside the carriage," Bill said, and as he did so, James opened the door and stepped out. She ran to greet him. He had grown so much, he seemed to be a couple of inches taller than when she'd last seen him at the wedding ten months ago. They spoke for a while, and then Rebecca turned back to Bill.

"What's wrong Bill? You don't look very happy."

He let out a long sigh. "I didn't want to ruin everyone's Christmas but it's young Hannah, the Doctor's wife. She was found dead last night..."

Rebecca's heart thumped loudly. "No...no...surely there has to be a mistake?"

"No mistake, I'm afraid." He shook his head savagely.

"What happened then, Bill?"

"She went missing yesterday morning. Doctor Owen couldn't find her when he went to pay his morning visit to the attic. It was most odd as she's refused to leave there for the longest time. Anyhow, the front door of the house was wide open. He couldn't find her, so a search party was sent out. Lots of people joined in, the police were involved as well. I felt ever so sorry for him when someone found her body on the river bank the following morning. Part of her was still on dry land but her face was submerged in the water. We don't know if she died like that, maybe stumbled, or she drowned and was washed up on that part of the bank."

Rebecca's heart went out to Mansell. "How dreadful! Are the Doctor and Hannah's mother all right?"

"Well as you can expect, both are in deep shock. There have been a lot of visitors back and forth to the house. I suggested I remain with the carriage in Merthyr in case I was needed, but the Doctor said he wouldn't hear of it. His friend has offered him a loan of a carriage and driver while I'm away. I won't be staying too long in any case, but it's put a downer on this Christmas for all of us."

"Those poor children..." Tears sprung to Rebecca's eyes.

James put his arm around her. "I know it's awful, Bec. I never met Hannah, but I heard a lot about her from you and felt as though I knew her."

"Although I never knew her when she was well, I'd only known her since her mental illness following the birth of a child, she seemed to have vitality for life, she was like a child really. A mischievous one at that!" she said between sobs.

"I think we'd better all go inside," Bill advised.

As soon as they entered the house, Rebecca's mother could tell something was wrong and Bill ushered her to sit down even before she had chance to greet him. Before long they were all sitting around the table while Rebecca and Gwyn regaled tales of Hannah. Gwyn being her uncle, had known her since she was a baby and he openly wept when he spoke of his niece. Rebecca worried this would be too much for him following the death of his wife, but she could tell he needed to talk.

He sat by the table twisting his handkerchief. "You see, I think that sort of thing was in Mable's family, her aunt had a mental illness and was found drowned in the duck pond at her home..." he said.

"I remember Mable telling me about that when I first came here to stay," Rebecca said. "If only there'd been a way to protect Hannah..."

"Unfortunately, there didn't appear to be..." Rhys took his wife's hand across the table. "If I could lay my hands on Tobias Cookson! I'd flatten him outright!" He roared as he thumped his hand down on the table violently. Some around the table flinched as he caught them off guard with his anger.

"I know what you mean..." Rebecca said gently, "but I honestly believe whilst what he did was a very wicked thing, that it was the birth of the baby that made her condition even worse."

"Aye, well that maybe so, but if he hadn't have knocked her up in the first place, there would be no baby!" Rhys added. "Sorry Gwyn, I am so annoyed..."

Gwyn held up his vertical palm and nodded. "Yes, you're probably right, Rhys. She was such a delicate flower."

"What was she like before she became unwell?" Rebecca asked Gwyn.

"Oh, a lovely young lady, full of fun. Very intelligent too. She loved her husband and children. She had been training to become a doctor herself but left the profession to marry Mansell. They met at a hospital in Cardiff."

Rebecca was surprised to hear of this, as it had never been mentioned before. "So did Doctor Owen put pressure on his wife to end her studies?"

"Oh no," said Gwyn, "nothing like that. Far from it. He encouraged her with her studies. She just felt it was the right thing to do to become a full time mother."

There was a silence in the room as if no one knew what to say. Then Gwyn rose from his chair and said, "I think we should all raise a toast to Hannah's memory and celebrate the little life she had. She wouldn't have wanted us to be sombre over Christmas."

"I'll drink to that," Rhys agreed.

Sarah brought some rum to the table for the men, which had been decanted into a glass jug, and a bottle of sherry for the ladies. They all raised a glass to Hannah Owen, who'd once been a fine doctor and a very charismatic young lady.

***

Rebecca awoke early on Christmas morning and it seemed a lot lighter than usual for the time of day, she went to the window and drew back the curtains to see there'd been a fall of snow during the night. Thankfully, the farmhouse was close by for them all to be together at Christmas. She got herself washed and dressed, then lit a small fire as they would be spending hours at the farmhouse, so wouldn't need to bank it up. By the time Rhys arose, she'd made him hot buttered crumpets with his cup of tea. "I'm not making a full breakfast today," she explained, "as we'll be over the house, but I do have a present for you. Merry Christmas!"

He lowered his head to kiss her cheek. "Oh I wasn't expecting anything, *cariad*," he said frowning. "I haven't had the time to buy you anything!"

She tried not to show her upset and swallowing a lump of disappointment, handed him the book which was wrapped in brown paper and tied with red and green ribbons, which he untied and then folded back the paper.

"Oh my goodness, Becca, this must have cost you a pretty penny! It's leather bound too!" He took his time to admire it and opened it to the title page, where she'd written in her best copperplate handwriting:

To My Dearest Husband, on our First Christmas Together. Love from Your Faithful Wife, Rebecca.

His eyes shone and she was almost certain she noticed the tears begin to form, but instead he just sniffed and kissed her again.

"Now sit down and eat your breakfast as we have a busy day ahead!" she exclaimed.

When she'd turned to pour his tea, she looked back at the table to see a small package in the middle of it. "What's this?" she asked, blinking several times.

"It's for you!" Rhys exclaimed. "Of course I got your something..."

The small package was wrapped in red tissue paper and tied with a gold bow, which she unwrapped. Inside was a narrow velvet box, she opened it and gasped in awe. "Pearls!" she said in excitement, just like Mable had from Gwyn.

"I remembered what pleasure Mrs Evans had from her husband's gift and wanted you to have the very same thing!" Rhys said. "Let me put them on you."

She undid the clasp and lifted her hair as Rhys stood and slipped the pearls around her neck, fastening it in place. She did feel grand as she fingered the pearls. "I wish Mable had the chance to have her jewellery returned before she'd passed away..." she said sadly.

"Aye, I know," Rhys agreed. "No one's seen hide nor hair of Jake Morgan recently, maybe he's upset too many people!"

"No doubt," she agreed.

They both sat at the table and finished their breakfasts before leaving for the farmhouse.

***

Christmas day was wonderful as they joined in and toasted one another's health. Two geese were cooked and an apple sauce made as an accompaniment. Roast potatoes, mixed vegetables, and all the trimmings were laid out, followed by a steaming Christmas pudding served with brandy sauce. Gwyn had given Mable's old family recipe book to Sarah and she'd faithfully followed the pudding recipe to the last letter. It including mixed dried fruit and nuts and everyone agreed it was a great success and laughed when Rhys bit on the silver sixpence buried inside. Sarah laughed hard and long though, making Rebecca feel somewhat uncomfortable. Rhys just smiled and took it in good part, joking and wagging a finger at Sarah warning her he'd half a mind to slap her backside. Sarah coloured up and left the room to make a pot of tea. Then a couple of moments later, Rhys drew back his chair and stood to excuse himself, saying he was about to check on the livestock. He had to pass the kitchen, so Rebecca knew without a shadow of a doubt, he'd exchange words with young Sarah, but she tried to push away the thought. He was old enough to be her father.

He returned to join in the merriment later and watch the twins play with their toys. Sarah immediately joined the trio, while Rebecca and her mother cleared the table and washed the dishes. Rebecca's mother looked at her.

"What's the matter, Bec? You've been quiet this afternoon."

"It's nothing," she lied. "Just thinking about Hannah." Which was partially true but what was really on her mind was her husband's behaviour with Sarah, but even above that, she fretted about Mansell and hoped he was all right.

***

When they returned to the cottage later that evening, Rebecca felt something amiss. It was in darkness as they'd left it, but the door was slightly ajar.

"I'm sure we closed this door!" Rebecca said.

"Yes, me too," Rhys agreed with his wife. Tentatively he pushed it open, there was no sign of any disturbance, so he sighed a breath of relief, and went to light the fire which was already set in the hearth.

Soon they had a nice fire going to warm up the place and Rebecca went upstairs to put on her nightdress and dressing gown. They sat together by the fireside supping steaming hot cups of cocoa.

Without warning, Rebecca heard something fall in the bedroom above them, causing Rhys to shoot up the stairs, but when he got there, there was no sign of anyone or anything. The place was beginning to spook Rebecca out.

"Don't know what that was..." Rhys said, when he returned to the foot of the stairs, might have been some snow falling off the roof, I expect."

Although she accepted his reassurance as a possible cause, she was left with a feeling of dis-ease.

The following day was Boxing Day but there was still work to be done on the farm, so after the milking and checking the animals were warm and fed, Rhys and Gwyn later joined them all at the farmhouse. Bill was in good spirits playing with the twins and their trains.

Rebecca interrupted him. "I suppose Hannah's funeral will be soon..." she said wistfully.

"Would you like to come back to Merthyr with me, Bec?" Bill offered, his grey-blue eyes looking full of concern.

She hesitated and looked at her husband for confirmation before replying, and when he nodded, she replied, "I think that might be a good idea."

And so it was arranged, the following day she left for Merthyr. A lot of the snow on the roads had began to thaw as the weather had got milder, and she ended up on her journey back to her old home town, promising to return to the farm in time for the New Year.

***

The journey back to Merthyr took longer than usual due to weather conditions, roads were quite passable in Cardigan, but when they got closer to Merthyr Tydfil, the snow was a lot deeper causing Bill to need to dismount and shovel some of it out of their way. But eventually, they made it home safely. She had the keys to the family home where she could rest for the night, and tomorrow would call to see Mansell and the children, and if she had time her aunt and uncle at Abercanaid too.

The following day found her trudging through the snow covered streets to get to her destination, although she was well wrapped up with a double layer of clothing and shawls and wore mittens, the cold beneath her feet permeated her weary bones, the walk seemed to take twice as long as usual, and by the time she arrived at the Doctor's home, she could barely breathe.

Tentatively, she was met by the Doctor's mother-in-law, Mary Jacobs.

"Oh my goodness!" the woman gasped, her hands flying to her mouth. "Come inside child and sit down!"

By now Rebecca was feeling light headed as she walked into the warmth of the Doctor's home where she was put to sit beside the fire in the drawing room, while Mary summoned the maid to fetch a hot cup of tea.

"She'll be wanting more than that, I prescribe a small glass of brandy to warm her up!" She turned to see the Doctor there, smiling at her with compassion, then when Mary left the room, he was beside Rebecca holding her hands, removing her gloves to warm them. "Oh my dear, you should not have walked all this way to visit us here..."

"Oh...but...I wanted to," she explained, as she began to feel the warmth of the room and the company seep into her veins. "I was so sorry to hear about Hannah." She lowered her head and wept not just for the woman herself, but her family too. Her heart went out to them all, particularly the children who would now be forced to live without her and to whom, one day she would be a dim and distant memory.

She stood and before she realised what was happening, Mansell was embracing her tenderly in his arms and it felt good, but she knew it shouldn't. He had awakened something inside her once more. Her head was swimming and she broke away as she heard the approach of footsteps.

Mansell turned suddenly and opened the door to allow the maid into the room, who had brought a tray containing a china tea pot, two cups and saucers and a sugar pot. She placed it down on the small walnut table beside them.

"Before we pour the tea," Mansell said, when the maid had departed, "I'll fetch you that brandy. He went over to glass cabinet in the corner of the room and extracted a crystal decanter and poured one for Rebecca and one for himself which they sipped in silence from bulb-shaped glasses, both seated in high back armchairs, either side of the fire place.

"I was so sorry to hear what happened to Hannah..." she said finally, breaking the wall of silence.

He looked up at her with glassy eyes. "It was awful, Rebecca. Since coming back here after the birth of the baby, we couldn't persuade her to leave the attic room. We could hear her wails downstairs, they seemed to reverberate around the house. It was scary for the children, mind you. Maria had to pretend their mother was playing a game. Finally I sent them to stay with my sister in Aberdare.

"And where are they now?"

"Still there. They are besotted with their new baby cousin. Of course the baby is really their half sister, but I can't tell them that."

"So it was a girl then," Rebecca brightened. "And what was she named?"

Mansell cleared his throat. "My sister and her husband named her, Myfanwy."

"Oh I love that name. Actually, the name means a lot to our family as my mother once sang the song of the same name for Doctor Joseph Parry."

Mansell blinked. "I didn't know that, Rebecca. I mean I knew your mother used to sing on stage, but what an honour to sing that song for the composer himself. Did you get to hear it being performed?"

She nodded. "Oh yes, but I was young at the time, ten years old, but it's something I'll remember all the days of my life."

"That's wonderful." She could see he genuinely meant it.

"But what about you, Mansell...how have you been?"

"Not quite as bad as you might imagine as I felt I'd lost the wife I knew a long time ago. Her illness was so cruel. It's the children I feel most sorry for and my mother-in-law. They've lost a mother and she's lost her only child."

When he put it like that, she realised how sad the situation was all round.

"What date is the funeral?" She asked the question she had been dreading to ask.

"The day after tomorrow..." He let out a long breath, as she watched him blink back the tears, almost as if the very mention of the funeral itself were making it all the more real to him somehow.

"I shall be here to support you all," she said firmly. "What time is it arranged for?"

"11 o'clock. The service will take place at St Tydfil's Parish Church. Hannah attended there all her life from a young child, we were also married there..." He swallowed a lump in his throat and then he was openly weeping with his head in his hands, and she didn't quite know what to do to comfort him.

She got out of her chair and patted his shoulder in reassurance. "It will be a difficult day that's for sure, Mansell, but we'll all support you. What about the children, will they be attending the funeral?"

He dabbed at his eyes with a silk handkerchief. "No, I thought maybe it was best if Maria takes care of them for the day."

"Maybe you're right," she said softly.

"I can't see any benefit in them attending with so much sadness throughout the day."

"I suppose there might be other ways of saying their goodbyes," she suggested. "What was Hannah's favourite flower when she was well? I know she loved flowers as she collected them in abundance whilst we were at Crugmor Farm."

"Her favourite flowers were roses. Yellow ones."

"Then I suggest when all of this is over, maybe in the New Year, you plant a rose bush in the garden and explain to them, so every year they can watch the flowers bloom and think of their mother."

"That sounds a marvellous idea, Rebecca," he said, taking her hand and kissing the back of it. Then he dropped her hand quickly as the door opened. Mary Jacob stood at the entrance of the room.

"Doctor Daniel Evans is here to see you, Mansell," she said quietly.

Mansell finished dabbing at his eyes and pushed his handkerchief out of sight in his inside top pocket. "Very well, please send him in," he said gruffly.

Rebecca wasn't quite sure what to do, having to encounter Daniel once more. "I'd better go," she said to Mansell.

"Very well, Rebecca. I quite understand and thank you for calling."

She nodded and said, "I'll call to the house just before the funeral."

"Thank you, you shall have a lift in my carriage. Speaking of which, have you a lift back home?"

She shook her head. "I'm going to see my aunt and uncle in the village. I might stay there a while."

"Very well, but if you change your mind, do call back here and Bill can take you home."

She nodded and smiled, then left the drawing room, almost colliding with Daniel in the hallway. His eyes flashed when he saw her. She couldn't quite make out whether he was pleased to see her or not.

"Rebecca?" he seemed surprised.

"Hello, Daniel," she said curtly.

"What are you doing here?"

Her chin jutted out. "I came to pay my respects of course!"

"No, I meant how are you back in Merthyr Tydfil, are you living here again now?"

She tossed back her hair. "No, I just returned for the funeral. I'm married now and living in Llandbadarn Fawr!"

He raised a questioning brow. "Oh...I see..." his voice trailed away and finally she had the satisfaction she sought. All this time he had treated her badly and thrown away their relationship for a little flirtation and she wondered if he regretted doing so.

"How's Jane?" she queried.

"Er I don't see her anymore, she's working at another hospital." His face was now a faint shade of pink.

He's embarrassed, she thought. Now for once she had the upper hand and she walked off with her head held high.

***

Once in her auntie's kitchen, she was able to let go and tell her Aunt Lily what had gone on.

"I heard about Hannah, of course I did," Lily explained. "Bill told us he would be informing you. We'll be attending the funeral ourselves."

Relief flooded through her veins to realise both Evan and Lily would be there, it reassured her. She told her aunt about Daniel being at the Doctor's home and their encounter.

"Well he had his chance with you, *cariad*," she said.

Her aunt was correct, he'd had his chance and had blown it away like petals in the wind.

***

The day dawned as slate grey clouds gathered overhead as Rebecca made her way to the Doctor's house. The streets of Abercanaid seemed sombre somehow, already, people had gathered to wait outside the Doctor's house to watch the funeral cortège.

Two carriages gleamed on the driveway in readiness for the procession.

Rebecca nodded at a couple of people she vaguely recognised, but did not stop to make conversation. Instead, she walked briskly up the drive and tentatively knocked the door. The door swung open and Mary Jacobs answered immediately.

"Do come inside, Rebecca, we've been expecting you." The woman's eyes were red-rimmed and raw looking, almost as if she hadn't slept in a month of Sundays. She glanced past Rebecca at the crowds gathering outside and quickly shut the door behind her.

As Rebecca entered the foyer, she spied the open door of the drawing room and behind it sat Mansell, upright in a leather Sedan chair. He was deep in conversation with someone, though she could not see who that someone was. Feeling like an eaves' dropper she followed Mary to the parlour, where a couple of people whom she didn't recognise, were seated.

"This is Mansell's sister and her husband, Bella and George Morris, from Aberdare..." Mary introduced.

Rebecca swallowed, so this was the couple who had taken care of Hannah and the baby.

Bella was sat on the sofa beside her husband. She wore a long black satin dress with lace white collar. On her head perched a small black hat with veil that partially covered her face. She sniffed loudly into a handkerchief. Her husband sat beside her, also in black: tailcoat, waist coat and matching trousers with stiff white shirt and black cravat. He sat stoically, from time-to-time patting his wife's hand as if to comfort her.

"I'm pleased to meet you both, though would prefer if it were in some other circumstance," Rebecca greeted, then sat opposite the couple.

They both looked at her and nodded. Then as realisation dawned, Bella said, "So you're the Rebecca who now lives in Llanbadarn Fawr?"

"I am indeed." Rebecca blinked.

"I've heard a lot about you from my brother..."

For a moment, she feared what Bella Morris might say to her. "Oh?"

The woman paused and drew in a breath before letting it out again. "He said you are an excellent nurse and was very good with Hannah. I understand how difficult it must have been as she was prone to fits of hysteria upon occasion. I, myself, was fortunate not to have cope with those as we employed someone to take care of her during her confinement, but the weeping and wailing was quite enough!" She snorted loudly.

Shocked by Bella's confession, Rebecca took an instant dislike to the woman, no doubt she was more than happy to have offloaded the woman back to Mansell following the birth of the baby, and pleased at last she had her longed for child.

At that point, Mansell, himself, entered the room. Feeling relief at his intrusion at what might have turned out to be an awkward moment, Rebecca made eye contact with him as he said, "Ah, Rebecca, glad you could make it. I see you have already met my sister Bella and her husband, George."

She nodded politely. "I have indeed. And what of Hannah's baby?" she found herself saying, and thought afterwards that she sounded a little too forward.

"The baby..." Mary Jacob explained, "was christened, Myfanwy, and she's very well. She's being cared for by Maria today at Bella and George's home in Aberdare, along with my other grandchildren at this present time."

Rebecca nodded. Of course she knew the child's given name and the fact the children were being cared for, but wondered if Mansell had done the right thing in handing the child to his sister and husband. Although, of course, in reality it was Tobias Cookson's child and not his own.

"Yes, she has a good home with us," George chipped in for the first time. "She'll want for nothing."

Bella sniffed very loudly and stuck her nose in the air, no doubt affronted by Rebecca's upfront manner about the child.

The maid entered the room and Mary whispered something to her, she returned a short while later with a crystal decanter and matching glasses on a silver tray.

"Sherry," Mary explained. "It will take the edge off our nerves today before the funeral."

Rebecca looked at the woman's eyes and knew she was putting on a front, no doubt after they'd all gone home, she would do her own private mourning. She was just too composed about it all.

When they'd partaken of the sherry, they boarded the coaches parked out on the driveway of the Doctor's home. A chill wind ruffled Rebecca's hair and a shiver skittered down the length of her spine, as she paused to gaze around herself: the trees surrounding the house were bowing in the wind, almost in reverence as if in mourning too. *This shouldn't be happening,* she thought to herself. *Hannah was too young to die.* Rebecca accompanied Mary and the Doctor, whilst Bella and her husband took the other coach. Mansell said very little as the carriage clattered along the streets as they made their way to St Tydfil's Parish Church. From time-to-time he turned his head to gaze out of the window and she wondered what must be going through his mind. Mary though, surprised her, it was almost as if she were going some place else, not her own daughter's funeral. Rebecca guessed the woman did somehow not comprehend the situation.

Rebecca was amazed as they approached how many people stood outside, congregating in small groups within the church yard, a sea of black, waiting to pay their respects to the good Doctor and his deceased wife. Rebecca wondered if Doctor Daniel were there somewhere in amongst the crowd.

When they entered the church, she wasn't quite sure what to expect, but it became evident that Mansell wanted her to sit in the front pew beside himself and Mary Jacobs, as he stood to allow her to pass. She seated herself between Mansell and Mary, taking hold of the woman's crepe-like hand throughout the service. Hannah's favourite hymn, before her illness took hold, was sang, 'Abide with Me'. Tears sprang to Rebecca's eyes and she had to swallow to hold them back to avoid them streaming down her cheeks. She intended to remain strong for Mary and Mansell's sakes. Then the vicar read from Isaiah 61: 1-3 which spoke of good news for the broken hearted. "To appoint unto them that mourn in Zion, to give unto them beauty for ashes..." She hazarded a glance at Mansell, who was gazing blankly ahead as if some place else and she guessed this situation bore no reality for him, as in essence he had lost his wife a long time ago.

Somehow they got through the service, but when Hannah's oak coffin was carried up the aisle covered in white lilies, it all got too much for Mary. The woman stood and shouted, "No! Not my precious child! Please don't take her away from me!" Her voice reverberated throughout the church, Rebecca shivered as it echoed and haunted the church walls. Mary pulled away and tried to bypass Rebecca and Mansell, who both fought to restrain the woman who by now was in hysterics.

"Please seat yourself down, Mary," Mansell beckoned. "This will do you no good..." He shook his head.

People were beginning to stare as Mary began to weep and wail.

"I thought she'd been too good," Rebecca muttered looking at Mansell.

He nodded. "I'll give her a sedative when we return home."

Rebecca somehow managed to persuade Mary to sit down and remained with her in the church, comforting her, as Mansell shook hands with people at the door as they departed. Being not customary for women to stay for the burial, she then ushered Mary away to the awaiting carriage and they departed with Bella Morris, whilst the other carriage remained for the men.

It was all a haze of confusion that Rebecca barely noticed the journey back home. When the Doctor returned a good hour later with some of the male funeral guests, Rebecca and Bella had managed to coax Mary into having a lie down in her darkened bedroom. Mansell brought his leather Gladstone bag and administered a strong sedative to his mother-in-law.

"You get plenty of rest now, Mary," he explained. Within a few minutes the woman was fast asleep and Rebecca tucked her in the bed and then followed Mansell back down the stairs.

Later that evening when the funeral guests had departed and all that remained was Rebecca in the drawing room with Mansell, while his mother-in-law slept soundly upstairs, he drew near to her.

"I'm really sorry, Rebecca..." he said softly. Their figures were illuminated by the flickering flames of the fireplace and all that could be heard was the ticking of the Grandfather Clock in the corner of the room, encased in its walnut shell.

"Whatever for?" she whispered.

"For bringing you here on this sad occasion and for ..."

"For what?" she replied, huskily.

He closed the distance between then and brought his hand to her face, then gazing directly into her eyes said, "And for loving you..."

He brought his head down as if about to kiss her, his warm breath on her face, but she pulled away, her senses reeling and her heart beat quickening. She drew in a breath of composure and let it out again. "I'm sorry Mansell, we cannot do this. I am a married woman and you've just lost your wife."

"I lost her a long time ago though, Rebecca. I know you're married but I love you so. I'm sure we would both be happy together if circumstances were to permit?"

She felt a sharp shard of anger course her veins and straightening her countenance replied, "Well circumstances do not permit. I am married, and your mother-in-law, who is sleeping above our heads, has lost her only child. I think it better that I leave!"

"I can see that you're annoyed, your beautiful eyes are flashing with anger, Rebecca. But you know as well as I do, that you love me too..."

She hung her head and allowed the tears to fall because there was truth in what he said. Then he took her hand and laid a kiss upon it and she was gone. She needed to get back home and tonight should have stayed with her aunt and uncle in Abercanaid, but instead chose to walk all the way home in the darkness and not for one single, solitary second, did Mansell leave her mind on the trip to her family home.

There was no doubt about it, she was as much in love with him as he was with her.

***

Thankfully her brother was in bed when she returned home, needing to get up early for work in the morning. It had been nice spending time with him, he'd told her he now had a girlfriend, but as yet, she had no idea who she was.

The following day Rebecca rose at 7 a.m. to cook for her brother. This wasn't even an early start for her, as living on the farm, she rose a couple of hours earlier than that to see Rhys off to work and begin her daily chores.

James came breezing into the kitchen, whistling some tune she didn't recognise, hands in his pockets. He stopped when he saw his sister. "Sorry, Bec, doesn't seem appropriate me whistling when you attended that poor woman's funeral yesterday."

She shook her head. "On the contrary, it's nice to hear you so happy. Come on, I've made you eggs and bacon, oh and fried bread too!"

He smiled and sat at the pine kitchen table whilst she placed the breakfast in front of him. Then ruffling his hair, she went to boil the kettle to make them tea. She didn't much feel like eating after the Doctor's declaration yesterday. It almost felt as though she was keeping some dark secret to herself and maybe she was.

When James had eaten his fill, after requesting another slice of bacon and hunk of bread and butter, she placed his cup of tea in front of him and took hers and sat opposite him.

"So..." she said finally.

He raised his brows. "Oh?"

"Who is this young lady you're stepping out with?"

His face flushed, then his lips curved up into a smile. "Oh Rebecca, Amelia is the most delightful young woman I've ever met in my life, apart from yourself of course!"

"How did you meet?"

"At work, she's Mr. Goldstein's daughter, the man I work for!" He announced proudly.

"Yes. I'm quite aware who Mr. Goldstein is!" she laughed. "So she's Jewish?"

"Yes. Don't worry, her father knows about our relationship, she hasn't gone unchaperoned or anything like that."

"But do you understand what this could mean if you were to marry, James?"

He nodded. "I'm still young, but I do understand I'd have to convert to the Jewish faith not to cause any problems for the family. Mr. Goldstein has treated me like a son. Better than my own father has actually."

Rebecca felt a little uneasy about it all, and felt in some way that although they'd already lost their father, maybe she was now losing her brother too. As if somehow sensing this he grabbed her hand across the table. "Don't concern yourself, Bec, it will not change me as a person and you shall always be my sister."

She nodded, but at the back of her mind was what had happened to her Aunt Lily many years ago, losing one brother to the Saints of Utah and the other to the demon drink.

***

That same day she paid a visit to Lily at Abercanaid and told her what had happened yesterday following the funeral.

"Hmmm I thought somehow he'd make his feelings known, Bec..." Aunt Lily said thoughtfully, as they sat in the kitchen. "Yesterday was a sad day. Poor old Mary was distraught, I'm glad to see you managed to calm her down. Now about the Doctor, it was an emotional day for him and maybe he felt under the circumstances, he should make his feelings known before you return to Cardigan."

"Doesn't make it right though, does it?"

"Maybe not, but you both can't help how you feel. I've told you this before Rebecca, in my opinion you should follow your heart for once not your head. You've married a man you're not truly in love with for convenience sake, and believe me, I, of all people, should know as it almost happened to me until I came to my senses."

Rebecca frowned. Deep down in her heart she realised her aunt was only being truthful, Rhys was a good man who'd make a fine father if and when the time came, but so far there was no success with him getting her pregnant.

"So what I can do about the situation, Aunt Lily? I would have to break one man's heart to make another happy, and surely that's not right at all."

Aunt Lily nodded. "It is already too late, *cariad*. I tried to warn you of this at Christmas before your impending wedding to Rhys, but you seemed set on marrying him. In the eyes of our Lord, you are now one, and that's a consequence you will have to live with I'm afraid." She stood and walked over to where Rebecca sat, then hugged her niece to her bosom as Rebecca cried, realising she had to go back to Llanbadarn Fawr and leave the man she loved behind.

***

The following day Rebecca left Merthyr early for Cardigan, with Bill taking the reins of the coach. She had deliberately avoided saying her goodbyes to Mansell, in case she should falter if he were to say he loved her once more. Now it was time to return to the farm and concentrate on her marriage.

As Bill helped her into the carriage, he looked at her for a moment, "Is all well, Rebecca?"

She nodded and smiled. "Yes, it is, I can't wait to return to the farm..."

"Me too, even though it will only be until tomorrow morning I love seeing your Mam and the boys."

"Doesn't it bother you though, Bill, that my mother will never divorce so you are free to marry?"

For a moment his eyes clouded over, then he shrugged. "Rebecca, I will take what crumbs I can get for now. Just to be in the presence of your mother is fine with me. You don't realise what a difference it has made to my life. I miss her so much now she's residing in Cardigan but I understand the reasons for it..."

Rebecca smiled, then Bill dismounted and closed the carriage door and climbed on the front of the coach and they were on their way.

Darkness had fallen by the time they arrived at the farm, but there was still an oil lamp glowing in the farmhouse kitchen window.

As they entered, Rebecca sensed that something was wrong. Her mother came to the door. "Oh Rebecca, I'm afraid that something dreadful has happened, you'd better sit down."

Rebecca felt her heart thudding. "Has something happened to one of the boys?"

"Please sit down, dear," her mother urged.

She did as told, then her mother reached out and took her daughter's hand. "It's Rhys...he's had an accident."

"W...what kind of accident?"

"He fell from the loft in the big barn and hit his head."

"But where is he now? I must go to him."

"He's being tended to by Sarah. The girl is beside herself, that upset she is. She found him and ran for help. The Doctor left about an hour ago and he says the next twenty four hours will be crucial."

"Crucial? You mean he could die?"

"I won't lie to you, but yes, that's what the Doctor has indicated to me, he fell a long distance. Gwyn has checked the barn and said it appears that some planks of wood had been disturbed in the hay loft, so when Rhys walked on them, he fell through. Though what he was doing there in the first place none of us know."

"I don't understand it. But who would remove the planks?"

At that point, one of the farmhands, Luke, entered the room. "There's talk that it might be that Jake Morgan who used to work at the farm," he announced.

"Surely not?" Rebecca said.

"Well it could be correct, Bec," her mother said. "The same barn went on fire some months ago. Looks like someone is out for revenge and we know he doesn't like Rhys."

Rebecca shook her head. "I need to get to my husband, right now, he needs me!" she exclaimed.

"Take her over to him!" Kathleen said, handing Luke a lantern. "Take care how you go mind, you never know if that Jake is around somewhere, watching what we're all doing."

Rebecca shuddered with apprehension.

Chapter Thirteen

When she arrived at the cottage, Rebecca found Sarah kneeling by the side of the marital bed, mopping Rhys's head which was beaded with perspiration, as he mumbled incoherently.

"Thanks Sarah, you may go now," she said. The girl stood, but seemed reluctant to leave Rhys's side, until Rebecca made a point of opening the bedroom door. Sarah was about to leave the room, but turned to take one more look at Rhys with tears in her eyes. He looked a sight with his head heavily bandaged. Blood had seeped through from the wound. Sarah rushed out of the room as if badly wounded by the fact she'd now been dismissed.

Rebecca glanced at the Doctor who just grimaced.

"Will my husband be all right?" she asked.

He shrugged. "There's no way of knowing for sure, for now rest is the best thing for him. Just ensure you come and get me if he vomits as that's a bad sign." He tutted and shook his head, then donned his hat and lifted his leather bag to leave.

She had nursed head injuries previously at the hospital but when it came to her own family, she became a nervous wreck. She fought to think what usually happened. She remembered that most, with time, became well again, but there had been the odd one or two who had slipped into unconsciousness. She so wished Mansell were here right now, he'd know what to do.

Her trust in countrified quacks was at an all time low. If this doctor were to offer her a tonic at a time like this, she felt she'd hit him over the head with the bottle.

When the doctor had departed, and both Sarah and Luke had returned to the farmhouse, she sat up all night by the side of the bed, holding her husband's hand. He'd stirred a couple of times during the night, mumbling something unintelligible to her ears. His fever had broken after she'd bathed him with cool wet flannels. And as the early embers of dawn broke, he opened his eyes, sat himself up and asked, "What happened?"

She broke down with tears of joy that he seemed well again.

The overwhelming sense of relief washed through her, but at the back of her mind was the fact she was guilty of mental adultery with another man and that didn't sit right with her at all.

During the next few days, Rhys was quiet. It was arranged that both farmhands would take over his jobs for now and Gwyn did whatever he could, but he was an elderly man, struggling with the most basic of chores.

It wasn't that her husband had lost his memory due to the fall, more that he didn't seem quite the same person any more, not the kind man she had fallen for. Now he became demanding and snappy.

It all came to a head when he returned the first day to work and his evening meal was not on the table on time for him as it usually was. She had been particularly busy that day and had been over to Mable's grave with fresh flowers, there she had spoken with a couple of villagers, which had made her later than usual.

When she arrived at the cottage, Rhys was there in his armchair, staring at her.

"I thought by now, my food would have been ready!" he growled.

She set her basket down on the table and removed her shawl and bonnet and hung them on a coat peg behind the kitchen door. "It won't take a moment, I only have to reheat the cawl and warm the bread..." she said brightly.

"Where have you been anyhow?" he glared at her.

"I took flowers to Mable's grave, no one's been there for a while and Gwyn told me it would have been her birthday today."

He got out of the chair and roughly grabbed hold of her arm, pulling her towards him so she had to look into his eyes, recoiling when she smelled the beery fumes on his lips.

"I...I thought you'd been in work today?" she asked, trembling from top-to-toe.

"Aye, I have, but I called into the Black Lion, if I'd known there'd be no food on the table, I'd have remained there. It was my first day back in work today and you make a fool out of your husband by not being here to greet him when he gets home!"

"I'm sorry, but as I said I was busy."

"Busy, huh? It's the living you ought to be caring for and not the dead!" She felt a hard slap across her cheek, which stung to high heaven and sent her tumbling backwards, but she managed to remain standing. Before she had chance to catch her breath, Rhys pushed her aside and walked out of the room. The front door slammed and she wondered where he was off to.

Rubbing her sore cheek, she went to get a cold wet flannel to put on it, he'd never done anything like that before and it disturbed her.

It was hours later when he returned and she guessed he'd been to the pub, so kept out of his way then went to bed, hoping this was a temporary setback, in what had been up until now quite a happy marriage.

About an hour later, she felt him crawl into bed with her and cuddle into the small of her back as if that earlier episode had never happened at all.

***

The following day, Rhys seemed to be back to his old self and she breathed a sigh of relief as she waved him farewell, meanwhile, she tidied up the cottage and set off in search of her mother to explain what had happened, first ensuring that last night's slap across the face hadn't left a bruise. Luckily her face didn't look too bad, though it was slightly swollen.

Her mother sat her down in the farmhouse kitchen. "I see what you're saying, Bec. It sounds similar to that time your Uncle Evan had a blow to the head and lost his memory."

"This is different though, Mam. With Rhys it's not that he's lost his memory, but he seems to be behaving in a strange manner, not like the man I married. More violent somehow."

"You have concerns?"

"Yes, I do. Last night, well, it was the way he was looking at me, almost as though he wanted to hurt me."

"He had better not or he'll have me to contend with, so he will!" Her mother held up a fist.

Rebecca smiled, her mother was quite some force to reckon with. "No, well, hopefully it won't come to that, but he did scare me. Today he seems to be back to normal again, almost as though last night never happened at all." She hadn't wanted to frighten her mother, so kept the slap across the cheek to herself.

Her mother relaxed her stance. "Well, just keep an eye on him Becca and if it happens again, we'll call out the doctor to him."

"I don't trust any of those quacks around these parts, they try to fob you off with a bottle of 'Doctor's Cure All Tonic' as good as look at you. Medicine in Merthyr Tydfil is much more advanced than it is in this back water!"

"I suppose you might be right. Pity Doctor Owen wasn't nearby..."

At the mention of his name, Rebecca felt her face flush and hoped that her mother wouldn't notice. "Yes...he'd know what to do."

"Look, Bec, just stick with it for now and see how it goes...I'm sure this won't last too much longer. He's had a severe blow to the head, 'tis bound to affect him somewhat. But he's not to lay a finger on you, you hear?"

She nodded. "Don't worry, if he gets violent I'll run over here to the farm house."

"Just give him some time, Bec. I had my problems with your father and his moods, but he never laid a finger on me."

"I know," she said wistfully. "Speaking of whom, there's been so sign of him coming back to Wales, so do you think you and the boys ought to go to back to Merthyr? Bill must be missing you terribly."

Her mother sighed heavily and ran her fingers through her salt and peppered hair. "Aye, maybe I should, but part of me wishes to remain here."

"I don't understand."

"I'm hoping Bill will eventually forget all about me, we can't marry anyhow in the eyes of the Church."

"I don't think he's liable to forget you, Mam. Go back, he's been a good friend to you and the boys."

"I will, Bec, I promise, but first I want to check all is right with you and Rhys."

A deluge of guilt washed over Rebecca. It hadn't been her intention to worry her mother, but maybe it was best she knew the truth.

***

The following weeks passed by without incident and Rebecca was pleased to see her husband had gone back to being his old affable self. Though it annoyed her the way Sarah kept hanging around to check on Rhys, almost as if he were her husband and not Rebecca's. She guessed the girl must have some sort of designs on him, maybe she was flattered by his attention, but one thing she couldn't get out of her mind was, the reason they were in the hay loft together. She pushed the thought away, it just couldn't be so. Meanwhile, her mother and the boys made plans to leave for Merthyr.

One evening whilst Rhys was out in the field, she became aware of the feeling of someone watching her. Shivering, she drew the curtains and waited for her husband to return. Every tick of the clock increased her heartbeat, every crackle, every noise the old cottage made, caused her to startle, so much so by the time Rhys returned, her nerves were fraught.

"What's the matter, *cariad*?" he asked, when he entered the kitchen.

"Rhys it's strange, I feel as though someone has been watching me here this evening. I can't get the feeling out of my mind."

He drew close. "Well I'm here now, I expect your imagination is playing tricks on you."

She nodded, not wishing to alarm him. "May be."

After supper, they spent some time by the fireside and then went to bed. Their lovemaking that night was frenzied and urgent. Making things all the worse was the fact that they'd been trying to conceive a child for so long but nothing was happening as yet.

When she turned over to see Rhys snoring gently by the side of her, she got out of bed and gazed out of the window. For a moment, she thought she saw the figure of a man down below. Then a dog barked and all went silent. What if it was Jake Morgan? She feared waking her husband in case he thought she was quite mad, but she was so sure there was someone there. It was so dark that she tried to reassure herself maybe she was mistaken.

The following day, the sun shone bright and early, the birds were singing, it was spring and almost turning into summer. All felt good with the world and she dismissed her thoughts as silly.

She spent the day baking at the farmhouse and helping Sarah with the washing and ironing. Then finally, she went to the small barn to check on the horses before she set about making the evening meal. The door was just ajar and she went in to see the horses were fine, so she threw in a bale of hay and was just about to turn around when a hand clamped over her mouth. Her heart raced as a hot breath bathed her as a rasping voice said, "So, what do we have here then!"

Was it Jake?

She tried to turn but felt unable to as the man had her firmly in his grasp and to her horror lifted the back of her dress.

She tried to cry out but his hand remained heavily clamped over her mouth. She felt him drag down her drawers exposing her bare buttocks as he pushed her over a low lying wall that kept the bales of hay in place.

"I know what a woman like you needs!" he sneered. "And it ain't no handling gently." He dropped his hand from her mouth, but held her down firmly with the other. She heard a sudden whip crack noise and realised in horror what he was about to do, he was lashing at her bare bottom with a horse whip. She felt the leather fronds scurge her skin, cutting into her delicate skin, again and again and again. In horror, she cried out, but that seemed to excite the man.

"Gee up, filly! He rasped and then he chuckled devilishly as he continued to lash out at her. She yelped, her breaths coming in short bursts till she felt she could take no more.

Then she felt his hard penis painfully enter her in a position she had never experienced before. He clamped his hand tightly over her mouth again, so she couldn't cry out, instead salty tears slid down her face as the man grabbed her breast and squeezed with his free hand. The act seemed to take an age as he pressed himself hard inside her, grunting and groaning, and when he was spent, he slapped her bottom hard and dropped the hand that had been holding her firm.

She spun around expecting to see either a stranger or Jake stood there, but bitter bile rose up to her mouth, when she saw it was her own husband who bore a glazed expression on his face. That voice just hadn't sounded like him at all.

She pulled up her undergarments and brushed down her skirt, then her stomach began to heave involuntarily from the shock of it all. When she had expelled the contents of her gut, she wiped her mouth on the back of the sleeve of her dress and rearranged her clothing. Sore between her legs and on the skin of her buttocks, she ran out of the barn as fast as she could, annoyed with herself that she had trusted him and sent her mother and the boys back to Merthyr. Who could she turn to now? She couldn't live like this for the rest of her life?

What had just happened would be a rape and physical cruelty if it were a stranger, but as it was her own husband taking his pleasure, the act wouldn't be seen as a violation. Yet, that's precisely what it was, a violation of her mind, soul and body. His voice had sounded so strange not like Rhys at all, almost as if he were the Devil incarnate. Fear took over her body, she had to get away to a place of safety.

She ran back to the cottage, gasping for breath, tripping over the hem of her dress on the way, and dragging herself back up on her feet again. When she got to the cottage, she ran up the stairs and then found an old carpet bag on top of the wardrobe. Trembling from top-to-toe, she packed it with anything she might need for the journey back home to Merthyr Tydfil. She dare not even tell Gwyn what was happening to her not to upset the old man, so would be unable to say goodbye and she was sad about that.

Her stuff loaded up, she was ready to leave and hoped to catch the early morning stage coach, but was stopped dead in her tracks as her husband entered the house.

"What's for dinner, Bec?" he asked, with a huge smile on his face.

She pushed past him gripping on firmly to the bag. He pulled her toward him.

"Don't you dare touch me again! Ever!" she cried out.

"I don't understand. Is this some kind of a joke, *cariad*?" Now he sounded like her dear Rhys once more. This was too much for her to bear. How could he be so rough and cruel one moment but normal the next?

"I'm going back to Merthyr!" she said firmly.

"But why? Aren't you happy living with me?" His grey eyes questioned.

"I was, but after what happened not yet an hour since in the barn, I can never trust you again."

"But I haven't been in the barn, I don't understand."

She pushed him out of the way as he stood there blankly. This really was all too much for her to bear.

"Wait, Rebecca!" he called after her, but it was already too late, as she strode off towards the village. She'd find a bed for the night and catch that stage coach first thing in the morning.

Initially she tried at the Black Lion to get a bed for the night. The place was packed, men were arguing inside and out, and she heard one of them call, "Jake Morgan! If I get my hands on that blighter!"

"What's going on here?" she asked the landlord.

"It's Cled Morgan...he was found dead this morning, clobbered over the head with a shovel he was. The villagers know who was responsible for his murder, it was that son of his. They're getting together to find him and string him up, should have been done a long time ago!"

A shiver ran the length of her spine, although Jake was a wrong 'un in most people's eyes, she didn't want to see a lynching party going after him.

"But how do you know he killed his father? It could be any one of his debtors who owes him money!"

The landlord's lips curved into a snarl. "It has to be him, he's a thief!" he growled. "He's held up a few coaches this past week or two!"

"But that's preposterous," she argued, "it doesn't make him a killer."

The landlord took a swig from a tankard and wiping the beery foam from his mouth, looked her squarely in the eyes. "Killer or not, he deserves a bloody good pounding, and these men here are going to see to it he gets one!"

Rebecca glanced around the pub, this was no place for a lady to be. She decided maybe it was best to ask Mrs Clancy who owned the tea room, if she could give her a bed for the night as she needed to bathe her wounds. Someone caught hold of her arm.

She turned to see the landlady, Blodwen, standing there. "You'd be better off getting out of here, swift as you go," she hissed.

"I was just thinking the same myself. I need a bed for the night though," Rebecca whispered, "I urgently need to get to Merthyr Tydfil. I'm hoping to catch a stagecoach tomorrow."

"Very well. I have a small room I can allow you to use, it only has a horsehair pallet on the floor, mind. 'Ere you look a bit frightened though, dear. Is all well?"

What could Rebecca do? She couldn't tell the woman what had happened earlier with Rhys. He was well known in the pub. She felt shocked to the core and at the moment was holding back her feelings, she daren't break down until she returned to the safety of home which wasn't Llanbadarn Fawr, it was Merthyr Tydfil. Tears were near the surface, she fought to hold them at bay.

"I'm fine, thank you," she lied, swallowing down her pain. She needed to say something that might explain her distressed demeanour. "I've just had bad news and need to get back to Merthyr, that's all."

The landlady nodded. "See that gentleman there?" she pointed at a man in black shiny top hat, nicely dressed, who looked around the place with much bemusement. Rebecca guessed he was about forty years of age. He appeared to be some sort of business man.

Rebecca nodded. "I do."

"He's something to do with the ironworks in Merthyr Tydfil and he's due to return there soon. I could ask him for you if you like. His coach and driver are outside."

"Oh, I couldn't impose on him..."

"Look, lady, you seem like someone in need to me," Blod rolled up the sleeves of her dress and wiped her hands on her already filthy apron. Before Rebecca had a chance to object, Blod had approached the man and appeared to be having some sort of conversation with him. He glanced across at Rebecca and nodded and smiled, then tipped his hat.

Blod returned with a big smile on her face, revealing the gaps where she had a couple of missing teeth. "All sorted she said!" slapping her hands together.

Rebecca fiddled around in her purse and gave her a shiny shilling for her bother, which the woman dropped into the pocket of her filthy apron.

"Ta very much, missus! He says he's leaving as soon as he's finished his ale so better forget staying the night here. He offered to buy you a drink, fancy a tot of rum?"

Rebecca guessed it was the same stuff left over from the shipwreck. She shook her head and held up her vertical palm in deference. "Thank you, but I'd prefer a glass of water."

The landlady rolled her eyes and returned with a glass of water, which she handed over to Rebecca. "You're a lady you are!" she exclaimed. "Not like some of those rough women we get in here. They're only after a man to buy them drinks all night or to take them to bed. Haven't I seen you before some place?"

Not wishing to reveal her identity, Rebecca replied, "No, I've just been staying at my aunt's farm and need to get back to my own home town."

Rebecca didn't know whether Blod believed her or not, but none of that mattered as soon she would be out of here for good. So when the gentleman was ready, she left the pub. He introduced himself as, Mr. Humphries. He did not have a Welsh accent but an English, Yorkshire accent she thought, she had once met a doctor at the Merthyr General with the same sort of accent and she liked it, so it had stuck in her mind. During the journey Mr. Humphries was polite, though did not question her motives as to why she should be going all the way to Merthyr Tydfil.

Inside, she was dying, thinking about what her own husband had done to her the night before and she was aching and sore, she really needed to bathe badly but her need to get back home was stronger than her need to stay and cleanse herself first. But who could she confide in about such a traumatic incident? She did not wish to worry her mother, she had enough on her plate. But who would believe her anyhow? She was her husband's property and all was legal in the eyes of the law. A man could not be found guilty of raping his own wife in a court of law.

The only person she would feel comfortable regaling all of this to was her Aunt Lily. She needed to get it off her chest. As soon as she returned she made straight to the home of her aunt and uncle. Luckily her uncle was out visiting his parishioners, so they were quite alone.

"Rebecca, what on earth has happened?" Lily asked, blinking several times.

"Is it that obvious, auntie?"

"I'm afraid it is. You look so pale and worn out, something has gone wrong?"

"Yes, I'm afraid it has." She seated herself, then lowered her head and wept bitterly as she recounted her ordeal in the barn.

"My poor child..." Lily said, when she'd allowed her niece to tell the whole sorry tale. She sat beside Rebecca and hugged her warmly. "I don't know what to say to you. Rhys is obviously not in his right mind, which is something I understand after what happened to Evan, but he would never have laid a finger on me. In fact, for him the reverse was true, he hardly came near me, which was very hurtful indeed. But this, for you, is different. Your welfare is at stake and for that reason, I think you have done the absolute right thing by coming home to those who love you, but you mustn't return, ever. You don't really love him anyhow—your heart is with Mansell and his with you." Her aunt's tone softened and then she rose.

"Aunt Lily..." Rebecca chewed on her bottom lip. "Might I stay the night with you? I don't wish to return to my family home yet, in case my mother realises something has gone dreadfully wrong. I couldn't bear to upset her."

"I quite understand. Now allow me to put on some milk on the stove to boil and we can put the world to rights..."

***

After Rebecca had warmed herself with the hot sweetened milk, and eaten some of Aunt Lily's fruit cake, which comforted her, they chatted some more. The woman had offered to cook a meal for her, but it was all Rebecca could manage for now. The shock had left her with a lump in a throat. Aunt Lily boiled some pans of hot water so that Rebecca could bathe in the tin bath in front of the fire. Rebecca slept fitfully that night in the spare bedroom, realising that Mansell was only down the road and she'd left someone far behind her. It would be foolhardy for her to go to him right now, and even more foolish to visit her mother for her to see the pain she was in right now.

Finally she drifted off to sleep only to be awoken by the sun shining in through the bedroom window. There were sounds downstairs of someone moving around, so she threw her old shawl around the nightdress her aunt had loaned her and softly padded barefoot down the stairs.

When she got to the bottom step, she was surprised to see Evan sitting at the kitchen table with his fountain pen in hand.

He looked up. "Ah Rebecca, it's good to see you. Lily told me you were staying overnight. I'm afraid I didn't get back until late as one of the members of my congregation was very sick and prayers have gone out for her. Unfortunately, I don't think she'll last the day." He stood and kissed her softly on the cheek.

"Where's Aunt Lily gone?" she asked.

"She's just gone to the shop to purchase some eggs for our breakfast, she won't be long. Come and sit by the fireside until she returns."

Rebecca nodded and sat in the armchair closest to the kitchen fireplace. "Thank you," she said, gingerly trying to get herself

194

comfortable as the surface scratches from the horsewhip Rhys had used on her, stung to high heaven. Her aunt had given her some soothing balm to use after her bath which helped a little, but if she sat awkwardly, the pain made her grit her teeth and she was embarrassed about her uncle finding out what had occurred.

"So what are your plans, how long will you be staying in Merthyr for?" He looked up from his sermon.

Not quite knowing how to answer, she was about to change the subject, when Aunt Lily breezed in through the back door with a laden basket of groceries.

Rebecca eased herself out of her chair and took the basket from her aunt's hand and laid it on the table.

Removing her shawl, Lily said, "The kettle has already boiled. I'll make us all a cup of tea and put some eggs on to boil. Rebecca, if you can slice and toast the bread over the fire for me, that would be a big help. The toasting fork is hanging up beside the fire.

Rebecca eagerly did as told and was pleased she hadn't had to answer her uncle's awkward question. There would be time enough for people to know she wouldn't be returning to Llanbadarn Fawr, but this wasn't the time nor the place as her mother needed to know first.

After breakfast, Rebecca got washed and dressed and made her way back home, giving her aunt a big kiss. Uncle Evan had already left the village for Troedyrhiw to see to a member of his congregation who was recently bereaved.

"I won't forget your kindness to me, Auntie," she said, as she stood on the doorstep to leave. "I don't know what I'd have done if I'd not had you to come to talk to."

"Are you all right now, Rebecca?" Her aunt's eyes were full of concern.

"I am, yes. And thank you for last night."

"I think you've done the right thing in leaving, Rebecca."

"But what will people say? When two people get married it's supposed to be for life, isn't it?"

Aunt Lily's eyes clouded with emotion as she wiped away a tear with the back of her hand, and sniffing loudly said, "It is supposed to be. Though I'm sure HE understands," she said, referring to the

Almighty. "Like I said, it almost happened to me and your uncle but thankfully, we were reunited once more."

"I wonder what your life would have been like if you had married Cooper Haines."

Aunt Lily smiled through her tears. "Let me tell you...Mr. Haines later came to this town and met a lovely lady called, Lucy Howells. They became very friendly and a year later, Lucy and her two children emigrated to Utah, so she could marry him. She also took up the Mormon faith. What I'm trying to say to you is, although I broke Mr. Haines heart at the time, it was all for a purpose. It was Evan I really loved after all. Lucy needed a good husband and her children, needed a father. Their real father had absconded and Lucy fell into a life of destitution. His body was later discovered in the Glamorganshire canal, where he had drowned under the perils of alcohol. Although a sad story, it enabled Lucy to freely marry Mr. Haines."

"And did you ever hear from Lucy or Mr. Haines again?"

"Oh yes. We keep in correspondence by letter. Lucy and Cooper went on to have three more children of their own. We are in regular contact as Mr. Haines is very friendly with your Uncle Delwyn."

Rebecca paused for a moment, "And my father, what of him?"

Aunt Lily's eyes creased at the edges. "I'm sorry Rebecca, but Delwyn said he left Great Salt Lake months ago, and no one has heard from him since." She bowed her head in a reverent fashion.

"I suppose he could be dead by now?"

"Possibly, but I won't think that way, and neither should you, Rebecca."

Rebecca's eyes misted with tears, then she swallowed a lump in her throat. "Although things turned out badly between my mother and father and he abandoned us all, I wouldn't like to think of him dying sad and lonely."

"And neither should you, *cariad*, as that just might not be the case."

"Goodbye, Aunt Lily."

"You take care, Rebecca." Her aunt hugged her closely to her bosom, then letting out a long sigh, Rebecca turned to make her way back home to The Walk.

***

Over the following months, Rebecca became used to being back at the family home and her mother had agreed wholeheartedly, that she should not return to Cardigan. Rhys had contacted her by letter claiming he couldn't understand why she'd left him, but she did not reply. Instead she penned a letter to Gwyn, who had been so good to her, explaining she had left for personal reasons and would always be grateful for the home he had provided her with and would be eternally indebted to him and his late wife, Mable, for making her feel so at home at the farm.

She did not receive a reply immediately and when she did it was from Sarah, explaining that Mr. Evans was not in the best of health and she had taken the liberty of opening the letter upon Rhys's instructions and read it to him.

Rebecca decided to reapply for her old position at the Merthyr General Hospital and was pleased to be summoned for a meeting with Matron Steed, who said she would be pleased to have her at the hospital once more, but she would need to be interviewed in front of the Hospital Board. She didn't mind that at all, after all, she couldn't just expect to walk back into her old position and carry on where she'd left off.

On the day of the interview, several members of the Board were seated at a long table, with Doctor Daniel Evans one end of the table and Matron Steed, the other. There was little indication whether she was welcome or not as Matron only politely acknowledged her, and Daniel Evans appeared to look through her.

Mr. Pritchard, who was head of the Board, looked at her over gold half-rimmed spectacles, "Ah, Nurse Jenkin, sorry I see here you are now married and your name is now Rebecca Watkins?" He gazed intently at her, his black moustache almost covering his top lip, what he made up for in facial hair, he lost to his crown, which was imperceptibly bare.

She hesitated for a moment, before replying. "Yes, it is my married name."

Daniel gazed at her making her face flush red.

"So how do you mean to go about your duties if you have a husband who needs looking after?" Mr. Pritchard persisted.

She cleared her throat. "M...my husband and I are no longer living as man and wife. I was living in Cardigan but I've since moved back to Merthyr Tydfil."

Mr. Pritchard steepled his fingers on the table. "And would you like to elaborate on that?"

Rebecca felt a surge of anger at his impudence. "No, I would not, as it is quite a private matter!"

Mr. Pritchard turned to confer to the woman beside him, who looked out of place as she wore a fox fur draped around her neck and a small hat with a veil, which covered one eye. Rebecca watched her whisper behind the palm of her hand to another man on her left. Daniel Evans did not give anything away with his expression, nor did Matron for that matter.

Mr. Pritchard nodded, and turning back to Rebecca said, "Well that's your prerogative, madam, but is the separation from your husband going to interfere with your work at this hospital? Will you be running back to Cardigan to be with him in the future?"

Rebecca shook her head. "Most definitely not, the marriage is well and truly over!"

For the first time she noticed the light in Daniel's eyes switch on, although his demeanour remained stoic. She glanced at the wall clock behind the panel of interviewers; it was five minutes past three. She had only been in the room for a few minutes.

The woman in the hat, looked directly at her and asked, "So, Rebecca, what do you think you could bring to this hospital as a nurse?"

She cleared her throat before answering. "Well, I once worked here for some time so know it well, having worked with Doctor Daniel Evans and Matron Steed. Also the board were previously impressed with me and that's how I ended up working on the Isolation Ward before leaving for Llanbadarn Fawr..."

Before she had a chance to finish, Daniel butted in, "But why did you leave such a good position as a ward sister in the first place? You weren't married then and you were recommended by the Board in the first place for promotion as a sister on the Isolation Ward. Don't you think that was a little ungrateful of you?"

She felt like shouting, "I left because, you buffoon, you betrayed my trust and when I had the chance to go there to look after Doctor Owen's wife I took it." But instead she heard herself reply, "I was grateful to the Board, but an opportunity arose to look after Doctor Mansell Owen's wife. I'm not sure if the panel are aware, but Hannah Owen had a mental illness and behaved often in a childlike and hysterical manner. She is since deceased."

The panel all nodded.

Rebecca continued. "Whilst I was staying at the farm I had a proposal of marriage from a gentleman who worked there."

"That sounds like a case of 'Marry in haste, repent at leisure'?" Mr. Pritchard said in a condescending manner.

She glanced at Daniel, who she could almost imagine was scoffing at her plight inside, but his expression spurred her on to explain herself further. "No, it wasn't that at all. It was months before I received the proposal, and even then I didn't marry him for another few months. It was not an overnight decision believe me."

Daniel shifted around on his seat and loosened his neck tie. "So what happened then?"

She bit her lip wondering how much she should say, but something needed to be said, that much was evident. "We lived as man and wife for a period of time but my husband had a nasty fall from the loft in one of the barns, hitting his head. His character changed somewhat after that, he became harder to live with."

"Are you indicating that he was abusive, madam?" Mr. Pritchard asked.

"I'm afraid I am, but out of respect to him, will speak no more of the matter."

Mr. Pritchard and Daniel Evans averted their eyes, as if they were both uncomfortable with such subject matter in any case. The silence was finally broken as the woman in the hat said, "We have some more nurses to interview. Thank you for your time, Mrs Watkins. We'll be in touch shortly. You shall hear one way or the other by post."

Rebecca stood and thanked them, then left the room, there were three other nurses in the narrow corridor seated on chairs as she passed by. One was already in uniform as if she had just finished her shift, the other two were very well dressed, making Rebecca feel quite dowdy in her dress and jacket. Maybe she wouldn't have much of a chance against the likes of those as she'd been out of the profession for more than a year, but she simply had to try.

As she was about to leave the hospital and had approached the exit, she felt a hand on her shoulder, turning, she saw Daniel Evans smiling at her. "Rebecca, why didn't you tell me it was all over with your husband?"

"Probably for the very same reason you didn't tell me it was all on with Jane." She watched as his face fell and the light diminished from his eyes.

"I am sorry about that, truly. I made a mistake. That friend of yours led me on, she was very free with her favours, what was I supposed to do?"

"Believe me, she's no friend of mine! You told me when we last encountered one another that she's gone to another hospital?"

"Yes, she left a few months ago. Got married to a chap and settled down. I think she might have left that hospital to get married. Most men don't like their wives working. That's why it never worked out with me and you. You thought too much of your job and would have had little time for a husband and family."

Rebecca sniffed. Daniel had made it sound as if he'd dumped her as he considered she'd never give up her job as a nurse to see to his needs, not like Jane had for her husband. Maybe she was more career-minded than that harlot. Cuttingly she said, "So Jane left for pastures anew when she got a better offer, just like you did to me?"

He fiddled with the collar of his shirt as if it were too tight for his neck. It seemed to indicate how he had difficulty facing up to the subject matter. "Yes, you are correct. She left me in the end but it wasn't my fault."

"No, it never is." She was enjoying watching him grow uncomfortable in her presence.

His face reddened. "So, I was wondering...would there be any chance of you and I stepping out with one another once again?"

"I'm sorry, Daniel, you had your opportunity with me over a year ago. You treated me badly. I think it best we don't resume matters between us, and if I am awarded the position at the hospital, then we have to keep things on a highly professional level, don't you agree?"

He stood there with his mouth agape as she descended the steps outside the hospital and walked towards the main entrance to go home. Now, she might have well and truly have scuppered her chances of getting that job, but the feeling she now had gave her a sense of satisfaction, which was priceless. There was no way Daniel

Evans was going to want her working with him whilst there were three other attractive nurses vying for the same position.

Although Rebecca realised that any chance she had of obtaining that job had now severely diminished, she felt she had evened the score between them. Smiling to herself, she made her way back home.

When she arrived home, her mother was waiting for her with a newspaper in her hands. Even before asking how the interview had gone, she blurted out, "'Tis on the front page, Rebecca! Tobias Cookson has been captured by the police and is to be put on trial for the rapes of several women in the town!"

Rebecca stood there, trying to take it in. She took the newspaper from her mother's outstretched hands and studied it. "Thankfully, it does not mention any victims' names," she said to her mother.

"I wonder how the Doctor feels about all of this?"

"I've no doubt, he will be glad the man is to be brought to justice and in a way he was a murderer too, as I feel that pregnancy led to poor Hannah's death." Rebecca's eyes filled up with tears.

Her mother nodded. "Yes, that was an awful business, maybe you should pay him another visit?"

Rebecca shook her head. "No, I can't do that, not right now."

"You've got feelings for the man, I've no doubt of that, Becca. Maybe it's best you don't then as you are still a married woman."

"I wish I could divorce my husband, I made a big mistake."

Her mother draped her arm around her daughter's shoulder and hugged her closely. "No, not at the time you didn't. You thought all would be well, it was that fall that did it, turned him into a beast."

"Yes, and the worst part about it is, he doesn't even realise it."

***

Deciding that she wouldn't get the position of sister at the General Hospital now that she had given Daniel Evans a piece of her mind, Rebecca carried on as usual helping her mother with the chores and looking after her young brothers. A few days later, a letter arrived for her written in elegant copperplate handwriting.

"Well go on," her mother urged. "Open it for goodness sake, Becca."

Trembling, she slit open the envelope to read:

Dear Mrs Watkins,

The board is delighted to offer you the position of Ward Sister at the Merthyr General Hospital...

"Mam!" she shrieked. "I've got the job! I can't believe it!"

"I never doubted you'd get it." Her mother smiled. "When do you begin work there?"

"Next Monday! That only gives me a few days. I'm to be measured for a new uniform. I handed my others in when I left for Cardigan."

"Well done! I'm so proud of you!" Her mother stared at her, then frowned. "What's wrong, Bec? I know you and there's something up, isn't there?"

She let out a long breath. "I'm thinking of filing for a divorce!" she announced, saying it before even realising what she'd said.

Her mother grimaced. "Don't be so silly. We don't know people who get divorced. Well not people around these parts. Any woman who does so tends to get talked about. It's just not seemly. Divorce is for the well-to-do, more common place with the nobility and such like, who are protecting their family wealth, not working class folk like us."

Rebecca's heart slumped. "Then what am I to do? Do I never marry for the rest of my life? Live in sin and risk getting gossiped about? Or go back to a man who treats me so badly? What choice do I have in all of this?"

"You do have a choice..." Rebecca turned to see her brother stood at the entrance of the parlour. "James, how long have you been standing there for?"

"Long enough to get the gist of it. Divorce is possible, Rebecca, though might be costly for you. Thankfully, these days the husband is no longer entitled to his wife's earnings. It wasn't so long ago that once you were wed and wished to divorce, if you had children, they would have been awarded to your husband, but that no longer applies. Wealthy titled women, have divorced and protected their rights, but I fear this would be costly for you. I think you should book an appointment to see Mr. Goldstein and seek his advice."

"Thank you, James." She could have kissed her brother as at least he could see some sense in her proposal.

"But...what sort of issues can women get divorces for these days, James?" she asked, eager to discover more.

202

"I need to check it out, but I think it's mainly for cruelty, bigamy, incest, and so forth."

"I think that might be a good idea under the circumstances, James," Rebecca agreed, feeling uplifted.

Her mother harrumphed and set about laying the table for tea. Divorce was an ugly word to Kathleen Jenkin, and because she felt so strongly about it, Rebecca felt it was preventing her mother from starting over again in life. That evening they ate a meal of roast ham, potatoes and peas from Bill's allotment and her mother, she noticed, had given him the largest portion. How she wished life could be better for her Mam. She so deserved to have someone decent as her marriage partner.

Even the boys were well behaved and Bill offered to read them a bedtime story, whilst Rebecca and her mother washed the dishes and James got ready to see his girlfriend, Amelia. He wasn't allowed to see her alone, Mr. Goldstein would never allow it. So they spent their time chaperoned, either by one of Amelia's brothers or elder sisters, who occasionally broke the rule and allowed them a few stolen moments together.

Rebecca noticed how her brother had matured and how manly he had become. He'd got taller and his shoulders had filled out. In some ways he reminded her of their father, headstrong and proud with a strong physique, though unlike their father, James had no intention of joining the constabulary.

And so a date was arranged for Rebecca to have an appointment to see Mr. Goldstein at his chambers, with a view to discussing a possible divorce from her husband.

**

Rebecca began work at the hospital the following Monday. Her stomach lurched as she walked onto the ward and knocked on Matron's office.

Matron Steed shouted, "Enter!" When she saw it was Rebecca, she smiled then asked her to sit down for a moment. Rebecca hadn't even had time to remove her cape, so sat awkwardly perched on the chair, hoping Matron would not keep her for too long.

"So, how are you feeling about coming back here to work?" Matron enquired.

Rebecca let out a breath, "To be truthful, I feel quite nervous..."

"That's perfectly understandable. You have been out of the profession for some time but you shall soon get back into the swing of things. Remember you are a good nurse. An excellent one in fact. Now I asked you to report for duty a little later than the rest of the shift as I want to hand the patient report over to you and will take you on a ward round with Doctor Evans, so you can familiarise yourself with the patients and the premises once again."

She was quite surprised at Matron's thoughtfulness and touched by it. "Thank you."

"First though, we shall take some refreshment together. Now if you can remove your cape and hang it behind my door and then make us both a cup of tea, I'll run through some items with you that you might be interested in. I'd also like to introduce you to some new members of staff."

Rebecca did as instructed. Soon she returned with a pot of tea and two cups and saucers with a bowl of sugar and small jug of milk, which she placed on Matron's desk. For some reason, this time around the woman didn't seem as formidable as she had more than a year ago, treating Rebecca more as one of her contemporaries.

After they'd finished their tea and spoken amicably, Matron drew a breath and spoke. "The real reason why I pushed for you to have the position here as senior ward sister is because in a year or so, I shall be retiring.... When I do, I'd like to hand over the reins to someone I trust..."

Rebecca swallowed. "You mean you'd eventually like me to become Matron here? At this hospital?"

"That's exactly so, Rebecca. So don't let me down. I trust you, but you still have a lot to learn and I will teach you. To be a Matron you need to be highly disciplined and you can't afford to allow your staff to get away with anything. I rule with a rod of iron as you well know."

Rebecca stifled a giggle, hiding it behind the palm of her hand.

***

After attending a word round with a less than enthusiastic Daniel Evans and Matron, she was introduced to the staff. Two of the nurses looked young enough to still be at school, *"I must be getting old..."* Rebecca thought to herself. They were helpful though and affable enough. The shift went by quite quickly. They had to deal with a woman who had been run over by a horse and carriage in Victoria

Street, thankfully, she wasn't too worse for wear, having a few bumps and bruises as the horse had only been trotting at the time, but Doctor Evans thought it best to keep her in for observation in case she had a head injury. He spoke only briefly and only when necessary to Rebecca, but then that was hardly anything new as his manner had often been curt before she'd got to know him.

Later, there was a crush injury brought in from the ironworks, but thankfully no deaths that day. She went home, tired, exhausted but happy after her first day back on the ward. Tomorrow afternoon, following her shift, would be her appointment with Mr. Goldstein with a view to seeking a divorce from her husband.

***

The next day, she brought her clothes to change into after her shift, before freshening up and making her way to the chambers of 'Johnson and Goldstein' on the High Street. Their offices, were above a draper's shop in the town, which were well painted and decorated both inside and out.

There were plush velvet chairs with ornate edgings for potential clients to use whilst they waited for an appointment to be seen by Messrs Johnson and Goldstein, or on the odd occasion if the appointment were on a minor scale, they spoke with her brother, James Jenkin, who by now knew the drill of whether he could give some advice to them or pass them on to his superiors sometime in the future to undertake legal proceedings.

On the windowsill in front of a large bay window, stood a marble bust of what appeared to be some sort of Greek god, and behind a small desk fitted into the corner of the room, sat a middle-aged woman who appeared busy. She was well-dressed in a high neck cream blouse which was fastened with a jewelled brooch, her long black taffeta skirt making a bustling noise when on the odd occasion she moved around the room. Her salt and peppered hair neatly scraped into a bun and whose manner appeared to be proficiency itself.

Rebecca hesitated at the desk before speaking. The woman was writing something into a ledger using a very fancy gold fountain pen which looked very much like the one Mr. Goldstein had gifted Rebecca's brother.

She cleared her throat to secure the woman's attention. The woman glanced up from her task-in-hand and peered above her gold-rimmed spectacles. "Yes, may I help you?"

"I'm here to see Mr. Goldstein. My name is Mrs Rebecca Watkins."

The woman sniffed. "Can I ask you to what it's regarding?"

Rebecca glanced around the room and noticed a man in a long woollen grey coat, reading a newspaper, absorbed in the daily dealings of Merthyr Tydfil, to his right was a young woman with an infant soothing him on her lap and to her right, a man in a filthy jacket, shirt, muffler and torn trousers, who she guessed was either a collier or from the ironworks.

She lowered her voice to barely a whisper. "I'm here to see him about a possible divorce..."

The woman coughed and raised an eyebrow, but didn't comment on the matter. It was almost as if she could hardly believe her ears. "I'll just knock and check if he's ready to see you," she replied curtly.

There was no sign of James, and Rebecca wondered where he might be. The woman rose from her chair and softly knocked the office door belonging to Mr. Goldstein; it was half-frosted glass, with an oak frame, a gold name plate adhered to it in the middle of the door.

"Enter!" boomed a voice, and timidly, the woman walked inside as Rebecca strained to hear the hushed voices inside. She wished she could hear the conversation but then guessed if she was able to, then that would mean when she discussed her business inside the room that would mean everyone else outside it would hear, so she was most glad that she couldn't hear anything of note.

The woman returned a couple of moments later. "Mr. Goldstein will see you now, Mrs Watkins," she advised.

The woman held herself well, straight-backed and slow-paced, which gave her a graceful countenance. Rebecca inwardly smiled to herself as she bypassed the prim assistant to walk into the solicitor's office.

"Hello Mrs Watkins, won't you take a seat..." Mr. Goldstein greeted her as he closed the door behind her. He looked about the same age as her father, his dark hair silvering at the edges by the side of his ears. He was a smart man, his hair was slicked back and he had a very trim moustache. He wore a grey silk cravat and his suit appeared well tailored. When he spoke, his piercing sapphire eyes shone and lines around them crinkled at the corners, which made it appear as if he smiled a lot. This reassured Rebecca somewhat.

She did as instructed and took a seat, taking in her surroundings. His office looked very plush. He had a huge shiny walnut desk which he seated himself behind.

"Thank you," she replied.

"Now your brother, James, informs me you are thinking of petitioning your husband for a divorce?"

"Yes, that is correct."

"How long have you been married?

"Almost sixteen months."

Mr. Goldstein's eyebrows shot up in surprise. "Oh, I assumed you'd been married longer than that?"

"No, we've been married for sixteen months, but for the past couple of months I've been living back in Merthyr Tydfil. My husband lives in Llanbadarn Fawr."

Mr. Goldstein let out a long breath. "Please could I ask you about the circumstances of your separation from one another?"

Rebecca swallowed as her eyes filled with tears. Taking a breath of composure, she said, "When I married Rhys, he was a good, kind man, but following a fall from the loft in the barn, he suffered a head injury. It seemed to change his personality somewhat, he became snappy and aggressive and the worse thing was what he did to me just before I left..."

"Go on, please take your time..." Mr. Goldstein said softly.

"He...he raped me!" The words were out making them sound more real somehow. She trembled as the horrible event came back to her in vivid detail.

"That's terrible, m'dear, though under the present law, a man cannot rape his own wife, I'm afraid, so it would be difficult for us to bring divorce proceedings on those grounds, also there's a question of evidence. How could you prove this? Were there any witnesses? Did you tell anyone immediately afterwards?"

She shook her head. "No. I had no one to tell. I only told my aunt when I arrived back in Merthyr Tydfil the following day. He also beat me with a horse whip!"

Mr. Goldstein's eyes reflected the compassion within. Softly he said, "You do have my sympathies, may I call you Rebecca? Your brother often mentions you."

She smiled. "Yes, of course you may."

"I've seen a few women walk through these doors who claim to have been raped by their husbands, but it won't hold up in a court of law, I'm afraid. Current law works on the side of the husband. It's only recently that a woman could be allowed the custody of her own children when she tried for separation or divorce. Also, only in recent years can a woman retain her own earnings if she divorces her husband. You have Caroline Norton to thank for that."

"Who is this lady you speak of?" Rebecca had never heard the name before.

"She's deceased now, but she campaigned over child custody and the conditions of divorce for women which helped bring about a change of the law, she fought for the rights of women. She was from a wealthy family and her own husband used to beat her. Caroline's campaign efforts were influential in the passing of the Marriage and Divorce Act of 1857. She even wrote to Queen Victoria herself!"

"What an amazing person!"

"Yes, she was. However, although we in the legal profession realise it goes on, there is basically no rape in marriage as the law stands. Now, although a divorce would be difficult to procure, there might be grounds for me to petition for a legal separation for you, but that wouldn't leave you free to remarry I'm afraid. The only items I could petition a divorce for you are: if your husband had committed bigamy, bestiality, incest or maybe if he hadn't consummated the marriage with you. I'm sorry it's not good news. If you had some evidence it could be a different matter."

In her heart it was what she had been expecting to hear. "I don't think there would be a lot of point in petitioning for a separation, though it might protect any assets I have I suppose."

"Well, I would strongly advise you to have a legal separation as who knows what might happen otherwise if you were left money in a will or property, it would be considered the property of both of you and your husband could make a claim, if he desired doing so."

"Oh, I can't see that happening, I don't own anything, nor does anyone in the family apart from my Aunt Lily and Uncle Evan in Abercanaid I suppose, but even their house belongs to the chapel, and in any case they have two children of their own who would be first in line as entitlement."

"You just never know though, m'dear. Have a think about it and we can arrange another meeting if you wish to proceed."

"I'll let you know after I have given it some thought, Mr. Goldstein. Thank you for your time." She rose to her feet and opened her drawstring purse. "Now how much do I owe you for your time?"

Mr. Goldstein stood and raised a vertical palm. Then he accompanied her to the door. "On this occasion, Rebecca, there will be no charge, but please think carefully and take my advice about that separation order. It will free you up financially."

But not free me up to remarry, she thought wistfully to herself. She thanked him once more for his kindness and left the building, stopping off at a market stall to purchase a leg of lamb and some crusty bread for the evening meal. They were well stocked up with vegetables from Bill's allotment. Briefly, she wondered what Mansell Owen was doing right now.

Chapter Fourteen

Rebecca thought about nothing else but the separation from her husband during the following weeks but instead of just going ahead with it decided to return to Llanbadarn Fawr to speak with him about the matter, she felt she owed him that much at least and it would enable her to see Gwyn one last time. Her mother wasn't happy at all about the idea.

"I have to go there, Mam," she explained. "It feels as though there is unfinished business for me, don't you see?"

"Believe me, I do understand, Bec, but what if you put yourself in danger? Take your brother with you!"

Rebecca had not wanted to drag James into her problems, but he said he was more than happy to accompany her. Bill said he'd borrow the coach from Doctor Owen. Rebecca hadn't wanted to procure a favour from Mansell either, but Bill had said he'd insisted on loaning the coach for a couple of days.

And so, it was just before Christmas that year, when the party set out to Llanbadarn Fawr. Rebecca had sent a letter to Rhys explaining she would be calling on him, there had been no reply but she decided to go anyhow. Snow hadn't arrived as yet and the weather that year was quite mild. As the coach clattered along the country lanes, she viewed all that was so familiar to her: the neighbouring farms, a patchwork of various shades of green, the glistening sea on the horizon, and the spire of St. Padarn's Church in the distance. She let out a sigh, in an ideal world this would have been a wonderful place to settle down and begin a married life with someone who treated her well.

As the coach made its way up the dirt track toward Crugmor Farm, the hairs on the back of her neck bristled, something was wrong she could sense it, but felt frozen to the leather squabs of the carriage unable to utter a word. From outside the coach window she could see the main barn had been razed to the ground. There'd been a fire that much was evident. All was black and charred.

"Rebecca, what's wrong?" James asked, his eyes wide and alert. "Speak to me please!"

She brought herself back to the here and now, almost as though someone had doused her with an ice-cold bucket of water.

"It's the b...barn," she said. "Look! It's been burned down. There was a small fire whilst I was living here, but now it's completely gone all together."

James moved past her to look outside his sister's side of the window as he'd been gazing out the other side. "Oh my goodness, I hope there's nothing wrong."

By the time the coach had pulled up outside the farmhouse, James was ready to leap out the carriage door and help Rebecca down. Her heart began to thud heavily.

There was no sign of life anywhere. No sheep, no dogs, no birds singing in the trees, not a sound.

James knocked the farmhouse door but received no reply from inside, so gingerly he pushed it open. The pine kitchen table was overturned along with the tables and chairs, he went from room to room calling out, but there was no one on the property. Bill helped too.

Then Rebecca shouted, "The cottage, we must check the cottage!"

James ran down the path towards the little cottage where Rhys and Rebecca had once set up home, with his sister following at his heels, holding up the hem of her dress so not to trip over. Bill went to search the other barns.

"Stay outside while I search the cottage!" James commanded his sister.

"No, I'm coming with you," she said forcefully. She followed behind him but he didn't resist.

The cottage looked just as she'd left it, save for a little mess here and there. James bolted up to the bedroom. "Rhys's clothes have gone from the wardrobe," he said, returning to the foot of the stairs. When he got to the fire grate, he knelt and touched the fireplace. "Stone cold, he hasn't been here in a while."

"But what about Gwyn and Sarah?"

James stood then shrugged. "I could ask at the Black Lion if you like?"

She nodded her head vigorously; she couldn't bear to leave here without knowing what had happened. "I'll ask Mrs Clancy at the tea room, too."

Bill returned from the barns. "Nothing I'm afraid!" he shouted.

"Come on," James said, "we'll set off for the village."

Rebecca's heart pounded so loudly she feared it would jump out of her chest. What if this was all her fault for leaving Rhys in the first place? What if he were dead because of her? And where were Gwyn and Sarah?

James took hold of her hand as if reading her mind for the first time. "Now don't go blaming yourself, Bec. Rhys treated you badly and that's why you left here."

She nodded sniffing back the tears. "Yes, it was the reason, I felt I could stay here no longer." Of course she hadn't told James the real reason why she'd left, that she had been raped by her own husband, she'd only confided that to Aunt Lily, her mother and the solicitor, all of whom had been sympathetic and said it was quite a common thing in marriage that people rarely spoke of. Her mother had muttered, "It's a man's world!" Whilst Mr. Goldstein had insisted the law needed to be changed, but he couldn't see it happening in his lifetime.

She admired her mother though for challenging her own husband and breaking free to do her own thing, to sing in the music halls of Merthyr and finally the London stage. She revered her for that, following her dream and even defying her father, who eventually had come around to the idea of his wife being on the stage and adored by so many. Some women would have not had the fight in them and bowed to their husband's will.

When they reached the village it was decided that James would head off to the Black Lion, Rebecca would call to see Mrs Clancy, Bill would call to see Rhys's widowed mother and they would meet back outside the church in one hour's time.

When Rebecca returned Bill was already waiting atop the carriage, he shook his head. "Rhys's mother was not at home," he said sadly. "Did Mrs Clancy tell you anything?"

She looked up at him. "Yes, she did. I am so upset, Bill. Gwyn died a month ago. His heart gave out. Mrs Clancy said he died of a broken heart. I should never have left."

Bill jumped down from the carriage and stood next to her. "Aye now come on, this isn't like you, Rebecca. I met him a couple of times and he looked very frail to me, also I don't think he ever got over losing his wife." He held her close while she sobbed into his chest, then they broke away as James turned up.

"What's the matter?" His eyes looked large and concerned.

"Your sister had a bit of bad news, Mr. Evans passed away a month ago, it was his heart."

"Oh dear. I did think he looked a bit thin and wiry last time I was here."

"See, Rebecca," Bill said kindly, "your own brother thought the same thing."

She turned to James and dabbed at her eyes with a lace handkerchief. "Did you find anything out at the pub?"

"I did indeed, I don't know how to tell you this, but your so-called husband has married young Sarah!"

"Pardon?" she blinked several times.

"Apparently it's true."

"But how can that be, the vicar at St. Padarn's would know he was married to me."

"It wasn't at St. Padarn's the marriage took place, it was somewhere in Aberystwyth, a chapel I believe."

"But he can't do that..." Bill butted in.

Rebecca was about to say something, when excitedly, James said, "Don't you see this is good news for you, Bec?"

"I don't see how that can be!" She looked at her brother in astonishment.

"Yes, it's good news because if we can prove he has made a bigamous marriage to another woman, you will be granted a divorce!"

Rebecca couldn't take in what she was hearing. "But how could he do that? And young Sarah too."

Bill shook his head. "From what I've seen when I've stayed at the farm, Sarah's family need the money so maybe she saw it as her chance to better her lowly status. Don't be too hard on her, she's only a young girl."

James shrugged. "Old enough to know better perhaps, what we need to do while we're here though is to find out the name of that place where they supposedly wed one another as if that's true, we can ask Mr. Goldstein to write to the minister for confirmation. I'm sure then you would be granted a divorce, Rebecca."

None of this made her feel any happier though, there was a lot of sadness in her heart not just to hear of Mr. Evans's death, but the fact her husband could forget about her so quickly and what they'd once had together. But then again, following his accident in the barn, he was no longer the man she had married. One other thing suddenly occurred to her. "That's all very well, but how did that barn raze completely to the ground?"

James looked her squarely in the eyes. "It was Jake, he knew the villagers were looking for him, the lynching party was led by Rhys, so he sneaked onto the farm and lit the fire. The men reckon the upset of the fire along with the loss of livestock caused Mr. Evans to have his heart attack, bringing on a premature death."

"That's absolutely dreadful. I wonder if that's why the farmhouse was left like that in such a mess. Maybe Jake tried to rob the place. Where's he now?"

"Safely behind bars, I've been informed," James said soberly. "He's also set to go on trial for the death of his father."

She shook her head. "So much has happened since I first arrived at Crugmor farm with Hannah..."

James touched her gently on the shoulder. "Come on, we need to find accommodation for the night, then first thing in the morning we can set out to find the name of that chapel in Aberystwyth where Rhys got married bigamously to Sarah."

Rebecca nodded. Suddenly she felt wearisome.

Bill suggested driving the coach into Aberystwyth to find rooms for the night as there'd be more chance of getting somewhere there. Eventually they found room at an old coaching inn near the sea front. Bill and James roomed together, whilst Rebecca had a small room to herself. The inn keeper and his wife were very accommodating even though they spoke mostly in Welsh and very quickly at that, but they made themselves understood. That night, the innkeeper's wife, who they were to discover was named, Llinos, served them up a supper of sea bass, baked potatoes and a selection of vegetables, followed by her own homemade apple tart.

Bill rubbed his belly afterwards, "My word your mother can cook, Bec, but that lady's meal really hit the spot!"

Rebecca had to agree it was the best fare she had ever tasted.

They complimented Llinos on her cooking and she blushed profusely. "Oh, it's nice of you to say but I think it's because all the food is so fresh living in a sea port."

"No, it's not just that," Bill said heartily, "you're a fine cook!"

For a moment, Rebecca feared Bill was flirting outrageously with the woman, but then he said in a hushed whisper to her, "Lovely couple Llinos and her husband, Berwyn. Sometimes when I see a couple so good together like that...I wish about me and your Mam that things could be different and we could wed one another."

"I know you do," Rebecca said softly. "Mam though, won't go against the teachings of the Catholic Church and you could only marry if my father were dead." As soon as she said it, she regretted it, to think her father might no longer be walking the earth.

After supper, they went for a stroll along the seafront. Rebecca wrapped her shawl tightly around her shoulders, as big breakers made their way toward the shoreline.

"Berwyn told me there's a storm on its way," James said. "Maybe we'd be better off getting out of here as soon as we find the name of that chapel where Rhys wed Sarah."

"I agree," Bill said. "The horses are getting anxious. Animals can always sense these things."

Rebecca could barely believe that at some point Rhys had taken Sarah to get married somewhere in Aberystwyth and she feared for the woman's physical safety. But what could she do about it? If she tried to warn her then she'd have to tell people he'd raped his own wife, but if she said nothing, then the woman would be at risk.

And the other question was, was it really the bump to his head that had turned her husband into a beast or had he always been that way inclined, but putting on an act? She thought back to her own wedding night with him and how he hadn't taken his time and been quite rough with her.

She made up her mind, she had to say something. "I need to speak with Sarah or at least her mother," she said forcefully.

"I don't advise you to do that," James said.

"Let her do it, if it helps," Bill butted in. They found a bench overlooking the sea and sat for a while, feeling the sea breeze on their faces.

"Can't see any fishing vessels going out in this tomorrow." Bill let out a long breath. "The sea is a savage beast that can't be tamed..."

"Very well then, Bec..." James said suddenly. "We'll find Sarah's family home tomorrow and you shall speak to her mother. I don't know what good it will do, but if it will make you feel better it shall be worth it. I don't suppose we'll be in these parts again. Do you know where she lives?"

"Yes, I do. She's from a big family and the house is overcrowded. To be honest, it was Rhys who got her employment at the farm in the first place. I'm wondering now if he had an ulterior motive. He told me she needed the job to help Mrs Evans and there wasn't much room where she lived, so her parents would welcome the fact she'd found employment at the farm. Maybe there was some sort of liaison going on between them whilst we were married..."

They rose and walked in silence back to the inn, where Bill checked on the horses to ensure they were comfortable for the night. There were a few other horses stabled at the back of the premises too, who also seemed a little distressed.

He patted Bess and Bertha and gave them some hay to eat that the innkeeper had told him he might use. The trough was full of water, so satisfied, he left them to it and went to bed.

The following morning the trio arose bright and early to find Llinos had a full cooked breakfast ready for them of sausage, bacon and eggs with fried bread and mugs of steaming tea. Although she hadn't been able to eat much last night due to the shock of everything that had transpired, Rebecca found her appetite returning once more.

They thanked Llinos and Berwyn for their hospitality before leaving and settled the bill, leaving a little extra as a tip for such good service.

Llinos was delighted at their generous gesture and stood at the doorway of the inn to wave them off before they left for Llanbadarn Fawr to find the home of Sarah Griffiths. The wind had picked up dramatically since last night as huge waves crashed up from the beach headed towards Marine Terrace.

"I wouldn't fancy living here on the seafront tonight," James said to Rebecca as the coach began to jerk away.

"It looks as if it could flood to me," Rebecca agreed.

***

When they approached the small street Sarah's family resided at, Rebecca insisted on knocking the door alone, the other two men remained with the coach.

216

The windows and door were grimy as if unwashed for years. Rebecca could hear a lot of noise from the inside.

Finally, a girl appeared at the door holding a young child in her arms, her clothing so grubby and torn that the clothes were almost falling off her slight frame. The young child's face and hands ingrained with dirt.

"What do you want? We haven't got no rent money," she said.

"I've come to see your mother, or is your sister Sarah in?"

The girl grimaced. "Haven't seen hide nor hair of her in a long time!"

She stood with her back pressed against the wall to allow Rebecca entry to the house. The small passageway was dark and gloomy, and smelled strongly of must and meat. Inside the living room where a small fire burned brightly, sat a woman who was probably no more than middle-aged, but the lines of time had ravaged her face. She looked up from her darning, when she saw Rebecca's approach.

"Come in and sit down," she said.

Rebecca did as told, removing a child's homemade stuffed teddy bear with one eye, from the armchair. The chair was hard as she felt the springs digging into her flesh. The family probably didn't have the money to buy a new one, so she wriggled around, until she got comfortable.

"I'm Rebecca Watkins who used to live at Crugmor Farm where Sarah worked," she explained.

The woman's face fell. "So? And what is your business at my home?"

"I wondered if I may speak with your daughter, Sarah?"

The woman shook her head. "She isn't here."

"Do you know where she is?"

The woman shrugged, but Rebecca sensed she was being evasive. "It's just come to my attention she has recently married my husband, Rhys Watkins!"

The woman's eyes narrowed to slits. "He's not your husband, never was!" The woman snapped, causing Rebecca to sit up straight in her chair. "You pair were living tally, over the brush. In any case, our Sarah said you couldn't give him the child he wanted so badly. Now she's young and healthy, she'll be the one to give him what he needs, a son and heir!"

Rebecca recoiled at the woman's harsh words. "That maybe so, Mrs Griffiths but we were not living tally, it was all official. No, we were married properly. I have the certificate to prove it and you can ask the vicar at St. Padarn's Church if you don't believe me!"

The woman threw her darning onto the small wooden table beside her and stood. "If I find out you're lying to me, lady!" she threatened as she loomed over Rebecca, causing her to stand herself and meet the woman eye-to-eye.

"No, I'm not lying. You can ask my brother and neighbour who are waiting in the coach outside. In any case, Sarah would have known this as she attended our wedding!"

Hearing those words the woman frowned. "What will this mean then? Sarah was led to believe by that husband of yours he was free to marry her?"

"It could be that he told her he'd divorced me when I left him, I really can't say. I don't think Sarah will be in any trouble though, Ma'am, but Rhys Watkins will be. If I can prove his bigamous marriage, I can free myself and divorce him. Will you help me, please?"

The woman seated herself. *"Galwch yr Heddlu!* Call the police! The man has ruined my daughter's good honour. No man will want her now."

Rebecca sat back down in the armchair, so she was looking eye level at the woman once more. "It's more serious than that I'm afraid, Mrs Griffiths. The reason I left..." Rebecca chewed on her bottom lip, "is because before I went to Merthyr Tydfil, my husband beat and raped me."

Mrs Griffiths shook her head. *"Fy ddaioni.* My goodness. We need to save our daughter from that man and he was so charming to me at the wed—" Realising what she had said, her hand flew to her mouth.

"So you attended their wedding then?"

The woman nodded, open-mouthed. "Yes."

"And where was it held?"

"A chapel in Aberwystwyth called, Salem..."

"And what date did the marriage take place might I ask?"

The woman shook her head sadly. "It was two weeks ago this very day."

"And did anyone know that Rhys was already married?"

She shook her head vehemently. "No, of course not." A child began to cry and she excused herself from the room out into the garden outside. Rebecca took it as her opportunity to escape. She had what she came for, the name of the chapel and the date, also she'd imparted information to the woman that her daughter might not be safe living with Rhys Watkins. Rebecca's job here was done.

She headed back through the dingy passageway and outside to the coach. "Quick as you can, Bill, please!" She shouted.

Bill tipped his hat and James descended the carriage to help her inside.

"What's the rush?" James asked, once both were settled back inside.

"I've got the information I need," Rebecca said breathlessly. "You're correct. It was a bigamous marriage and I know the date and name of the chapel. I took it as an opportunity to leave when Mrs Griffiths went out into the garden to attend to one of her many children. I feared the family might turn on me when they realise I've spoiled their daughter's future dream of being Mrs Watkins."

"Very wise," James said, patting his sister's hand. They sat in silence for a while, then Rebecca fell asleep with her face pressed against the window as the coach rode out of Llanbadarn Fawr and back towards home.

Chapter Fifteen

As soon as Rebecca had rested the night after arriving back in
Merthyr Tydfil, James took her to the chambers with him the
following morning, to see Mr. Goldstein. She hadn't an appointment,
so waited whilst he saw his first client of the day, then she acquired a
ten minute slot to confer with him. On hearing that Rhys Watkins
had committed bigamy, his eyes lit up.

"M'dear, you shall get to go to the ball!" he boomed.

Although the solicitor was jubilant, Rebecca was not. She'd have
given anything to have what she saw as the mild mannered Rhys
back as he was, but she had to admit, even then there had been
something lacking in the marriage and that thing could be summed
up in one word, passion. There was a distinct lack of it on her part.

Mr. Goldstein took details of the date of the wedding and the
venue and then said he would set about writing to the minister of the
chapel to confirm the said marriage took place.

Feeling slightly sad, she left his offices and went straight to work.
She'd used all her time off that week to go to Aberystwyth so now
felt a pang of guilt that it would have been time she could have
helped Mam and the boys.

Later as she entered the ward at Merthyr General, it was as if all
hell had broken loose, so she had no time to think about her own
troubles. Three males had been brought in with burns from the new
Bessemer department of the Lower Works, Dowlais. Things had
proceeded in the usual manner until shortly before 10 o'clock that
morning, when by some unaccountable means the machinery got out
of gear. The workers had to run to get out of the way of the molten
iron that was splashing over the sides of the vessel. Similar accidents
had happened in the past where men burnt to death, although in this
case the injured failed to escape unscathed even though they had
desperately tried to get out of the way. Most of the men, when they
saw the molten metal splashing out of the converter, rushed here and
there, and some of them actually rushed, in their fright, right in the
path of the burning liquid.

The injuries were a severe gash over the eye caused by the fall in
the rush to get out of the way to one man, a young boy who was
injured on the hands and around one of his eyes, and a man burned

around the hands and arms, but fortunately, no injuries were life-threatening.

An Accident Unit had been opened at the hospital, so Rebecca was despatched to help out there, so fortunately didn't have to remain on the ward with Doctor Daniel Evans who might ask her awkward questions about her marriage to Rhys and Llanbadarn Fawr.

The young lad in the accident was crying for his mother, so Rebecca had to calm him down. Fortunately the injury was to the side of his eye and not inside, he could have been blinded for life. The two older men were more stoic and accepting of the situation. Fortunately, the men would only be kept in for a couple of days then allowed home. She thanked her lucky stars that her brother wasn't working in such a dangerous profession. And would do all she could to keep Benjamin and Daniel out of the pits and ironworks. Of course, Daniel had been named after Daniel Evans as he'd delivered both twins. She thought back to that time and how different things had been back then. She'd enjoyed the Doctor's company until he betrayed her trust. But still, he didn't seem to be giving up, as later that day when she bumped into him leaving Matron's office, he asked her out for afternoon tea later that week. She just smiled and said she'd think about it.

***

When she arrived home after her shift, Rebecca sat down with her mother in the living room, the boys were in bed and James was visiting Amelia.

"How did things go at Mr. Goldstein's office?" her mother asked.

"Very well. He's going to write to the minister of Salem Chapel in Aberystwyth to confirm the marriage took place, and if that being so as we know it will be, then the police have to be informed. Oh Mam, I would hate it if Rhys were to be sent to prison because of me!"

"Don't be silly, Bec. The man brought this on himself, he wasn't forced up the aisle for a second time, was he?"

She supposed there was a lot of sense in her mother's words. "No, you are right."

"How about a nice cup of cocoa? You look dead beat."

Rebecca nodded wearily, it had been a hard shift for her. Eventually the young lad had stopped crying for his mother, but when she eventually arrived at the hospital she seemed to be more concerned that now there wouldn't be another wage coming in than the welfare of her own son. That had made Rebecca extremely angry and she'd taken the woman to one side to warn her to go easy on the boy. He was one of seven children and whilst she appreciated that times were hard for the family, the boy could easily have lost his life. After the ticking off, the woman became mild mannered and Rebecca wondered if it was the shock that had made her react that way.

By the time Rebecca had drank her cocoa and gone to bed, she was ready for sleep but when she did drop off, her dreams were full of Rhys chasing her and calling her names intermixed with Daniel Evans telling her he would rescue her. She woke in a cold sweat and opened the bedroom window. Down below all was quiet, the street swathed in darkness, except for the moon. Then she saw it, a figure in the distance, standing watching the house. It reminded her of what happened in Cardigan when she thought she saw a man watching the cottage.

She shivered and was about to call her mother when the figure realising he'd been glimpsed, quickly turned and walked off down the road.

***

The following morning, Rebecca mentioned what she'd seen the night before to her mother, who in turn told Bill next door about the mysterious figure. He offered to keep watch over the next few nights, which relieved Rebecca as she was working a run of night shifts which meant she was away from home.

Nothing happened for a while, but by the third night, Bill had accosted the man and marched him around to Rebecca's home.

Rebecca, who had just finished her night shift at the hospital and was sitting at the kitchen table with her mother, startled as Bill pushed the man into their kitchen.

The man was younger than she thought, maybe in his mid twenties, reasonably well dressed and his eyes were darting back and forth, nervously.

"Here's the blighter that's been watching your house. I've been up all night looking out for him, was about to get to my bed when

222

about twenty minutes ago, just before daylight, caught him peeping over your hedge. He ran off and I gave chase..." he puffed. "Won't tell me what he's up to, I was wondering if he'd taken a shine to you, Rebecca!" Bill said boldly.

Rebecca shook her head. "But I've never seen this fellow before in all my life!"

The man, who appeared out of breath, took a large gasp of air and said, "I am a married man, I'm not like that at all... I've got two young children, mouths to feed. I only did it as *he* paid me. I recently lost my job and I'm finding times hard. So it was a way to get some easy money."

"*Who* paid you?" Rebecca asked.

"A man about your age..." he turned to look at Bill.

Bill narrowed his gaze. "I bet you'll tell any old tale to get off the hook!"

"No, please believe me. A couple of weeks ago, a man came on to me in the Vulcan Inn in town and said he was looking for someone to do some private work for him and he'd pay handsomely."

"Oh, and what might that 'private work be' I might ask?" Kathleen glared at the man as she stood and poked a finger in his chest.

"I...I was told to keep an eye on the comings and goings of this house. He asked me to record specific things..." The man swallowed.

"Specific things?" Rebecca furrowed her brow.

"Yes. He wanted me to record who was coming in and out of this house. Particular descriptions. He seemed most concerned with your whereabouts, Missus!" The man addressed Kathleen.

"Mine? I wonder why? I don't owe anyone any money or anything. Oh I know what it 'tis, my family spying on me. My father has never got over me leaving them behind in Utah after they emigrated from Ireland!"

The man shook his head. "Don't think so, Missus. This man didn't have an Irish accent. He was most interested in what you were getting up to and those two young boys of yours!"

Kathleen's eyes glinted dangerously. Rebecca knew this would be a red rag to a bull to come between a mother and her children, she was fiercely protective. Her mother raised her fist, closing the distance between herself and the man so that her knuckles almost made contact with his chin, as Bill restrained him from behind. The whites of the man's eyes gleamed as he showed his fear for the first time.

"No, you've got it wrong!" The man blurted. "I didn't get the feeling that he wanted to harm any of you, quite the reverse in fact. He seemed to want to protect you and make sure you all came to no harm whatsoever! He's concerned for your welfare..."

Puzzled, Kathleen dropped her fist to her side. "No harm, you say?"

"Aye!" As Bill released his grip, the man turned to him and said, "And you, Sir, he wanted to ensure you weren't cohabiting in this house!"

"That's preposterous!" Bill said. "There's nothing like that going on!"

"I know," the man smiled. "I kept reporting that all was well. I haven't seen anything untoward."

"This man..." said Rebecca, "what did he look like?"

"Oh a good six feet tall, broad shouldered, hair greying at the temples. Skin looks a bit weather worn for a better choice of words..."

"You know who I think it is!" Rebecca exclaimed suddenly. All eyes were now on her. "Dad! It has to be!"

"I can't see that myself," her mother said, shaking her head.

"But who else would want to check on your welfare and the boys too?" She made a point, then turned to the man. "This gentleman, when do you get to see him again?"

"Well, there's never a specific date or time, he just finds me in the pub. I give him the information and he pays me for my time and what I'm able to tell him. I'm keeping out of this from now on. I'll stop drinking in the Vulcan for a while, but you'll no doubt find him there."

"I can't believe it!" Kathleen shook her head.

"Oh, I can," Rebecca said firmly. "We knew he was on his way back from Utah and we knew he wanted you and him to reunite!"

"The lass is right," Bill chipped in, and was about to say something else, when the man spoke.

"Can I go now, like? I need to get home, haven't seen my own kiddies since yesterday afternoon."

"Too busy spying on us, that's why!" Rebecca said bitterly.

224

Her mother touched her arm gently. "Now, Bec, there's no need for that talk. The young man was only trying to provide for his own kids. Would you like to stay for something to eat?" she offered.

He shook his head. "I really must be off and don't worry, it shan't happen again. I can see now how upsetting this must be for you all. He seemed such a nice man that's why I agreed to do it."

"Yes, he is..." Kathleen said sadly. "I mean was..."

The man nodded, then turned and walked away, leaving Bill looking at Kathleen as if to say, "What now?"

Kathleen sat herself back down at the table, it was as if a tornado had hit them all.

Wordlessly, the three sat in silence at the table until, Rebecca rose and said, "Well I'm pouring us all a glass of brandy, there's some left over from Christmas, think we've had a bit of a shock, don't you?"

Bill nodded in agreement.

***

After Rebecca had slept ready for her next night shift, she got dressed and wrapping a shawl around her shoulders, donned her bonnet, then made her way to the Vulcan Inn in the town. The premises was bustling that evening as she edged her way towards the bar, her eyes darting back and forth this way and that in search of her father, but there was no sign. She asked a couple of men at the bar if they'd seen a 'Dafydd Jenkin' lately, but they shook their heads. She even went as far as giving the men a description of him and was just about to depart, when one of them took her by the elbow and guided her towards a quiet alcove.

"I think I know the man you mean. He's got a drink problem, love—you don't want to go bothering with the likes of him!"

It became apparent that maybe her father had returned to the drink since landing back in his hometown. She wondered if he'd been in touch with his sister and brother-in-law in Abercanaid.

Rebecca nodded and thanked the man but did not tell him he was her father. Feeling deflated, she left the inn and headed back up the town in the direction of the General Hospital.

Daniel Evans was waiting for her when she arrived, even before she'd had time to remove her cape.

"Thought any more about my proposal, Nurse Jenkin?" he asked, as he followed her in the direction of Matron's office.

"What proposal?" she asked, not in the mood for speaking with him right now.

"About me taking you out some time?"

"Oh that. I haven't had time to think about it to be honest with you..."

He exhaled loudly and she realised she had taken the wind out of his sails. She turned and said, "This isn't the best time to discuss such matters, we'll speak later when I'm on a break, if you are around?"

"I shall make it a point to be..." he said, brightening up. Then whistling, he wandered off down the corridor.

The shift was a busy one and when things had finally calmed down, Matron sent her to the canteen to have a break. There was no sign of Daniel, so she sat at a table with a glass of milk and a slice of fruit cake in front of her, minding her own business and wondering what to do about her father. Would it be in her mother and young brothers' best interests to reunite with him or not? Her mother didn't know she'd gone in search of him that very evening.

Yet, she felt as though he were a lost soul. To have taken to drink again he had to be, as it went against the teachings of the Mormon faith. Aunt Lily had told her that Mormons could be excommunicated from the religion for that very thing. Several had attended Temperance meetings in the town.

She became aware of a presence in a white coat and looking up, saw Daniel Evans standing there with a cup of tea in his hand.

"Mind if I sit with you?" he asked.

"Not at all," she replied truthfully. It was a welcome respite from her troubled thoughts.

They chatted for a while, then he quite suddenly stretched his hand across the table and touched hers, causing her to flinch as she had not expected that at all.

"I'm truly sorry Rebecca..." he said earnestly.

"Sorry for what, Daniel?" she blinked several times.

"For upsetting you and spoiling what we once had, I was foolish, arrogant even, and there was no excuse for my behaviour."

"Truthfully, you did us both a favour, Daniel."

"But I don't see how?"

"Well you obviously were not entirely happy with me or else you wouldn't have been looking for another to step out with."

"Oh, but I was happy with you, it was the attention your friend gave me, it went to my head somewhat and she was extremely free and easy."

"Please do not refer to Jane as my friend!" she said, feeling affronted. It had been a double betrayal really, as she'd thought of Jane as trustworthy. "So, it was all because I kept my honour, whilst Jane offered hers on a plate to you!" Her chin jutted out in defiance.

"Sorry..." he gazed down into his tea, and then stirred it as if to distract himself, to give himself something to focus on.

"No need now to apologise, I am truly well over that business, there has been a lot of water under the bridge since that time. What I was going to say to you is, I will go out with you sometime, but only as a friend, we could never resume what we once had."

He nodded. "I understand. Perfectly."

"Well I hope you do. Some things can never return to what they once were!"

"Yes, well it's a start. I do miss you, you know."

She finished the remainder of her cake, then stood. "I have to get back to the ward," she said, standing and brushing the crumbs from her apron, then she patted him on the shoulder and he took her hand, no doubt feeling regretful for what he'd lost due to his own stupidity. She felt he'd learned a valuable lesson.

**

The following day her mother spoke no more about the fact her father was in Merthyr and just went about her business as usual which mystified Rebecca, yet she never doubted for one moment that her mother still loved him.

Aunt Lily was shocked when Rebecca told her what she knew and said she'd go with her to search for him herself. At one time brother and sister had been very close and Lily had spent a lot of time searching for him herself after their mother died. Rebecca had to admit that her father was the sort of man who found it hard to cope with his feelings and how she missed him so.

When James returned home from work that evening, he brought a letter with him for Rebecca. "It's from Mr. Goldstein," he said. "He

227

now has all the evidence necessary for your divorce, Rebecca..." Her brother grinned as he handed her the letter.

"Wanted to save himself a stamp, did he?" she said, ripping it open and it was as her brother said, confirmation of the impending divorce, her heart began to race.

"How do you feel about it, Bec?"

Her mouth was dry. "To be honest, I don't know whether I'm excited or anxious, maybe a little of both."

"Soon you shall be a free woman though!" he expounded.

She chewed her bottom lip. "I am very wary of the financial cost though, James."

"Not to worry. I've spoken to Mr. Goldstein on your behalf and he said it shall be affordable and he's willing to take part payments. At least you are in full-time employment, Rebecca."

That was true, she dreaded to think how she'd have coped if she'd had a houseful of children and no job, she was in a powerful position in reality. She knew her mother didn't really approve of divorce, but in this instance, knowing the awful event that had happened to her daughter, she was most understanding.

***

The following day, Rebecca agreed to go for a walk to Cyfarthfa Park with Daniel Evans. He was very gentlemanly and she found herself relating a lot of what happened in Llanbadarn Fawr to him, though she did not tell him about the rape.

"I'll always be here for you, you know," he said.

She nodded and believed him when he said so, he seemed to have learned his lesson.

They stopped for a while to watch a couple of squirrels bounding up a large oak tree and watched in amusement as one dropped its stash of nuts.

"Have you heard about Mansell Owen?" he asked.

"Heard what?" She frowned not quite knowing what to expect.

"He's moving to London!"

Rebecca's heart missed a beat. "No! Where did you hear of this?"

"From the horse's mouth, himself. He informed me when we were last at a medical meeting together."

"But what are his reasons for leaving Merthyr?" She was truly shocked.

"He's been offered a position at Bart's Hospital and feels it would be a good chance to make a new start after all that's happened."

Suddenly, she felt a sense of impending danger. It was the last thing she wanted for Mansell to leave the town, though she felt guilty she hadn't been in touch with him of late, but there'd been good reason for that. Her mind was messed up and she'd had a lot on her plate with divorce on the horizon.

"What's the matter, Rebecca? You've gone quite pale?"

"N...nothing..." she stammered. "I'm quite surprised that's all!"

"I think it's more than that!" He stopped and stood in front of her, blocking her path. "Please tell me..." His eyes were full of genuine concern.

"There's nothing to tell." Her face grew hot and she just wanted to escape. A man and woman, walking with a young child with his small wooden sail boat clasped to his chest, walked past as if on their way to the lake.

Rebecca took in a composing breath and let it out again. "Very well, the Doctor and I have feelings for one another!"

"I just knew it!" Daniel scoffed. "So, that's why you haven't been so keen to take up with me again!"

"No, that's not true. Even if we didn't have those sort of feelings, I wouldn't wish to resurrect anything between us ever again!"

He softened. "Then if you feel that way about Mansell, you need to see him as soon as possible, Rebecca." He looked at her in earnest and for once, she realised he had her best interests at heart.

"But I think it's too late, he's obviously made plans, wheels appear to be in motion."

"That's true. He told me about his intention about a month or so ago. He's not been at the General hospital very much of late as he's been back and forth to London, making plans to move."

Sadness flooded her veins, shooting an arrow of despair towards her heart. No wonder she hadn't encountered him when she started back working at the hospital; she assumed it was because they were on different wards and worked different hours that their paths hadn't crossed. If only she had gone to see him and tell him she would soon be a free woman and now it was all too late, she couldn't disrupt his life now he had made up his mind to leave believing she was happily married, it just wouldn't be fair.

"Come on," Daniel said kindly. "Let's go to my digs, my landlady will allow us to speak there in private. It will be warmer."

Gratefully she accepted his offer, but swallowed down her disappointment at the thought of never seeing Mansell Owen again. As if understanding her plight, Daniel took her by the arm and led her back to the nearby house, so she could warm herself and recover from the shock of it all.

***

The following evening Rebecca told her aunt about Mansell.

"But you must see him whilst you are in Abercanaid..." Lily urged.

"Can't you see though, Auntie...it would do no good, it would put pressure on him and might confuse him. I don't want that for Mansell."

"Very well, you must do as you deem fit, but meantime, we need to track down your father."

"I've already tried the Vulcan Inn where that man said he met him now and again. Do you think it best I return there?"

Lily nodded. "Yes, but this time I shall come with you. It's not safe in that sort of place on your own."

Rebecca guessed her Aunt was right. She hadn't liked the looks some of the men there had given her, almost as though they were undressing her with their eyes. "Yes, I'd feel a lot safer if you were with me."

Lily smiled. "Well, that's sorted out then. I don't know what we're going to do if we find him mind. It sounds as if he's had some sort of relapse that might require our help. Even worse of course is if we can't find him at all."

Rebecca had considered that, but figured what they hadn't had this past few years, they wouldn't miss.

They searched the Vulcan Inn and surrounding public houses, but to no avail. No one seemed to have seen him at all, it was almost as though he'd vanished into thin air. Defeated and despondent, both women made their way back through the town, stopping off at St Tydfil's Parish Church. "Come on," Lily said firmly, "let's go inside and pray about these matters."

The door was open as they stepped inside and several candles were already alight in front of the altar, their flickering flames soothed Rebecca somehow. There was no sign of anyone around, so they quietly knelt in a pew as Lily prayed aloud with all her might.

"Dear Heavenly Father,

We petition you now in the name of your son Jesus Christ, so that we can find my brother, Rebecca's father, Dafydd Jenkin. We prayfully ask that you save him from any harm he might incur. He has been a lost soul for such a long time. Please help us to reunite him with his family who need him. Keep him safe and well and help him to avoid any temptations that might befall him.

Also we petition that if it is THY will that my niece, Rebecca, find someone to love her and take care of her as she deserves, that she will do so. Please if that person is someone she has already met, who is now free to love her, then let him show it before it is too late.

We ask you this in the name of the Father, Son and Holy Spirit. Amen."

Rebecca then said 'Amen' too.

"There," said Aunt Lily pulling herself into a standing position by holding on to the wooden pew, "it says in the bible in Matthew 18 verse 20, *"For where two or three are gathered together in my name, there am I in the midst of them."*

Rebecca nodded and following suit, pulled herself up into a standing position. They both lowered their heads before the altar cross before leaving the church, then deposited a small donation in the wooden slotted-box by the main door near the exit.

Praying was all they had to rely on right now. Rebecca realised Aunt Lily was referring to Mansell in that prayer, a sign was needed that Rebecca and Mansell ought to be together in this life.

"I don't think it's safe for us to walk home alone Rebecca, we'll take a cab," Aunt Lily advised.

Rebecca nodded. She was exhausted anyhow, all this worry about her father and the latest run of night shifts had taken it out of her, she was ready for her bed. They shared the cab fare home. Aunt Lily would be dropped off first at Abercanaid. Rebecca felt a shard of excitement as the Hansom cab rattled past the Doctor's home which was up the hill set into the Canal Bank. There was light on inside the house and she wondered what he was doing right now. Noticing her niece, Lily said, "Why don't you stop off and call in to see him, Rebecca?"

"I can't, Auntie. It's been such a long time. I can't mess with his emotions."

Lily smiled and nodded. "Very well, but if it's in God's will for you two to be together, it shall come to pass..." The cab pulled up outside the chapel and the driver got out, assisting Lily's descent.

"Goodnight, dear Aunt!" Rebecca shouted out of the cab window as Lily waved.

Then she closed her eyes as the cab left Abercanaid in the same direction from whence it came, she couldn't bear to see the Doctor's house again, knowing that he was there, so near and yet so far away.

***

The following morning, Rebecca went shopping in Merthyr Town with her mother. They strolled around the market place, her mother stopping at a second-hand stall to admire a fur stole, which she wrapped around her neck as she gazed into the full length mirror at the end of the stall.

"You really like that, don't you?" Rebecca said, as she watched her mother beam with a dreamy look on her face.

"'Tis just like the one your father bought me many moons ago when I returned home to Merthyr from the London stage. 'Twas only a short time I was home for, but your father wanted to buy me something special."

It was the first time her mother had mentioned her father's name in a long while. As if grounding herself in reality, Kathleen removed the russet fox fur from her neck and placed it back to hang with the rack of clothes. It was a memory that seemed to fade away with the passage of time.

As they approached Graham Street, they heard a shout go out and a police whistle being blown as a group of policemen went running past, people were beginning to stare. Kathleen recognised one of them as being one of her husband's old colleagues who was an inspector at the station. "Jim, what on earth's happening?" she shouted.

"It's a young lady who's got into difficulties by Jackson's Bridge, she tried to throw herself off to do away with herself. We're going to search the river, apparently some man jumped in after her..." he explained. "Sorry I have to go..."

He ran to catch up with the other constables, leaving Rebecca and her mother feeling flummoxed.

Her mother frowned. "I have a bad feeling about all of this," she said.

Rebecca shivered. She hated to hear of such things, but living in this town people sometimes found it hard and sometimes they tried to end it all rather than live in poverty or work the gruelling hours spent in the ironworks. She wondered for a moment if it was one of the prostitutes from 'China' as that was nearby. A few working girls over the years had been found floating in the river, sometimes by accident and sometimes by design, if they had a particularly brutal pimp or client. One had once been brought into the General Hospital with her head caved in, another beaten so badly she almost lost the sight in one eye, but still she would not name the person who did it to her.

After they'd finished their shopping, Rebecca decided they should take a walk near the bridge, it wasn't too far out of their way and they didn't have a lot to carry home. At Jackson's Bridge, Rebecca heard male shouts and a couple of women shrieks sending a shiver down her spine.

As they approached the scene, quite a crowd of onlookers had gathered as the policemen had removed their tunics and rolled up their sleeves and trouser legs.

"What's going on?" Rebecca asked a nervous looking young woman who appeared to be biting her nails to the quick.

"A young lady jumped off the bridge and a man passing by jumped in the River Taff to rescue her. They're both still in the water and the police are trying to save them both!" She exclaimed, then her eyes rolled back in her head and she collapsed in a heap on the ground.

"She's fainted!" Kathleen said.

"I'd better hang on around here, Mam," Rebecca said, "Just in case I'm needed as a nurse." Rebecca helped the woman back onto her feet and asked an onlooker to keep an eye on her.

"Good idea if you help out, Bec," her mother nodded. "I'll get this shopping home. Here give me your basket."

The woman who'd fainted was now back to life and feeling a little foolish to have passed out in front of the crowd.

Rebecca handed her mother the wicker basket of groceries. "Thanks."

"I just hope that young girl and the man will be all right..." her mother said, tutting under her breath. "Well I'm not going to stand gawping like some of those old biddies around here, only looking for something to tell their friends and neighbours about!" She raised her voice and glared at a group of women, who were muttering and shaking their heads. They stopped mid flow to glare back at her. Kathleen had always hated gossips since the days of Maggie Shanklin of Abercanaid, who had made her life a misery with her devious and most malicious behaviour.

When her mother had departed, Rebecca approached a young policeman who was pushing back a large horde of people. "Excuse me, but I'm a nurse from the General hospital, is there anything I can do, constable?" she enquired.

When he saw her he smiled and let out a long exasperated breath. "You're an angel. The man and woman are on the river bank down by there, the man is all right but they're having trouble rousing the woman. Think she might be dead."

"I'll go and have a look now."

"Let the lady pass by!" The constable shouted at the crowd and it parted to allow her access to the grassy verge below. The ground was very slippery, so the policeman called to his colleagues to help Rebecca down to the riverside.

When she arrived at the scene, there were two policemen attending to the bearded man, who by now was sitting up on a rock near the river, recounting his tale to the men. The woman though was lying on her back, her clothing stuck to her skin as it had absorbed so much water. The worst part was looking at the blue tinge to her skin and bloated appearance.

Without saying a word, as the officers had obviously given up hope of her living, Rebecca turned the woman onto her back and tipped her head back, then swept inside her mouth with her fingers and pulled her tongue out of the way to clear her airway. Then she knelt behind the woman's head and lifted her arms above her head, bringing them back to her side several times, it was exhausting work and she was about to ask one of the policemen who was watching, to take over as she'd been trying for a couple of minutes, when the woman spluttered violently and water oozed from her mouth.

"Quick!" Rebecca shouted to the constable, "Give me your tunic to keep her warm."

Without question the constable handed it over to her and she covered the woman's cold body after turning her on her side.

One of the older policemen observing, scratched his head. "Well I don't believe it, Miss. We'd given her up for dead! How did you learn to do that?"

"It's called 'Silvester's Method'. I was taught the technique by one of the doctors at the hospital. It might be an idea if your men learned how to employ it. It helps to increase lung capacity and expel water from the lungs."

He nodded. Then she turned back toward the woman, who was now trying to say something to her. "I...I...fell. I didn't really mean to do it," she croaked. "That man saved me, got me out of the water." She began to shiver.

"Can I have another tunic, please!" Rebecca shouted. One of the other policeman stared at her, but made no move to disrobe. "In your own time of course!" she barked at him, causing the policeman to flush with embarrassment as he removed his tunic, and passed it to her. "Thank you! But we have to keep her warm until we get her to the hospital or she might develop hypothermia."

"I'll see if anyone has a horse and cart or carriage," the policeman suggested, as if trying to make amends.

Whilst he was gone, Rebecca attended to the woman and made about to check the man out, when he stood and walked towards her, his eyes locking with hers. The grey straggly beard and wild looking salt and peppered coloured hair, did little to belie those piercing blue eyes staring out from behind that weather beaten skin.

He walked towards her and said her name, "Rebecca!" and she fell into his arms as he hugged her tightly. She sobbed uncontrollably, with the policemen looking on in astonishment.

"What's going on?" she heard one of them say.

Rebecca pulled away and through her sobs said, "My father, my father is home!"

"You're looking wonderful!" he said, his voice sounding raspy, but she guessed that was because he'd swallowed so much water.

She didn't know what to ask him first, if he was all right, what had happened, or why he was back in Merthyr. "So what happened here?" she finally asked.

"That young woman fell from Jackson's Bridge. I don't know for sure if she tried to jump or if it was accidental. I saw her and tried to grab hold of her, but she slipped from my grasp, so I went in after her, but the current was so strong we got swept along with it. Luckily someone witnessed what happened and the police arrived."

"Don't any of them recognise you?"

He shook his head. "New lot this bunch are. I do, though recognise the Inspector, but he hasn't recognised me yet with this beard!" He laughed.

"Why did you leave us, Dad?" She said suddenly, and the words were out of her mouth before she could stop them.

His eyes misted with tears. "I'm so sorry, Bec. I just couldn't live with myself after what I'd done. I needed to get away from the situation I'd created. How's your mother and the boys, and James too?"

"They're all very well, but then you already know that!"

Her father's face flushed as she made it clear she knew he'd been keeping an eye out for them all.

The Inspector arrived back at that point and they made to carry the woman to the bank where a horse and cart was awaiting to transport her to the hospital.

"And how are you, Sir?" the Inspector asked her father.

Her father grinned. "All the better now, Jim, for seeing my daughter again!"

The Inspector stared at him as if wondering how the man knew his name and then realisation dawned. "Dafydd, Dafydd Jenkin is it really you?" He closed the space between them.

"Yes, it's me, I know I look a bit rough, been travelling for months."

"But what happened to you?" The Inspector blinked.

"I took off for Utah to visit family, but I'm back now!"

"Gentlemen!" The Inspector turned to his team and shouted, "This man here is not only a hero for saving that young lady today, but he was the policeman, who years ago, brought the infamous, 'Twm Sion Watkin', to task. The bully from China, a brutal killer!"

The men began cheering and then applauded.

"We must get you back to the police station to warm up!" The Inspector said when the noise had died down, then turning to Rebecca, "And you, young lady, did a fine job as we'd given that woman up for dead!"

"That's my daughter," Dafydd said proudly.

"Not young Rebecca who used to call into the police station with Kathleen?"

"The one and the very same same!"

Rebecca smiled, she could not have been happier at this moment than she was right now, realising that both she and her father had played a part in saving that lady's life.

**

After they'd both got warmed up at the police station and the Inspector had loaned Dafydd a pair of trousers, shirt, socks and boots, and he'd got a shave, they were both given a small glass of brandy.

"Well I never thought that when I set out this morning I'd end up drinking alcohol at the police station with my father!" she said.

They both sat either side of a roaring fire in the rest room. The Inspector chuckled. "It does sound somewhat strange, Rebecca, but on a serious note, and I know a little of the story why your father left, but how will your mother take it now he's home?"

"She knows! Bill next door apprehended this young man who had been watching the house for days, he said you'd paid him to keep an eye on us, Dad?"

Her father nodded. "Aye, I'm not proud of what I did, but I did so as I had to reassure myself you were all fit and well!"

Rebecca nodded, quite understanding her father's concerns. Reassuringly, she rose and hugged her father. "Well, you're back home now where you belong, I want you to come to the house with me."

"Right now?" he frowned, as if worried.

"Yes, why not now? You've been away long enough. Now is as good a time as any!"

Her father frowned and then rubbed his chin as if mulling over her suggestion. "But what will your mother say?"

"Leave her to me!" Rebecca said with some authority.

Her father's eyes clouded over for a moment, then he let out a breath. "She's never found anyone else in all these years?"

"No, she hasn't, always said she'd never remarry, her faith won't allow her to do so anyhow whilst you are still alive."

"Faith?"

"Oh you wouldn't know, she has recommitted herself to her Catholic faith. And what about you and the Mormon religion? Rose wrote to Mam and told her you'd converted. It sounded as if you were a fervent believer."

He shook his head. "It wasn't for me. Delwyn and Rose tried to get me to convert, taking me along to services and meeting various people, but although I believe in God, I didn't agree with some of the practices in the end."

She narrowed her gaze. "I see, so what brought you back to us?"

His eyes misted up and she detected a catch in his voice. "It's not that I ever wanted to go in the first place, Rebecca... I just felt torn, didn't know what to do for the best. Leaving Merthyr was my way of coping, thinking everyone would be a darn sight better off without me around."

"Well you've got two young sons you've yet to set eyes on..." she said soberly.

His eyes lit up. "Ben and Daniel, aye I know, Delwyn and Rose told me and I received a couple of letters from you all."

Rebecca softened as she listened to her father's reasoning. "How did you feel during that time?"

The Inspector took it as his cue to leave the room at that point.

"Lost, so very lost..." her father shook his head and then, quite unexpectedly, put his head in his hands and wept.

***

The Inspector insisted on sending for a Hansom cab to take the pair home to The Walk area, even though Dafydd insisted he felt well and better than he had in weeks. Rebecca realised her father was getting older, he'd aged considerably this past few years, so she went along with what the Inspector said. As they got into the cab, the Inspector shouted, "Dafydd, if you ever wish to return to the constabulary, we'd be more than happy to have someone with your mettle. You're a hero to many of the men at the station!"

Dafydd just smiled and nodded, then followed his daughter into the back of the cab.

238

Rebecca guessed he was too weary to contemplate that right now. Her heart began to race. What would her mother say? Was this such a good idea bringing her father back so unexpectedly?

Chapter Sixteen

When they arrived at the house they walked quietly in through the kitchen door, all was quiet, the wicker basket still on the table as if Kathleen had put away all the shopping they'd both purchased earlier.

"Sssssh!" Rebecca put her finger to her lips as her father followed her into the living room. She pushed back the door to reveal her mother fast asleep on the settee, the gentle rise and fall of her chest rhythmically moving with each heart beat. Rebecca thought her mother still looked beautiful, and despite the emotional pain and suffering her father had put her mother through, it was Kathleen who had aged the better of the two.

Dafydd stood there for a few moments, staring at his wife with tears streaming down his face. He reached out his hand just inches from her face as if she were a fine piece of china, then he was on his knees by her side whispering, "Kathleen, my beautiful Kathleen."

Kathleen's eyes flicked open and she sat up in astonishment and rubbed her eyes. "Is this a dream?" she asked in bewilderment.

"It's no dream. I'm here, I'm back for good, if you'll have me."

It was several seconds before Kathleen responded, almost as though time had stood still. Then she was crying too and both were locked in an embrace, silently Rebecca tiptoed out of the room to fetch her brothers who were at Bill's house next door. She was going to have to explain to the man that her father had finally returned home and hoped he'd understand. It wasn't going to be easy for any of them. The twins had yet to see the man who'd deserted them. Of course, she also feared a reaction from James who had been the most upset when their father absconded. No doubt, in time her mother would get angry with her father for leaving in the first place and that was only natural. For now though, she was so pleased to have her Dafydd back under the same roof as her.

After Rebecca had explained all to Bill, quietly, so the twins should not hear, he just nodded and said, "Don't worry, Rebecca, I always realised your mother's heart was with your father all along and I hope in time I can be a friend to them both."

It was then Rebecca realised just how much Bill cared for her mother that he was more concerned with her happiness than his own.

"If you'd only both met at a different time and place, then I think it would have worked out for you..." she touched his shoulder gently.

"Don't go worrying about me, Becky," he said. "Your mam and the boys have been great company since my Edna passed away and that has been enough for me to brighten my days."

She smiled and nodded, then turning shouted, "Come on then!" Rebecca collected the twins and they followed her back to their own home next door. "Thanks for taking care of them, Bill!" she called behind her.

"Why are we going back home?" Ben, who was always the spokesman for the two, asked.

"I've got a nice surprise for you both," she said calmly.

"Surprise, like a toy!" Daniel hopped from one foot to the other.

She stopped a moment before opening the gate to the family home. "No not a toy, it's better than that!"

"Sweeties!" shouted Ben.

Rebecca smiled, it was a surprise that she hoped would eventually be better than any toy or sweets for the boys. Although they were too young to fully understand as yet.

Both boys looked wide-eyed as she turned to open the gate and walk them up the path. It might not be easy, she realised that, but they needed to meet their father and he needed to meet them too.

***

The afternoon family union had gone well, the boys had taken to their father without question as their mother had previously related stories about him and shown them photographs, so within minutes he had one son on his shoulders and the other in his arms, the trio overjoyed. Now all that remained was to gauge James's reaction.

At a quarter to six the front door opened and her brother entered the room, blinking to see the sight in front of him, as if realising they needed to be quiet, the twins stopped running around and stood quietly as father and son stared at one another.

"I've missed you, James!" Dafydd said softly. Then James was wiping away a tear. "You've become quite the young man!"

Then both were shaking hands and hugging one another, before breaking away as it didn't seem the manly thing to do.

After a family meal of roast chicken and vegetables and then rice pudding for dessert, they all sat in front of a roaring fire while Dafydd told them tales of his adventures in Utah.

Rebecca thought it was the happiest day of her life, so far, except for the time her mother performed in front of Doctor Joseph Parry at the Temperance Hall so many years ago.

***

Life settled back down and all the family were under the same roof again as if they'd never been apart. Mary Kinney and her young family had thankfully moved from the Brecon Road, but no one knew where. One of the neighbours said they thought she did a moonlight flit as she owed months of rent money. There'd been talk of her going back to family in Ireland. So thankfully, there would be no embarrassment of bumping into the woman and her father's other child.

Life at the hospital gave Rebecca a routine and she found herself now comfortable in the presence of Daniel Evans as he no longer pursued her, just treated her like a colleague and friend with the utmost respect.

One particular day, she was amazed at how he smiled throughout the entire shift, almost as though he had some secret she wasn't privy to. Puzzled, she just went about her business as usual and then went home to put her feet up, exhausted.

At a quarter past eight, after the twins had been put to bed and the rest of the family were about to settle down to a cup of cocoa together, there was a knock at the door.

Seemingly irate at having a family moment destroyed, Kathleen rose and said, "Who can that be now?"

"Don't worry I'll answer it, Mam," James said. "It's probably one of the neighbours who want to borrow something again..."

Straining, Rebecca could hear male voices by the door, then James returned to the living room. "There's someone to see you, Bec..." he announced his eyes wide with surprise.

Puzzled, she went to the door to see a familiar figure with his back toward her.

"Mansell," she said as he turned, a big smile on his face.

"Hello Rebecca, is there somewhere we might speak to one another?"

She nodded. "We could go into the parlour. One moment..." Her heart thudded as she went to speak to her parents and explain who was at the door.

Her father's blinked several times in astonishment. "Is that Doctor Owen's son from Abercanaid?"

"Yes. You wouldn't have known but he was widowed months ago," Rebecca explained.

"I remember him when he was a young lad," her father said.

"Well call him inside Rebecca, don't keep him waiting on the doorstep!" Her mother added.

"Very well, but first I would like to speak to him in confidence."

Her parents both nodded their consent. "I'll put the kettle on then!" Her mother said enthusiastically.

Beaming, Rebecca went back to the doorstep where she brought the Doctor inside and she took him directly into the parlour which was the best room, whilst their mother made tea for them both and the rest of the family remained in the living room.

Mansell paced the room for a while, then Rebecca said, "Please sit down, you're making me feel anxious."

He smiled. "I'm sorry, Rebecca." He sat in the armchair and she followed suit on the settee. "It's just I have something to say to you. I've heard that you've separated from your husband and that it shall be legal soon."

"Yes, that is correct. Actually, it shall be more than a legal separation—I've applied for a divorce on the grounds that Rhys married someone else bigamously."

He nodded. "Even better!"

She looked at him in amazement. "How can it be even better?"

"Better, as in you shall be completely free as I have a proposition for you?"

"Are you still moving to London and how did you know about my business?"

"Let's just say a mutual friend informed me!" He tapped the side of his nose.

"Daniel!" she exclaimed. It all made sense now, he must have known Mansell planned on calling to see her that evening before he left for London, that's why he'd been grinning all day.

243

Mansell nodded. "Yes, it seems to me, although Daniel Evans did you wrong, Rebecca, he wants you to be happy in life. In answer to your question about London. Yes, I am still going to Barts Hospital to work, but I'd like you to come with me. I'm sure I could get you a position as a nurse there."

"Oh?" Her breathing became shallow and rapid. He wanted her in his life, that much was evident, but what about the life she had planned in Merthyr?

"You sound thoroughly disappointed, Rebecca. Think what this could mean for your career!"

"It's not that, Mansell, it's just that Matron Steed has plans for me to take over her job when she retires. I wouldn't like to let her down."

"Just a moment, I haven't told you of all my plans yet. I mentioned the nursing position first and I suppose, what I'm trying to ask you, in my own clumsy way is..." He let out a long breath, "will you do me the honour of being my wife?"

She closed her eyes, she had been hoping he'd say those words to her, opening them she said, "Yes, I'd love to! But of course, we'll have to wait until my divorce is official. I could not do anything untoward before then."

He smiled, looking relaxed now he had said the words and she'd accepted. "Of course, I wouldn't expect anything else from a lady such as yourself. I am more than prepared to wait, I have waited this long for you. But what about the nursing position at Barts if I can secure it?"

"Well I suppose that would be a wonderful opportunity and Matron would understand."

Both stood simultaneously, then Mansell closed the space between them, his lips met hers and he was kissing her with a passion she had never felt before. Her head was swimming with desire for him. For them to be one. They broke apart breathlessly, and when she had regained her composure once more, she said, "I haven't had chance to tell you, my father has returned home, I'll explain all later, but first we need to speak with my parents about this."

Mansell beamed as he took her hand and they walked towards the living room to announce the good news. She didn't know if her parents would understand or not for sure, but they had both been through so much themselves that something inside told her if anyone would understand the course of true love never running smoothly, it was her parents, Dafydd and Kathleen Jenkin. During all the dark days of the past few years, there were now at last blue skies over the heads of all of them.

Books in the Seasons of Change series:

1. Black Diamonds
2. White Roses
3. Blue Skies
4. Red Poppies

Books are available from Amazon in both paperback and Kindle Formats.

Printed in Great Britain
by Amazon